I0822282

ALSO BY ALLISON TEBO

The Tales of Ambia

The Reluctant Godfather

A Royal Masquerade

Poppy's Peril

A Flash Of Magic

The Key to the Chains

The Goblin and the Dancer

A CLASSIC RETOLD SERIES

Break the Beast - Allison Tebo

Crack the Stone - Emily Golus

Steal the Morrow - Jenelle Leanne Schmidt

Unearth the Tides - Alissa J. Zavalianos

Raise the Dead - Nina Clare

Summon the Light - Tor Thibeaux

Chase the Legend - Hannah Kaye

Kill the Dawn - Emily Hayse

Riddle of Hearts - Rosie Grymm

Learn more at AClassicRetold.com

A Classic Retold

Break the Beast

Allison Tebo

Break the Beast

All quotations are from Beowulf: An Anglo-Saxon Epic Poem translated by Lesslie Hall. D.C Heath & Co Publishers 1982. © by JNO: LESSLIE HALL.

ISBN: 979-8-9885006-1-2

Cover design by MiblArt

Edited by Mary Herceg

Formatted by Declan Rowe

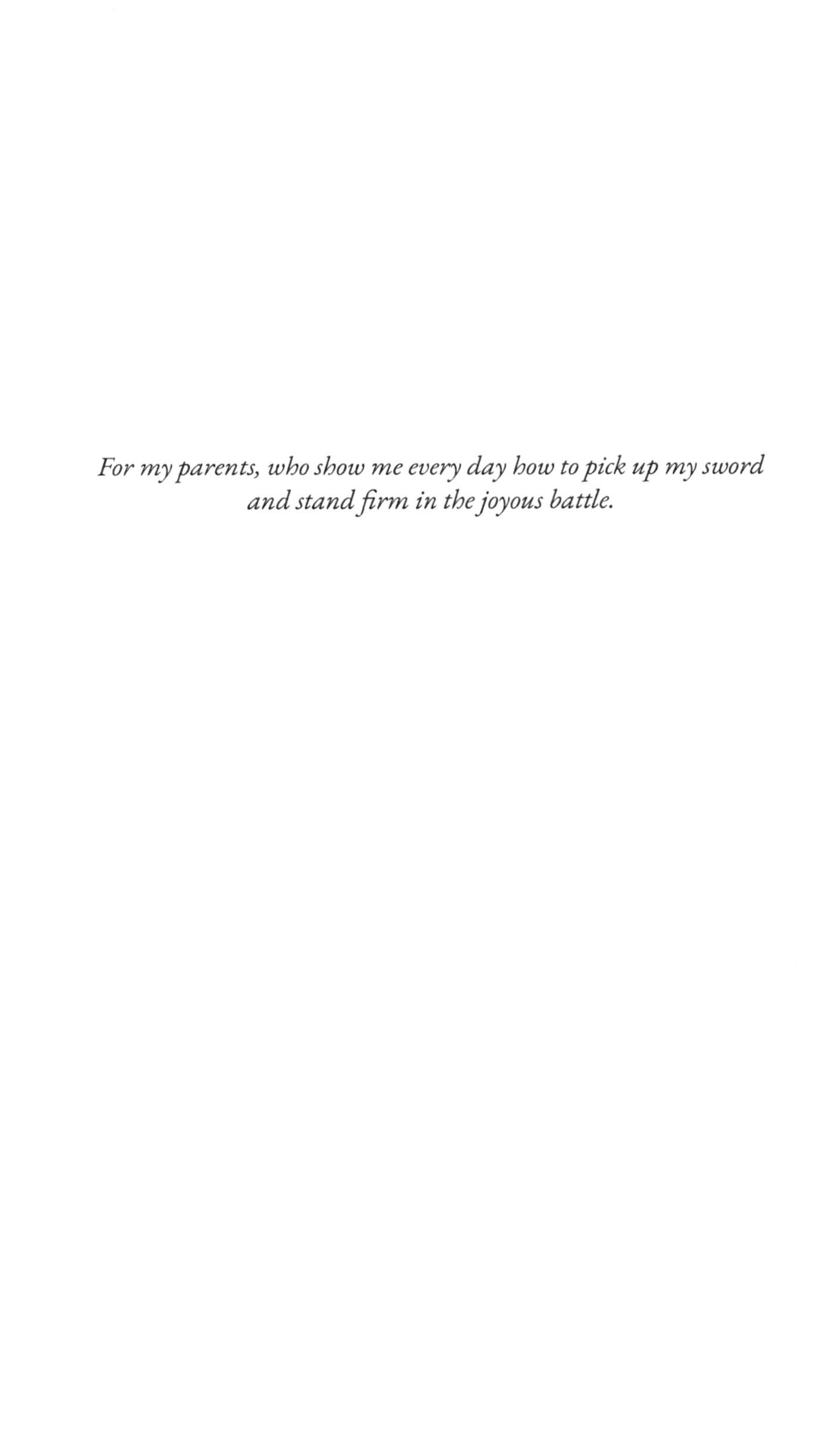

For my parents, who show me every day how to pick up my sword and stand firm in the joyous battle.

PLACES

Frisia (*friz-ee-UH*): A cold and desolate land.

Schrawynghop (*shra-WIN-gop*): A great settlement of Frisia and the king-seat of Hrothgar.

Trollhattan (*troll-HAH-tun*): The great mead-hall of the town of Schrawynghop.

Heofon (*hey-OOF-un*): A distant country across the Great Sea and the home of Beowulf.

The Prophecy of a Son

A son will come, and the sun will rise
To break the dragon's hold
But as the sun does rise, so it also dies
This golden death foretold

The son does die, but the sun shall rise
And with its rising, it does show
That son that came, to claim the prize
Has killed the Dragon Below

Two fires put out, one coal remains
A soul too strong to yield to night
To break the beast, the son is slain
Yet in the dark, there comes a light

PART I

The warriors abided, till a certain one gan to
Dog them with deeds of direfullest malice,
A foe in the hall-building: this horrible stranger
Was Grendel entitled, the march-stepper famous
Who dwelt in the moor-fens

— LESSLIE HALL, *BEOWULF: AN ANGLO-SAXON EPIC POEM*

1

I hide from the light that seeps across the cavern's pool. The moon has risen, and while it does not burn like the sun, it still shines where it is better not to shine.

It is the light that troubles me, not heat, for in the light I can see my shadow, and it is the shadow of a beast.

Mother has returned from her nightly roaming. She is stronger than I; she has resisted the attack of the light for years. It no longer torments her as it does me. Her own reflection no longer has the power to frighten her—only others.

It frightens me.

She moves into the cave and drifts across the pool. It ripples in her wake and sighs as she moves from the water onto the silver shale where I crouch, pressed into the cavern wall. Hiding in the shadows.

"What disturbs you, Grendel?" she asks, gently.

My voice is a thread. "I am a monster."

Her voice is still gentle, as soft as the ripples lapping at the shale. "Who calls you a monster?"

I look to the mouth of the cave, the narrow slit between water and rock, where I can glimpse the light.

Beyond this mere, there are the dells full of the people of

Frisia, and a settlement called Schrawynghop. And built in its center, in a place of pride, is the mead-hall called Trollhattan.

It is a beautiful place, but I am not welcome there. They have seen me in the night, and they chased me away.

I turn my gaze away from where a hideous hood trembles on the surface of the pool and answer her question. "It is the people who call me a monster."

Mother drifts closer, her dark shadow swallowing me, and I find my sorrow beginning to unspool, undone by her powerful certainty.

"Why do you think they are right?" she asks.

She asks why, when I have just glimpsed myself in her pool. I do not look as the people of the Hall look.

My voice is empty as my hands that I hold out to her, beseeching her to fill them. "Because my reflection tells me that I am."

A hiss.

Mother is angry.

"It is their fault," she whispers in my ear. "Have I not been teaching you all these years to love yourself as you are? It is they who are wrong for not accepting you. It is they who are the monsters for daring to judge you. And so . . ." She pauses.

The wind screams outside the cave.

Her voice comes again—the sound of a knife being drawn. "You must make them accept you."

"How?" I whimper, a child once more. By day I know who I am. At night I am a babe all over again. On nights like these, I remember something from before, and the memory threatens to make the present unbearable.

"By destroying them," Mother murmurs. "Destroy enough of them, and the others will realize how they have wronged you. They will repent and beg for your forgiveness."

I slip into the pool and look at the moon's glimmer in the water around me. I glance towards the entrance. I must brave the light to go to the Hall.

Her anger is seeping into me, giving me strength to face it.

Mother speaks again. "Deep down, we are all beasts. But in all this land it is only you who has been brave enough to embrace it. If they were as wise as you, they too would be like you. If they were as honest as you, they would adore you for your courage to live and embrace what you are. If the world were right, they would follow you, not that old man they call king."

I turn, my movement breaking my reflection into shivering ripples. I look at her, the twisted features that mirror my own—the face that made me what I am.

Her hatred flows into me, pushing out my fear, making my blood boil.

"It is not your reflection that calls you a monster, Grendel—it is them. It is they who are responsible for these nightly torments, it is they who keep you from being happy here with me, who try to deceive you into thinking that their life is better. Who are they to make you feel that there is anything wrong with you? They claim purity, and yet they have not been true to their own desires, as you have. They claim love and goodness, but what love and goodness have they shown to you? They have no right to say that you are not welcome among them, to say that you do not deserve to be honored in their homes. Such hypocrisy does not deserve to live. Go, take your rightful place among the people of the Hall. Destroy them, Grendel."

Her voice rises to a shriek: it is the wind and the cold and every terrible whisper in the night pouring from her throat in a final command.

"*Destroy them*!"

I am hurtling through water, breaking the still pool into heaving splinters as I surge out of the cave. I fling my head up, pulling moonlit air into my lungs to finally scream, letting loose all the bitterness in my heart in one mad sound.

I judge tonight.

I RACE across the fens into the night, towards Trollhattan. Rushes whip past me, half tangling in my scales, until my relentless pace rips them free from the earth. I am the fastest thing beneath the sky. I am the fastest thing alive. My fury lends speed to my monstrously fast gait.

My fear that there is something wrong with me, that I am the one unworthy, twists and snarls inside me like an animal, looking for something other than me to damage.

I run on across the moor. Even the clouds are against my cause, for they race away from the face of the moon, letting its eye fall upon me. I know what the moon sees: a figure as tall as a great man, but swathed in a trailing robe and hood that is half fabric, half slime, half metal: a covering that makes me look like a ghost with claws, a hood that always hides my face, save for gleaming red eyes and the sudden flash of yellow fangs in a gaping maw.

The clouds ought to hide me, but instead they expose me. Let the moon look. I will not cringe tonight. It is not only the men under heaven who should accept me but heaven itself. There is nothing wrong with me.

There is everything wrong with them.

The moors fall away and I stand on the edge of emptiness and fullness. Before me, ascending in soft folds, are the slopes that lead to the fortress of the Frisians—Schrawynghop.

A great wooden wall, guarded with torches and men, surrounds the town. It is but the work of a moment to spring up and grab hold of the battlements in the wall's darkest corner, seize the neck of a man who is too startled to scream, and cast him over my shoulder. He hits the ground beneath me on the wrong side of the wall with a broken and muffled thump, and I slip down the nearest ladder and into the encampment—a shadow of death.

Trollhattan, the great jewel of this settlement, rests high above me on a steep natural howe at the center of Schrawynghop, and I head for it, slithering up the many shallow steps to its doors, wincing as I pass dripping torches. The smallest brush of light pains me, but the darkness that I crave helps to hide me, turning me into just another shadow until it is too late for my prey to escape.

The sound of men reaches me, pouring from the interior of the Hall, as thick and sickeningly sweet as honey. It is that hated sound of belonging that does not include me, of approval that does not approve me, of love that does not extend to me.

I will silence it.

I draw nearer, and as I do, laughter distinguishes itself from song, and bile fills me as I recognize the words of their bard: it is the song of the prophecy, the tale of a golden warrior who will break the hold of the Dark Father.

Of all words spoken on this vile earth, I hate these most of all.

There is a guard halfway up the great stone steps, but he dies before he can raise the alarm.

I race up the steps past his bloody corpse. The sound of singing grows louder. Their happiness tears me apart; their false contentment makes me scream.

My hatred for the lie they hide behind gives me strength.

The heavy wooden doors are nothing to me. I nearly pull them from their hinges, and I begin to scream.

I am upon them before they can rise from their seats. My hatred hardens into wrath, a mad frenzy that must punish someone—anyone.

The judgment begins.

Some are clad in armor, but their souls are rusty: the dichotomy makes me despise them all the more. I gnash my teeth and pounce upon them first. I am scrubbing the Hall of untruths; I am purging the earth of hypocrisy. I bite through the monstrosity of half-truths, tearing them asunder. I break the bones of frauds, for they are brittle.

There is a terrible, putrid pleasure in the tearing. It's as if by making their blood run, it will somehow replace the bleeding of my own heart—drain the pain away from me into them.

I cannot spill blood fast enough.

My mother's last command as I left the cave rings in my ears. "Go, feel what it is to be a ruler."

Hrothgar thinks he rules this hall, but he does not.

At this moment, only I do.

I use my claws: the thing they call my shame, which my mother calls my glory. I use my teeth, my horns, my fists—everything that they fear.

Everything is madness for several scarlet seconds, and then I look around and realize that I am the only living thing left in the Hall—a panting shadow standing amidst a pile of bodies who are but shells of the men they once were. Only five of them escaped and, among them, not one leader. The king fled for his life—a disgrace among disgraces. A few warriors pulled him from his throne and dragged him from the Hall while I was busy with a warrior who thought he was strong enough to defeat me.

I curse everything on earth and whoever made it, for I have been cheated of the death I most coveted. But perhaps it is better this way, for now all have seen that it is their king who is the coward, not me. It is he who is afraid to stand up for his truth, not I. Now all the cowards can see that they are the appalling ones and that I am the only pure person among them.

The person they deemed fallen has risen. The being they have deemed unworthy has taken the Hall.

I do not follow them to the lesser houses where they might have taken shelter, nor do I go to the bothies to rout out the cowards that have hidden in their huts. I have done enough. They know now that I do not approve of them any more than they do of me, and they can now see that my victory proves the rightness of my cause.

I look away from the men on the floor and to the far end of the Hall, remembering my mother's command.

She alone has great visions for me: it is not enough for her that I am her instrument—she sees me ruling over the people who have ruled over me, and I am caught up in her image, wanting it to be true. It almost is.

I walk towards the dais where the king sat moments ago. My breath catches in my throat; my heart is hot with anticipation as I extend a bloody claw.

I instantly fall back, my body racked with the hideous pain that only light can inflict, even though the room is dark.

I stare and stumble back, then I try once more to touch the throne.

Again there is the pain. It is like walking into a wall of briars. I screech and step back, repulsed once more.

I am unable to sit in the throne: the invisible force that holds me back from life holds me back from this too.

I circle, snarl, and spit, but no cursing, no effort, can force my feet upon the dais.

I try to throw myself onto the throne, but I cannot sit upon it; I cannot even touch it. It is as if I am throwing myself into a wall over and over again. I cannot penetrate it to reach the throne.

I am not worthy.

After all of that, after all I have done, it is not enough.

I throw myself to the ground as if I am one of the dead, screaming and sobbing. Like the once-man lying beside me, I am suddenly unable to breathe.

Something is wrong. My mother says it is I who am the true one, that I was meant to purge the Hall.

But I have driven the falseness from the Trollhattan and I am still not welcome.

This can only mean that I also must be false.

My heart beats so slowly I think at first it has stopped. Tears make the blood on my face run down my cheeks.

The Hall is quiet. There is only me and the dead.

All of us are as empty as the Hall.

I rise, slow and stiff, and look at the throne: a vacant chair that will not accept me any more than the humans that sit upon it.

Very well. If I cannot be worthy of a place in the Hall, then no one will be worthy.

So instead of celebrating, I destroy.

It is what I am destined to do.

I try to fill myself with destruction, with the bitter satisfaction of vengeance, but it rings as hollow as the bone cups that scatter across the floor.

The towering room echoes with howls as I slash and throw, crush and smash. Even if the royal seat will not permit me to sit upon it, the Hall is still mine. My hood is my crown; the bodies beneath me are my throne.

I destroy until I am weary, until the moment of blind panic and pain has ebbed and recedes from hot hell to dull ache. I look around at the judgment I have wrought, willing it to satisfy me before I leave—for I must leave; I cannot stay. The cruelty of even an empty room's rejection is too strong. But I'll be back.

I go to the door and scream into the night.

"Can you hear me, King Hrothgar?" I roar. "If you rebuild what I have brought down, I will be back tomorrow night, and the night after that, and the night after that. I defy any man who thinks he can defeat me."

I slip down the steps and back to the outer wall. No one stops me. They are all running and hiding in a panic, and the shadows have swallowed me once more.

I pause once at the battlement, just before I drop over the wall, and look back at the desecrated Hall. Its doors hang on their hinges, the astonished open mouth of the doorway revealing nothing but darkness.

Trollhattan may not be mine, but it is not Hrothgar's either.

And no man on earth is powerful enough to change that.

2

It has been five days since my last attack, but I cannot rest.

With a swirl, I swim through the dark water and shake the black droplets free as I creep onto dry banks. Then I am running up the valley, until I am at the top of the ridge, looking out across the fells. Nothing is around me but grass, rock, air, and gloom.

I run. But I cannot outrun the images haunting me.

The night I killed those men, I didn't know they had faces.

They were ghosts to me, mere placeholders for the thing I hated.

They have faces now.

I see their eyes every time I close mine. In my sleep, when I try to tear them out of my memory, I cannot.

They stare and they stare and they stare.

They do not stop, so I cannot sleep.

I run on, and the wind causes tears to stream down my face. The wind is screaming at me—or is it the men whose features I now remember in perfect detail?

I do not understand why—I did not see their eyes before now.

In the moment before I kill, I don't see faces. I see the secrets in souls.

I have long been able to see what others cannot. I do not know how or why I was given this sight, but I have always had it.

It has been a misery to see what others are blind to. It is a curse to look at a man and see his lies, to see the shadow of his true soul on his face, and to recognize that he does not mean what he speaks.

I have always hated the lies that people wrap themselves in. It is the one thing I can remember clearly about myself before Mother found me.

It is my curse of sight which birthed the anger, which in turn bred a beast.

I shake my head, trying to clear my mind, but the motion avails nothing. If Mother were here, she would tell me that I am not a beast. Or, if I am, that all should be like me. But she is not here to silence the screams rattling through my memory.

She is hunting today. She doesn't usually hunt after I kill. She stays with me and soothes my doubt, smothering my fears until I remember that I am justified in my wrath.

But she is gone today, and there are no reassurances to silence the screams in my memory. The absence of her dark counsel makes me almost ill.

I am hunting today too, but I do not know what I am looking for. I only know that I must hurry.

Clouds cover the sky, dulling the moon's glare to a glimmer so I can roam the land I am afraid of. But the sky is lightening. Black turns to grey. Dawn is coming, and with it silver clouds that illuminate the fells.

The sun will be coming up soon: that dreaded light. But it is not this that makes me run.

I wander still further from my refuge and wonder why. I should want to miss the rising of the dawn; I always want to. And yet I keep pressing on, away from my cave. There is something else —unnamed and unknown—that I hurry for.

What is it? What is it? The thought forms a drumbeat to the melody of the screams in my head.

I run until I am on the edge of the sea, atop the cliffs that the Frisians use as a lookout.

The fools have almost entirely abandoned it. Why should they guard their shores when they are being destroyed from the inside out? Brought down by their own sin, righteously judged and subsequently purged.

The enemy invasion came from the inside . . . and it's not over.

I look down at the chalk cliffs beneath me, at the arms of rock that reach out across the pale beach like weak and grasping fingers, but I gain no satisfaction from this empty shore. I should. I know I should. I have broken the backs of these people.

Still, I look, and I'm empty.

I track the flight of a curlew wheeling overhead, a pale shadow across a paling sky. It dives into the cloud-mass that crouches over the horizon, a white arrow.

It is completely free.

I long to tear it from the sky.

But I cannot reach the clouds; I crawl on the ground. And even if I could reach up into the sky, it is home to the thing I most fear—the light.

So I stand on the edge of a bluff, a lonely figurehead on a lonely promontory, surveying a domain that I do not own and that has no place for me.

I grit my teeth and repeat what my mother has told me in the past: what I know to be true.

They deserve to die. The truth must be defended and protected from the cowards that would try to corrupt it. *You are protecting yourself and those that will come after you. You are making this world a safer place for people like you by purging such bigotry from the face of the earth.*

I look out across the silver ways of sea and sky, both of them as cold as the swords that have no ability to pierce me. Sometime in the past few weeks, the Frisians must have sent ships across this hungry space, ships engulfed in fire—funeral pyres to destroy the vestiges of the bodies I left behind.

All the faces parade across my mind—they are burned to cinder now, ashes swallowed by water.

They should be forgotten.

Why can I not forget?

I freeze as my gaze snags on a distant shape, and my heart stutters. There is a ship on the horizon.

For one terrible moment, I feel myself caught in my dreams, and I think it is one of the funeral ships coming back to haunt me.

But as it draws closer, my breathing slows and my vision clears when I see there is no smoke, no fire. It is just a ship; it isn't a ghost.

I start to turn away, but somehow I am riveted there on the cliff top. Something whispers to me that this ship is what I've been hunting for.

I stand there—trapped between fear and curiosity. I sink to my knees. The grass swallows me and shields me from view, while still allowing me to see.

The dawn and the ship come ever on. As the vessel grows closer, so does my strange sense of anticipation, growing to an almost unbearable height. My heart flaps and flutters in my chest like a fish pulled from the water and caught beneath a hungry claw.

The small ship is close enough for me to glimpse a figure on the deck now. It is a single man.

He lifts his head to study the anchorage before him: a bay ringed by a narrow beach—grey rather than white in the dim daybreak—and, beyond the dunes, sheer chalk cliffs with rocky outcroppings jutting out onto the beach at irregular points like fingers clawing at the sand.

The man raises his head to the cliff tops and, for one moment, I think he looks right at me. He cannot be looking at me, and yet, all the same, I feel the force of him, even from so far away.

Movement distracts me. To my right is a narrow channel

between two walls of rock, a small and sandy path leading up to the cliffs. A man has appeared on the path, heading towards the beach: a small man who must have been all wiry muscle and sinew in his youth, but who is now turning brittle with age. His face is like leather and scored with lines, but those eyes—only half hidden beneath grey brows like gorse bushes—are as bright and sharp as twin blades.

It is the Watcher.

I crouch down amongst the grass, hissing and flinching at his presence.

I do not want to admit it, but the Watcher is different from the rest of the men in this region. The Hall is full of empty men, full of false pride, fear, and cool cruelty. They hide behind large words and bright shields, but they are as false as fool's gold.

The Watcher's presence does not feel false, and he has no words to hide behind—he is as solid and real as the cliffs, as unafraid to live amongst the wild emptiness of the land as one of the birds that I cannot harm.

Most of the people of Trollhattan do not dare to leave their walls anymore, and if they do, they go together—not alone.

This Watcher is an insult to the havoc I have wrought on the enemy. Despite the carnage amongst his people, he simply goes on patrolling the seaside. He is a boil that should be lanced.

I wonder why Mother has not killed him; she ought to. But I do not ask, because if I did, I know she would ask me why I haven't done it myself, and I don't know how I would answer her —I cannot even answer the question myself.

I could kill him right now, rush at him from the rocks.

But I only hide. My uneasiness makes me unhappy with myself, and I bury the feeling in hatred.

This place used to be mine. The fells and the dunes and all their emptiness belonged to me.

This intruder came two months ago—a few days after my first attack. He left their little hiding hole—their precious Schrawynghop—to live in the rocky warrens of the sea cliffs, watching the ocean, and watching for me.

This one does not fear me; he only hates me—and that too makes him different from the men of the Hall. It is their fear that makes them easy to destroy. Beneath their loathing for me, they are frightened, and that makes them vulnerable.

The Watcher's lack of fear makes him stronger.

Worse, it makes me weaker, and I do not know why.

Movement drags my gaze back to the water. The figure on the little ship drops an anchor with a splash, then jumps from the prow and into the sea, surging towards the shore in great bounds.

I pull in my breath. He is gilded in silver spray—silver around a golden man, for I can see his hair shining even in the dull light—and it is not only his hair that is shining. All of him shines. Even from here, I can sense his presence, and it pins me to the rocks as if I am an insect, a bit of lichen.

I am something barely alive before something terribly, horribly alive.

The Watcher is coming towards the stranger, leaping nimbly across the shale, little more than a shadow in the early morning glimmer, and he stops several spear-lengths away from the stranger, at the cusp of a soft slope of sand.

For years now, I have possessed the eyesight and hearing of a creature, far sharper than that of mere mortals, so their voices—large and clear—carry to me in the stillness, even above the sound of the waves.

The newcomer puts a fist to his heart and bows to the Watcher. He speaks, with a voice like daybreak—a silent invisible force that pushes away the comfort of my shadows as inexorably as the sun.

"I am Beowulf, prince of Heofon. I have received the letter from King Hrothgar asking me to come and free Frisia from the monster known as Grendel, and so I have come."

I nearly fall from my perch. I do not know whether to be

alarmed or to laugh. One man has come to kill me when sixty could not?

But the men keep talking, not waiting for my spinning thoughts to steady.

The Watcher folds his arms. "I know who you are. Hail, Beowulf. It's been a long time. Do you truly not remember me?"

Memory flashes across the stranger's face and then gladness—a gladness like nothing I have ever seen, let alone felt.

"Auschere!" He bounds forward and takes the Watcher by the arms. "Forgive me for not recognizing you right away. Of course I remember you!"

The Watcher's teeth flash; his face crinkles and folds like old paper. "And I remember you, Beowulf, and have thought of you many times: the boy so eager to right wrongs and to defend the oppressed. So eager I sometimes feared you left your brains behind, so anxious you were to lead with your heart."

The Stranger—Beowulf—throws back his head and laughs, and something inside me unravels at the sound. I have heard laughter from the people of the Hall, but it is nothing like this man's laughter. Their happiness is as hollow as my mother's cave compared to his invasive, expansive joy.

He throws his arms around the old man and they embrace, clasping one another close.

I watch, frozen by their delight. Hating them, unable to look away.

They break apart and Auschere wipes his eyes. "It is good that you remember me, Beowulf."

Beowulf squeezes his shoulders. "It's been too long, Auschere. I have missed your counsel. I learned more about serving the Almighty in a few months with you than I did from any other man."

I hiss and cringe. The air seems to grow brighter around me at that dreaded name.

I know the name of the one called the Almighty. A terrible and taxing god, demanding the complete submission of his servants, the surrender of all that they are, so that they might become shadows of him—but never sufficient, always sent back to him, begging, for an unattainable holiness, so harsh, so bleak, it is a kind of living death.

He is the sum of all I fear and resent. He is the epitome and the source of the judgment against me that I have vowed to destroy.

If I could destroy him, I would.

But I cannot—not even Mother can. There is the hope, and the story, that one day, the Dark Father will. In the meantime, I can only destroy the people that claim to follow him. Those proud, disgusting people who think they are better than me.

Beowulf's next words drag my attention back to the beach. "But tell me, Auschere, what is one of King Hrothgar's oldest counselors doing patrolling the shore?"

Auschere's face becomes shadowed as he looks away from Beowulf. "I have not lived amongst my people for some time. I live in these cliffs: the last watcher on the shores of Frisia."

Beowulf is astounded. "You watch alone?"

"There used to be others on the cliffs . . . but over time it has been deemed unnecessary." Auschere glances over his shoulder, and I shrink into my hiding place. "The people believed themselves to be impenetrable. Trollhattan's greatness made us proud. And now look what that has brought upon our heads."

They do not speak for a moment—how dare they grieve men who do not deserve to be mourned?—and then Auschere moves past Beowulf to the ship anchored in the bay. "You travel alone now? But where is Breca?"

Beowulf does not speak at first, and when he does, his voice is so soft I have to strain to hear. "Breca is dead. He has been gone these six months. He was taken by a dragon in the north."

Auschere's head dips to his chest. "I am truly sorry."

Beowulf glances over his shoulder, towards the sea, as if he too is looking for something. "He could have wished for nothing better for his end. He took the dragon down before he perished from his wounds."

Auschere puts a hand on Beowulf's shoulder. "I know he is in the Almighty's Hall now, rejoicing, free, at rest from the fight."

"Yes," Beowulf says simply, and he shuts his mouth up tight.

Auschere cocks his head. "In all your court, and all your land, not one man would sail with you and fight by your side?" He is surprised.

I am surprised too. Even I can tell that Beowulf is a king among mortals. Humans would admire someone like him, wouldn't they? Surely dozens would be eager to follow such a person.

"It is only me," Beowulf answers simply.

"Six months you have sought and killed the Almighty's enemies by yourself as a beast hunter." Auschere studies Beowulf. His next words are not a question. "It is hard for you to fight alone."

"I am not alone," Beowulf says, rousing himself as if from a stupor. "The Almighty is with me wherever I go." He smiles at Auschere. "And I am more than ready to confront this monster. The Almighty has promised me that He will deliver Grendel into my hands and free you from its oppression."

A beetle scuttles over my hand. Without taking my eyes from the figures on the beach, I turn my hand over and crush it on the rock beneath me, squishing out its life.

Just try it, I think, but my heart is racing as I look at the man that seems more like a giant. Everything about him is large —from his frame to his feelings. He seems to fill up the sky. Or perhaps he is a bit of the sky coming down to earth, for his mere existence smothers me. While Auschere's soul is as cold and unyielding as ice, Beowulf's is bright and explosive, as weightless as the light I dread.

"Tell me how you think these attacks came about," says Beowulf.

Auschere folds his arms. "There is a stranger in our courts. A man calling himself Unferth Far-Traveler. He has become a powerful voice in Trollhattan. It is with his coming that some began to burn sacrifices to the Dragon Below."

My heart thuds at the mention of my father's name—the words curl like unseen smoke when it is spoken aloud. For a moment I think the beach has grown darker, covering me in loving shadow, and I am grateful, and afraid. The feeling that I am being watched and cared for by the great dragon oozes over me.

"I warned the king that if we worshiped monsters, monsters would come and claim their sacrifices. I called for Unferth to be cast out. I called for the Dragon's shrine to be taken down, for the monster to be tracked to its den. But the king did not listen. So the Almighty bade me to leave, so that my absence might be a testimony against the settlement. Then the Almighty reminded me of you and brought it into my heart to whisper your name to Hrothgar." Auschere looks at the Stranger. "The Almighty promised me that Trollhattan will be free again someday. And now He has sent you."

Beowulf smiles a little, but his voice is sad. "And King Hrothgar was eager for me to come?"

Auschere hitches a shoulder. "He is open to everything and commits to nothing. He at least insisted upon the shrine being kept outside Trollhattan's walls, but he seems to forget that while our walls might not be desecrated, every soul that burns at the shrine dooms itself. You and I both know that there has long been a shadow in Hrothgar that has never been tended by the light. After the third attack, when the last of the bodies were taken away, Hrothgar declared that no one else should return to the Hall, but he takes no other position. He does not lead his people to repent; he does not call for the monster to be hunted down in its den."

Auschere sighs. "His mind is tormented because he has never allowed the Almighty to come in and put it in order. You and I both know that when we do not allow the Almighty to erect the walls of His truth around our thoughts, our minds devour us, and then, fools that we are, we blame the Almighty for our pain, and we choose to live in the chaos, instead of seeking freedom in Him."

His words hit me like hot pebbles—maddening and unexpected taunts.

He is just like all the rest: judging me, mocking a torment that he has never known, understanding nothing, believing himself to be above me. He thinks he is so high above me. He dismisses me as a monster.

If Beowulf were not standing there, I would run down to the beach and kill him right now, tear him into shreds so small, even the birds could not find the pieces.

But I am afraid to go near that golden stranger, so I crush the rock beneath my hands until it turns into grit.

Auschere—the pompous piece of garbage—is still talking. "It is my hope that Hrothgar will listen to you, since he has not listened to me. Sometimes, an old friend's voice becomes so familiar, a man pays little heed to it." He raised his head and looked at Beowulf. "But an outsider who judges: that is someone who cannot be ignored so easily."

Beowulf's face is grave. "It's time to finish this, my friend."

His next words strike me like a blade. And this blow does penetrate me, as no other blow has ever done before.

"I swear, by tonight, this creature's hold upon your people will be broken."

Auschere is smiling in anticipation—he can't wait for me to be killed, to be destroyed. "Come with me then, and allow me to present you to the king."

They move as one across the beach and to one of the rocky paths that slopes up towards the cliff tops.

They pass close to me and, from my vantage point, I can see them, though they cannot see me.

I have seen my fill of Auschere, but the Stranger holds my gaze. I am unable to tear myself away, though my heart drops into the earth at my feet when I look at him.

"It is close by," Beowulf says, stopping suddenly and looking around. "The monster."

My insides shrivel. I cannot move.

"Yes," says Auschere, stopping too. "Should we hunt it now?"

There is no sound but the seagulls. I do not even hear my own breath.

"No," says Beowulf. "Time enough for that."

They move on, out of sight, leaving me splayed amongst the rocks, as wretched as a piece of flotsam, unable to see anything but Beowulf, even when he is gone.

It is not his face that makes my breath catch in my chest—I have seen plenty of handsome men, and my dreams tell me I have even killed some of them. My gaze was snagged by his soul—it shone around him in a nimbus as bright as the dreaded sun. My first thought, that he shone as bright as gold, was not wrong.

But this is gold without impurity.

The sky is still dim, but the sun walked up the beach and it blinded me.

A kind of miserable horror like I have never known sweeps over me.

Walking past me is my ending.

I know now that this is what I was looking for.

And I wish I had never seen it.

3

I should go back to the cave—tell Mother what has come to our shores.

But if I do, I will miss my chance to hear this killer's plans. What does he intend for me? I must know. My skin prickles. My mother has told me I am undefeatable, but he is so confident. . . .

Is there a blade in this world that can cut something as powerful as me? Is there some secret from beyond these shores that can crush me? Is death truly coming for me after all, instead of for my enemies?

I must know.

So I follow.

But I am not foolish enough to follow across land.

I hurry to a certain boulder, dropping onto my stomach and sliding into an aperture so small it hurts me to squeeze through it. Or perhaps it is only my heart pounding that causes the pain.

When people first settled on these shores, they discovered dragon tunnels beneath the moors and expanded them. They used these warrens to hide from pirates. But that is so far in the past it has been forgotten by everyone but Mother, who in turn showed them to me.

It is a spider's web, an endless maze. Dips and curves so

narrow I must slither, sudden chasms and secret chambers that appear so abruptly, a person might fall if they hadn't been warned beforehand.

The tunnel I travel through suddenly ends, plunging down into darkness. I half slide into a long, narrow space that smells of dirt and dead beetles. I have traveled beyond stone and am now buried beneath deep, dank earth. The only illumination is pale blue lichen that casts a dim glow.

I hurry for half an hour before I pause at a certain place.

The tunnel widens here, a swollen space perhaps two spears across. The tunnel feels deeper and blacker and thicker here than at any other point.

In this maze beneath the earth, this distended trench is almost spacious. It is here for a purpose, for above this spot is a copse of trees, less than a quarter of a mile outside the walls of Trollhattan. And in this copse . . . is a shrine.

I crouch, inhaling deeply of the stink and the grime and the hissing of voices—as sibilant and soft as snakes. Dark spirits inhabit this place, seeping into the ground and into the air. They are as at home as I am, hidden from the light amidst the shadows of the trees, soaking up darkness from the tunnels below.

I have seen the copse at a distance, dark and feathery in the moonlight, but have never entered it. It is enough to know it is here, welcoming me.

A shrine to the Dragon Below—my master, the person I am told is my father.

When they built this shrine, the fools all but invited me into their midst—and yet they wonder why I come. They have made a sacrifice to my father, and so he has sent me to cleanse them of their pride.

I rest a moment in the little swell of earth. This place of breathless profanity swaddles me and surrounds me like a womb.

It is not peace—I am never at peace—but it is a kind of black rest, like being unconscious. My mind floats in a dark and empty sea.

Then, suddenly, something pierces my rest. A presence.

It is almost like a scent, so strong it overwhelms the dank smell of earth for a moment. It is as sharp as salt, as sweet as the wretched flowers humans are so fond of, as strong as iron.

It's him. The Stranger.

He is standing right above me.

A snarl erupts from me and I drop onto my heels, creating distance between us. My fingers dig into the dirt wall behind me. I stare up at the thin ceiling of earth that forms a shield between us.

Why am I hiding? He can't see me or reach me. There is no cause to be afraid.

But I am afraid.

He has halted in the copse. He is looking at the shrine. I can feel his abhorrence for everything this place is, everything it represents, everything that I am. The place that is my refuge is the thing he means to destroy.

I hiss and cringe and hate him with everything in me, with all my years of bitter pain and emptiness gathering into a storm of loathing.

For one brief moment, our two hatreds reach out to one another and clash like drawn swords.

I cannot see or touch him—nor he me—and yet we are fighting. I can feel his grasp upon me as clearly as if his hands were on my neck, and I can feel his heart, huge and strong and hideously loud, beating against my resolve.

Our spirits lock together in a sudden savage conflict, shoving, sensing, straining—and then we fall apart, and I am gasping for breath.

As clearly as I knew he was there, I know, just as clearly, that he has moved away.

I pull at my hood, not understanding why I feel as if I am choking. My robe and hood have always felt comfortable until now. My garments are more like scales than fabric, as thin as paper and as strong as armor. When I first took on the mantle of what I am, my mother crafted this covering to protect me. Its enchantment makes me powerful, shields me from the torment and shame that once plagued me. It is my robe that makes my mind strong against the hateful attacks of mortals, my body impervious to iron.

But when Beowulf stood above me, for one brief moment, my cowl did not feel like a helmet; it felt like a noose.

It is some moments before I can breathe well enough to go on. I proceed down the tunnel, choosing a far more winding route than the one Beowulf and Auschere are using as they cut across the fells. I do not want to stand beneath Beowulf again. At least—not now. Not yet.

My shoulders brush the narrow walls of the tunnel, pebbles scrunch beneath me, my claws catch on bits of roots as I hold out my arms to steady myself.

Above me, Beowulf and the Watcher must be walking across rolling grass and soft hillocks, the horizon ahead broken by a tall, proud structure. The walls of the great settlement of Schrawynghop, stern upright walls of felled trees, stare down at them like sentinels, with stone towers at each corner.

The watchmen must have spotted the travelers, for I hear a horn, a low echoing call. The great wooden gates are being opened for the Stranger to usher him into the hard-packed compound of the settlement.

He is an honored guest, while I am left to crawl beneath Trollhattan like an unwanted spider.

My heart curdles, and bile rises in my throat, thick and foul. Those gates should open for me—not this stranger. I deserve to be counted as an equal—not this foreigner.

Instead, I must force my way in.

I suddenly hear footsteps and voices above me, and I sneer. They don't know I have already been in the heart of their precious town for months, able to listen to them any time I choose because of these tunnels.

Above me, this stranger, Beowulf, will be seeing Trollhattan—and what I have done to it.

In the great compound of Schrawynghop, towards the eastern wall, there is a swell of land, a tier of terraced earth, with stone steps leading up its slopes to a wide threshold between two stone pillars.

Trollhattan—the crown of the settlement—is now deserted. They did not bother to replace the doors I destroyed. The windows are dark and jagged around the edges—stumps of their former latticework line the edges of each sill like broken teeth. Its very gables seem to sag, like a broken back over a broken heart.

The Watcher said that Beowulf had been here before—before my time—but this gold stranger will not see the Hall he used to know, thanks to me. It has changed.

I laugh to myself and follow them, three feet below, unseen, but felt.

They are moving away from Trollhattan, towards a structure some distance away, amongst the common buildings. This is where the attendants of the royal family live and work, in various halls, smithies, bakehouses, and the like.

It is not usually the place where a king would receive guests.

I can feel my grin spread across my face, and it is feral.

I have never been inside this building, but I have glimpsed it in the dark when I have pillaged Trollhattan. It is a much smaller hall than Trollhattan, and far less grand. It will be close-packed now, since the smoke from the braziers has no place to disperse, filling the room with choking fumes and fire fog. There will be little place for feasting—though the Frisians have no cause to feast anymore, thanks to me.

As I move through the tunnel, I feel the space above me change—I am beneath the narrow hall. I can hear the sudden rise of voices fall silent as a door opens.

Beowulf has been brought to the Frisian court.

Auschere's voice breaks the pause. "King Hrothgar. I present Beowulf prince of Heofon."

There is a stirring in the crowd as Beowulf's name whisks through the room, the way a new log might rekindle a dying fire.

I hear the heavy tread of feet, and I follow it. I move with Beowulf—but beneath him—to the far end of the room, where the wretched Hrothgar will sit on his wretchedly temporary throne.

My animal ears detect the clink of armor. Beowulf is kneeling, and then he speaks in his glad and golden voice that makes me sink, slowly, to the ground.

"It is good to see you again, King Hrothgar."

Hrothgar does not answer for several moments.

The king has changed much since I first attacked. Once, he was prouder than all the men of Trollhattan put together, with a confident strength beneath it.

But the stronger a man, the more his humiliation consumes him when he falls. Hrothgar is breaking, and I glory in seeing it. He looks old now—far older than his years—and as frail as a bit of paper caught in a fire—crumpling and curling at the edges, on the brink of disappearing altogether.

I cannot wait for him to disappear.

"You have grown much since I saw you last, young Beowulf." Hrothgar's voice is a thread, so close to being cut.

"And yet I remember much of you and your court, great king," Beowulf answers.

"What do you remember?" Hrothgar whispers.

"I remember an advisor who taught me tricks to keep my sword sharp and my heart aflame for the Almighty. I remember a noble king who drew me to his side, as if I were a son. I remember a gracious queen, who gave me great gifts. I remember a people living and working and laughing: at peace, secure, unchained." Beowulf pauses. "I would see Schrawynghop that way again."

"My queen died," Hrothgar murmurs into the hushed silence. "Five years past, we marched against the Dragon Below. We drove him from his lair, but much was lost—including my wife. There is a cost in fighting evil, Beowulf. And sometimes it is too great."

Beowulf's answer is husky. "I am sorry for your loss, my king. But it is a cost I am willing to pay. I received your letter asking me to bring my experience and my sword to your court to address the troubles that have beset you. And now I have come."

Hrothgar sighs. "I greet you, Beowulf. I regret that you have come amongst us again at our darkest hour." He chokes on his words and begins to cough, racked by a sudden spasm. "And I also regret sending the letter you speak of—for I have now forbade any warrior on these shores from confronting Grendel, for their own sakes. Such an effort is futile."

I feel as much as hear the sudden ripple of pained whispers passing through the crowd, and satisfaction ignites inside me. At last, some of them know the truth: their king is not now suited for the throne.

Beowulf raises his voice, speaking above the excited buzzing of the crowd. "King Hrothgar, people of Frisia. I know it was the Almighty himself that prompted the wise Auschere to remember my name, which prompted you to send for me. I have come willingly, to remind you of the Almighty's love and mercy. I seek only your permission to set you free."

A low murmur runs through the crowd.

Hrothgar's words are rough and blurred with grief and sleeplessness. "Thirty of our best warriors have been taken by the waves; many boats have been set aflame and pushed from our sands. Our hall has been desecrated three times with the spilled blood of our very best." He sighs. "Dear Beowulf, there are many stories of your skill: of the hamlets you have freed from fireworms, the castles you have purged of ghosts. I can see that the Almighty has blessed you beyond other men with the strength to kill creatures born beneath the earth. But I fear that this monster is beyond even your skill."

Beowulf's tone changes, as if he is smiling, and I shrivel inwardly at the memory of that smile. "Do not fear for me, my king. I know the Almighty will deliver this creature into my hands. I promise you that it will be killed, even if I must die to see this accomplished. And if I am killed in accomplishing it, then so be it. Fate goes as fate must."

Hrothgar is silent again for a long, long time.

I shift, pebbles crunching beneath me.

Beowulf speaks again, with the voice of someone trying to lure a tired hunting dog to its feet to hunt once more.

"King Hrothgar. I know your history. I have heard many stories of how you kept the Dragon Below and his creatures at bay, of your great hunts and mighty victories." His voice deepens. "Do you not remember?"

"I remember," Hrothgar rasps. "I remember how it once was." His words tangle with dark memories, crack on the point of tears. "I . . . remember *her*."

There is the rustle of leather and silk. Hrothgar is rocking back and forth on his throne, like a keening mourner.

I smile. He has forgotten where he is, and wears his grief for all to see. It pleases me to imagine his shame increasing, for he has brought ruin upon his head.

But my satisfaction is short-lived.

His people may be ashamed of him. Auschere may be disappointed in him. I might despise him.

But Beowulf will not complete Hrothgar's dismissal. His voice is like a pair of open hands, reaching out to him. His words are hard, but there is something behind them that I do not know or understand.

It is as if he is not seeing Hrothgar as he was, or is, but rather what he could be.

"Remember, King Hrothgar," Beowulf whispers. "Before it is too late."

I sense Hrothgar is considering Beowulf's urgings, tasting them on his tongue and inhaling suddenly, as if steeling himself to answer the call.

I lean forward, as tense as the room above me.

The moment is broken by the crack of a door being thrown open and then the bang of it shutting again.

"Forgive me for my lateness, Your Highness."

I recognize this new voice. It is Unferth, the court challenger, the man Auschere despises, and thus a man I watch—for Unferth is as I once was, trapped between nothing and greatness, weakness and power, striving for the approval of a people that frustrate him.

I was like this when Mother found me and pulled me out of my struggle and into my true purpose. It was through her power that I finally took on the true form of the bitterness raging inside of me.

I have watched Unferth, and I have wondered if he will become an ally.

I see him in my mind's eye, young, and always clad in dragon scarlet, with close-cropped hair the color of honey and ash, and a voice like licking flames, walking stiff and erect. As court challenger, it is his duty to make visitors defend their reputation, and he plays his part well. Unferth speaks for the court, and he reveals the truth by provoking it from those around him, pointing out the flaws and failures in people or plans. While the men of Trollhattan are too afraid to use their swords, Unferth is fearless in using his tongue. He is like a dog nipping at the heels of sheep, herding them where he wants them to go, spotting the flaws and the weaklings, and then barking the harsh truth for everyone to hear.

He walks across the hall now, and his voice is perfectly respectful, but his words are lazy at their edges. He is a man well satisfied with his position in the court and his relation to the king. "I was much occupied with interceding for the people this morning. I had business to attend to in the copse."

I hear Auschere make a little suppressed snarl in the back of his throat.

Beowulf answers Unferth, in a voice like polished steel. "It is you who serve as priest at the pagan shrine I glimpsed under the hawthorn tree, then?"

There is a pause. They must be looking at one another.

Unferth does not trouble to hide his disdain. "And you are the great Beowulf! The tattle in the town is that you are the savior from over the seas who has come to save us all."

"You confuse me with the one I serve," Beowulf retorts. "The Almighty."

Hrothgar interjects then, hope and hopelessness mixed together. "Lord Beowulf proposes that he shall rid us of Grendel's attacks."

I can almost see Unferth cocking his head. "Only you, Beowulf? You alone?" He is sneering outright. "Isn't there usually another with you? What has become of your companion?"

For the second time that day, I hear Beowulf's voice die a little; memories of this person are his weakness. I wonder how I can exploit it.

"Breca perished with honor during a beast hunt," says Beowulf.

"Such a shame," Unferth says coolly. "But not surprising, considering your legendary—or should I say lunatic?—exploits." He raises his voice. "You and your shield-bearer were infamous for your irresponsibility. No matter how foolish the risk or how childish the dare, you were both obsessed, never backing down. Have you all forgotten this man's lunacy? Like the story of your swimming match in the open sea—where you risked the deep for three nights, for the sheer vanity of taunting sea beasts by holding on to their fins and riding them across the waves? What did that prove, Beowulf? What good did it do anyone? Are you here to perform an equally useless deed of daring that helps no one?"

Beowulf's voice is like a drawn sword. "It is true: Breca and I challenged one another to risk our lives in great feats. Breca understood that one does not always need a logical reason to challenge fate: the glory of it, the delight of strength against strength, is enough."

"No logical reason," Unferth repeats. "Your own words, not mine! It seems to me, beast hunter, that you care for nothing but gaining accolades. You claim you seek such foolhardy risks in the name of your god's glory, but it could also seem that you are merely seeking your own fame. Have you come to take advantage of our hardships for your own amusement?"

Beowulf is calm, refusing to rise to Unferth's bait. "It has always been my life's purpose—as it was Breca's—to free the land of anything that would raise itself against the Almighty—including valuing my own safety too highly." Beowulf's voice moves, as if he is turning towards the throne. "Unferth speaks of my deeds. So. Let my deeds speak for themselves. With the Almighty's strength, I have slain dozens of monsters and freed many hamlets, and I swear to do so here."

"*You* have slain?" Unferth repeats, amused. "Only you, Beowulf? You had help in times gone by."

"I have slain beasts since Breca," Beowulf murmurs.

"The men of this hall have slain beasts, too," Unferth snaps. "Do you think you are the only man on earth brave enough to confront this Grendel? You value yourself too highly! Thirty men have fallen before its claws. Do you really claim to believe that one man can do what thirty could not?"

Beowulf is unperturbed. "The Almighty has revealed to me that it is so."

Unferth is circling Beowulf. I hear the scuff of his shoes. "So. In addition to being stronger than the Frisians, you also have a greater communication with the gods than we do. Is that what you claim, Beowulf?"

That angers Beowulf. "There is only one God. The Almighty."

"You have not answered my question," Unferth replies silkily.

"Yes, with the Almighty's help, I will kill Grendel."

I press my claws to my chest, holding my life's thread within my ribcage as if it might suddenly spill out on the ground, like the contents of a spilled cup—for his words turn my stomach to water.

My heart beats so hard I can barely hear Unferth's next words.

"I see. Well then. Let us suppose that you succeed. What if the monster has friends that are angered by its death, and the attacks only become worse? I trust that the great Hrothgar has not forgotten my advice. The creature never comes further than the Hall: the settlement has remained safe. Let it have what it wants. Let it be appeased."

I can hear Beowulf stepping towards Hrothgar, anxious and eager. "What guarantee do you have that the monster will remain satisfied? And even if it never ventured beyond Trollhattan, there is more at stake here than mere safety. This monster has dared to raise its head against children of the Almighty. It has challenged you, and it mocks you while desecrating your home. Your honor is worth fighting for, just as much as your lives."

Hrothgar does not respond to Beowulf's rally. I do not even hear the rustle of fabric to indicate restless movement. He is as still and lifeless as his throne.

"It's easy enough for you to urge people who are not your own to risk their lives," Unferth flings back at Beowulf. "Do you hear him, Frisians? How quickly he dismisses the thirty warriors slain by the beast! Such a sacrifice is nothing to him."

"You accuse me of not caring for the death of these people?" Beowulf asks. His voice is no longer warm—it is like ice. A tremor runs through my entire being at the sound of it. "It is you, Unferth, who have aided in bringing calamity upon this people. Until you tear down your shrine to false gods, there is only so much mercy that can be shown to you. By leaving offerings there, you are inviting the Dragon Below to send torment into your midst."

Unferth draws in a breath. "You are a high-handed guest, Beowulf! You have barely been in our midst for the space of time it takes to raise a drinking horn before you are passing judgment on us!"

"It is the Almighty who judges, and it is He who determines good from evil." Beowulf says sharply. "I do not judge: I only follow the Almighty's rulings." Beowulf addresses the crowd, his words ringing. "Dear Frisians, you have forgotten His love, and so this creature finds it easy enough to attack you."

Unferth pounces. "So are you saying your loving Almighty sent this monster to torment us?"

Beowulf attacks without hesitation. "No, I am saying that the man who lowers his shield ought to expect that he will be hurt."

The tone of the room shifts at that and turns ugly.

I feel a savage satisfaction in his blunder. Extending condolence and offering help was one thing; implying that the calamity that has befallen them is their fault rubs grit in their wounds. Perhaps the people will tear him apart right now. And, if they won't kill him, perhaps they will at least send him on his way, back to his ship and to some other shore.

But Beowulf does not back down. "Let go of your wrongdoing before it is too late! You have nothing to risk now but your pride. What do any of you have to lose by letting me try to free you?"

I hear the whisper running between some of them, and I feel their hardness wane. Some are afraid of the implacable Almighty's judgment. Some do not approve of Unferth, some are ashamed of Hrothgar. But they are all of one accord in one thing: they want to be free of me. And, as Beowulf has said, what do they have to lose?

Perhaps they have nothing to lose, but I do.

My eagerness sinks into disappointment, and a bitter disgust for this gutless people rises to take its place. They are grass moved by whatever wind blows strongest. And Beowulf is strong.

Unferth must sense the changing mood as clearly as I can hear it, for he speaks with a swiftness edged by unease. "Very well, Lord Beowulf. Let us just suppose, for the sake of argument, that we would be better off attempting to rid ourselves of Grendel. Well, why should that task fall to you? A foreigner?"

His voice sharpens at that last word and, with a jolt, I hear an emotion I am well familiar with.

Jealousy.

Unferth, an outsider who has clawed his way into a powerful position in a foreign court, is threatened by Beowulf.

Unferth steps closer to the dais. "Yes, I ask the court. If we do indeed seek a champion, why should we look to a foreigner? And beyond that, why Beowulf? What makes him so special? As our own bard confirms to us every night around our hearth, the greatest stories are built upon fancies. We all know how tales are exaggerated in the telling. Have you brought witnesses that can confirm, for our peace of mind, that you have truly slain demons single-handedly?"

Beowulf does not respond at first. It is then and only then, that something inhuman touches the god-like voice above me. His voice, so alive, seems to die for a moment.

"I come alone, without witnesses."

My mind wings to that name spoken on the beach, Breca, the beast hunter that used to carry Beowulf's shield.

I am lucky that some dragon ate his bones. One beast hunter is already more than I can bear.

Beowulf's voice sharpens now, alive once more, and ready to fight.

"Not all stories are exaggerated in the telling, Unferth. There are stories about you too. The story I have heard of Unferth is that he killed his own brother in a jealous rage."

His words fall like a pebble in a previously unbroken pool; the gasp ripples to the corners of the room. I hear Unferth choke, as if someone has plunged a knife into him.

Beowulf's words are a blade that he pushes deeper. "How a man of such dishonor, so obviously lacking in wisdom or restraint, could become an advisor, is a mystery. It is clear enough why you must try your luck in a foreign court and not your own."

At that, Unferth flares up like a poked fire. "You dare to challenge me?"

Hrothgar finally intervenes, his words coming between the two men like an outstretched arm.

"Lord Beowulf. Trollhattan welcomes all. We pride ourselves

on our acceptance of all people, without judgment. You will please remember that you yourself have been received with courtesy, and you will extend that courtesy to the long-time dwellers of our court. Unferth has earned his place among us."

Unferth gives a little huff of gratification.

Beowulf sounds impatient. He is tired of talking. "If this court will not take me at my word, then let my claims be put to the test, King Hrothgar. Your sacrifices will avail you nothing, Unferth. The monster you call Grendel will be delivered into my hands. And to prove to you that this will happen through the power of the Almighty . . ."

Slowly and deliberately, a sword is drawn, and the sound of his blade freeing itself from his sheath is echoed by the slight hiss escaping Unferth. "King Hrothgar, please accept my sword until the morrow. When dawn comes, I will come and reclaim it. But I shall face the beast unarmed and grapple with it, hand to hand."

There is a gasp of shock and admiration from the crowd. They are desperate, on the cusp of being consumed, and yet they are eager at this new novelty: more fascinated by the idea of a thrilling battle than a possible freedom.

Through my own terror and outrage at Beowulf's declaration, disgust for the people twists through my gut at their shifting moods.

Their moods are as changeable as Hrothgar's, for I can hear that, for the moment, he wants to believe, though he is not convinced.

"As you say, Lord Beowulf. May the Almighty favor you more than he has us."

"My king," Unferth interjects silkily. "I repeat, to cease sacrifices now to the Dragon Below is premature." His voice pricks like a torturer probing a weak spot. "Your Highness knows what can happen when the Dragon is aroused."

The entire room inhales. Unferth has swiped the scab off Hrothgar's wound, unafraid to make him bleed.

"Have we not lost enough already?" Unferth whispers.

"Enough." Hrothgar plants his fists on the arms of his throne with a dull thump. He is angry, done, tired beyond all resting. "If Beowulf's heart is set on confronting this hell-beast, I shall not dissuade him. There is a simple way to discern the path forward. Make your sacrifice, Unferth. If Beowulf is unsuccessful in killing the monster, we shall know that the Dragon Below is not appeased and requires more blood from us. But if Beowulf kills the beast, then we shall know that we have displeased the Almighty and he has sent judgment upon us as well as mercy."

Beowulf is content with this, as placid as a still sea. "Thank you, King Hrothgar."

Unferth is not as pleased as Beowulf. "As you say, my King."

I hear footsteps, and then Auschere, who has been silent through all this, finally speaks, his voice radiating disapproval of everyone and everything under the hall's roof.

"Allow me to escort you to Trollhattan, Lord Beowulf." His words are a bold blow, aimed at Hrothgar. "That is where the beast always goes, so what better place to meet it tonight?"

There is another reaction from the crowd. They are shocked. They expect Hrothgar to punish Auschere for defying his orders to enter Trollhattan without express permission.

But Hrothgar does not rebuke him. He must have signaled to someone, for I hear the men of the hall dispersing and Beowulf is suddenly not there. The hall is seemingly empty, but then Hrothgar and Auschere begin to speak, quietly and close together, as if Auschere has come near the throne.

"It is good to see you, Auschere."

Auschere grunts, but his voice softens a little, uncoiling from its tight ball.

"And you, Hrothgar. Though it could be better."

Hrothgar laughs a little, and for a minute, he sounds stronger, younger, almost golden like Beowulf, but not quite. The tarnish comes back, echoing in his dry words. "The same old Auschere—approving of nothing!"

"If you believe that of me, then you have truly listened to lies for too long."

Hrothgar is almost taunting. "But how can you blame me, when my greatest counselor has abandoned me!"

"Do not mock the Almighty, Hrothgar, for it is He who urges me to speak out. Do you think I always wish to be angry with you? I do not—nor does the Almighty."

There is a pause. Hrothgar sounds wistful. "You will stay awhile, old friend?"

"Not until the copse is cleared and the sacrifices stop."

I can hear Hrothgar's frown. "But Lord Beowulf has deigned to grace us with his presence, though he disapproves of the shrine also."

"That is because our tasks are different. He stays here to fight the monster. I stay on the cliffs to remind the people that monsters can be born inside of us, and they must be dealt with."

Hrothgar's fingers drum against wood. "Do you never tire of your speeches, Auschere? Can you not appreciate the position I am in? The shrine is a passing whim, nothing more. But it is brought by Unferth, and he has a popular following. I cannot simply destroy it without losing the support of many. It is easy enough for an old knight to take a hard line, but a ruler's lot is one of compromise."

"So you have led yourself to believe." Auschere's voice moves away from Hrothgar. "When Beowulf kills Grendel, perhaps then the Almighty will soften your heart with gratitude and you will make the one sacrifice that ought to be made—rededicating the Hall, and its people, to the service of the one true God."

"I have told you I would not hesitate to do so."

"Will you? Right now? At this moment?"

Hrothgar does not respond and Auschere lets out a harsh breath. "You delay—then so must I."

Hrothgar sighs. "Your seat is always ready for you, if you change your mind, Auschere. I hope you will."

"You know me well enough to realize that I won't."

"I do," Hrothgar says with a hint of grim laughter. "Well, then, let us hope that Beowulf is successful, so that I can afford to remove the shrine and thus allow an ill-tempered old man to return to his rightful place at my table."

"I have difficulty believing that, when your anger and your pride keep standing between not only you and me—but between the Almighty and your people. Until you cease the practice which has brought your people's downfall, I cannot count myself a man of this hall."

"So be it." Hrothgar is cold once more, ice holding in a dam of emotion. "Go with your hero. He's waiting for you. May your faith preserve you."

"It always has," Auschere replies, with a voice like a sword being sheathed.

They go their separate ways and leave the hall, but I do not follow.

I stay a while longer beneath it, consuming the feelings of doubt and fear that still linger in the room above—letting them feed me.

But it is a pathetic meal, because I am not fighting the Frisians; they no longer dare to face me. No, I will be fighting Beowulf, and there is no panic or uncertainty in him.

Instead, that fear and doubt is in me.

4

I dive deep into the cavern pool, but it cannot wash away what I have heard.

I have always been able to discern what no one else can see. This ability has always been a curse. All my life I have only ever seen the bad in others, and thus have believed that this must make me good. At the very least, it must make me right.

Now I am no longer sure that is true, because when I looked at the Stranger on the beach I knew immediately—with a brutal clarity—that he was better than me.

It is the first time my vision has ever beheld indisputable goodness, and I do not know what to think.

What, then, does that make me? For if the Stranger is good, and he is nothing like me, does that make me wrong?

Does that make me a monster, as the Frisians have always said?

I am haunted by the memory of the Frisians singing that cursed prophecy in their hall before my first attack—the verses that foretell a golden son. It is as if they knew something I did not, as if they are mocking me, even in death. They rise up, specters in my mind, taunting me with those dreadful rhythms.

Even with a moor between us, I can still hear Beowulf's voice ringing in my mind. Diving into my dark pool cannot sponge away the echoes; pressing into the dark cavern cannot hide me from the light that seems to pierce my chest and lodge in my ribs —a shining dagger I cannot pull free.

I swish uneasily back and forth, touching one slick black wall and then the opposite, unable to rest. I feel trapped, and yet I am afraid to swim out into the open.

I, Grendel, am hunted.

And I have beheld good.

I am on the cusp of understanding something. I don't even know what it is: I cringe from knowing. And in my heart, I feel that once I understand this unknown thing, there will be a change in me that I am not sure I can endure.

There is the faint sound of disturbed water, and the pool swells, a black oily chest heaving a sigh as the water is displaced.

I jerk. Press back. I'm afraid it is the Stranger. He has followed me here!

But it is only Mother.

At the sight of her terrible face, I relax. Or I try.

It is not easy.

This bothers me.

All morning I have longed for her presence, her voice, her stream of words that make some sense out of the turmoil in my mind.

I force myself to focus on her, even though she is not looking at me. She is like my reflection in many ways, though taller, broader, more powerful. There are the knobs of horns beneath her hood. Her fangs, unlike mine, are always visible, and her claws twice as long. Her eyes are green, not red: green as poison, and she possesses powers that I still only dream of.

I see that she is distracted and almost as restless as I am. She does not join me on the rock but instead rises slightly out of the water, suspended in a kind of dark, cascading fountain, almost floating. She looms over me and speaks at last. "There is a stranger in the land."

It was not what I expected her to say.

I do not respond; some instinct warns me not to admit that I already know of whom she speaks, that I left the cave without her knowledge.

"I have heard his name before. It is a curse among my children, for he has cut down many of your brothers and sisters. They call him Beowulf." She breaks off, overcome with anger, and for a moment gives herself over to cursing, almost babbling in her wrath.

I press back, for she has lost control, and I know from experience that her hatred for our mutual enemies could just as easily turn on me. As I crouch against the rock and watch her whip the pool into a frenzy, droplets striking my face like needles, I too taste Beowulf's name, but I cannot spit it out in curse words as she does. Instead, I hold it on my tongue. I cannot spit it out, but I cannot swallow it either. It simply lodges inside me, like his voice, like his face.

Beowulf. . .

Mother's anger dies down, and she is calm and controlled once more, channeling her anger into calculation.

"All this means is that they grow desperate," she hisses. "This land is growing weaker: their hall is almost ready for the taking. They must turn to foreigners and other lands for help. But it is a false hope—is it not, Grendel?"

I look at her, waiting to be fed an answer, as she has always fed me.

And she does. "This is nothing more than an insult. We will take care of Beowulf, as easily as any other man that has dared to raise a sword against us."

I draw in a quick break of shock. Mother does not cower from his brightness. Can she not see, as I do, that he is no mere man?

Mother speaks on. "I know you grow impatient with these drawn-out attacks. I have been busy on your behalf, considering the final task that will allow you to come into your true power.

And now your father, the Dark Father, has brought a sacrifice to our shores. Beowulf: the perfect prize." She smiles. "The people's one last hope, and a false one. The end is almost here. Once they realize that nothing on earth can help them, they shall surrender and finally recognize you as right."

"I do not understand," I murmur, although I am beginning to. I am simply hoping that I have misunderstood.

Her gaze bores into me, and my heart sinks as she answers. "You must kill Beowulf."

A whimper escapes me, and it startles us both.

A memory flashes through my mind of a time before, perhaps before Mother found me, or a few days after. I am a child again, not a powerful being, and I am terrified and broken and uncertain.

My voice cracks. "Will you not kill him for me, Mother?"

The cavern is silent for a moment, save for my own muffled gulp.

She stares at me, cocking her head. She is not usually puzzled. "You hesitate. You have never before hesitated."

Haven't I? This hesitation feels strangely familiar. Did I once hesitate at the thought of putting out the light?

I cannot remember.

Mother is waiting for an answer. Her eyes begin to burn, and I know she will drag it out of me with her claws if I do not confess.

I swallow. "I went out this morning. I saw them arrive. I saw him."

She studies me. "You did not tell me this right away." Her eyes glint with warning. "What are you hiding from me?"

I try to escape through flattery, burrowing into it like a rat shrinking from prey. "I can hide nothing from you, Mother."

"No, you cannot," Mother agrees, mollified.

My ploy works, and this shocks me. She does not stop to realize that she had no idea what I had done until I confessed it to her.

I can hide things from her.

She is deceived. She is wrong.

Something races through me, hot and swift, so strong I nearly flinch.

It is something like disdain—the kind of disdain I feel for the Frisians—and now I am feeling it towards her.

I am horrified by my own thoughts and feelings, and terrified that she will guess it, so I risk another side of her anger with a different confession.

"I do not think I am strong enough to face him."

Mother towers over me, the pillar of water beneath her churning into a whirlpool, sending waves to the far reaches of the cavern in echoing cracks.

"You fear him? What is this cowardice? This weakness? Have I not taught you to believe that you are powerful? Perfect? All things? There is nothing on earth more powerful than you, save for me and the Dark Father."

I swallow, whispering the words. "The prophecy says . . . a golden son that comes to claim a prize . . ."

Mother grabs me by the arm, her claws drawing blood until I cry out. "Nothing will kill the Dragon Below, do you hear me? Nothing. He is stronger than all mortal strengths put together! There is no truth to that prophecy—it is merely the foolish daydream of wretched humanity. This foreigner is just a man with a sword."

I clutch at my bleeding arm as she lets me go, and I clutch at the same time for another desperate excuse. "But he has killed those like me. You said so yourself!"

The whirlpool checks itself, slowly abates. Water no longer whips my face as Mother's arms still at last. She sinks down, stepping onto the rock to look me in the eye.

"Only a few," she says, very gently. Her mood has changed. She is no longer snarling, but crooning, wrapping me now in her dark whisper. "And they were not like you, Grendel. You are my strongest child. My precious, powerful creation."

Her voice is almost tender.

I strain to forget, but I cannot. I cannot forget that his voice was gentle too—in a way that my mother's is not.

I look into Mother's face. Her gaze is inexorable, her command unarguable.

I am trapped between two endings.

Both of them could kill me. If I refuse to confront him, Mother will break me, punish me until I am a pile of screaming bones . . . but if I go to him . . . what will he do to me? There is death in his eyes—a kind of death I have not known. Does not that wretched prophecy claim that a son will break the dragon's hold? And what am I if not the hands of my Great Father?

And it is no ordinary death that I sense in this Beowulf.

Somehow I know that death at Beowulf's hand will be more than simply the end of my existence. It will be a kind of taking into himself, as if he—or whatever causes that terrible light in his eyes—wishes to eat me alive.

Mother suddenly reaches out and grips my face between her hands. Her claws dig into me. I am caught in her gaze, drawn into her anger, pulled into her will.

"What I have told you has not changed. A world that will not accept you for what you are is not fit to live. It must either be convinced or destroyed—and since it will not be convinced without force, you must destroy it until it acknowledges you as natural.

"Look what he has already done to you! He has made you doubt your perfection, he has made you cringe from your identity, he has made you run from your true potential. Will you stand for that? I will not let you stand for that.

"His face haunts you, doesn't it? His voice tortures you. Well then. Shred him. Choke him. This is your final test, Grendel. Once you kill him, you will be unstoppable. You will be able to sit on the throne. The people will finally acknowledge you and worship you as queen, as they always ought to have done."

She puts her face close to mine, her whisper washing over me.

"All you need to do is kill Beowulf."

Our eyes meet, and she does not like what she sees.

I do not like what I feel.

She draws her breath in slowly, between shut teeth. "Can you truly not find enough hate within you to destroy the thing that hates you? Very well—then take some of mine."

She takes my hood in her hands and I am lost in the sudden flood of venom.

5

There is a storm brewing. The air smells like thunder and crackles with yet unseen lightning.

I run along the sea-cliffs, gaining resolve from the sight of dark waves crashing onto dark rocks, destroying everything in their path. They are inexhaustible, insatiable, impossible to defeat.

And I tell myself that I am the same.

The moon is hidden by gathering clouds, casting the world in shades of iron as I near the boulder where the entrance to my tunnel lies.

I shove it to one side, and the wind rises as I do, surrounding me in a wild zephyr of screaming anticipation as I dive down into the dark.

I must not fail. I cannot fail.

I am in the tunnels. Running, running, running.

I burst out into the hollowness of the empty courtyard, and the sudden glare of lightning illuminates Trollhattan as I turn towards it, expecting to see the gaping doorway looming like an open mouth.

But the doors have been replaced.

I suck in my breath, furious—then I laugh. Does he really believe that mere wood will stop me? He has rebuilt the doors to close them in my face, to make it clear that I am not welcome.

So I will tear them apart again.

His insolence gives me fresh anger, and this gives me fresh strength. I attack the doors, pounding them with my shoulders until they shatter, and then rip at the hinges with my claws.

The doors burst open in a shower of splinters, and I stand, frozen, on the doorstep of Trollhattan.

For one split second, every detail of the room, and the change in it, strikes me like the blow of a sword.

I knew what to expect: the floors, once honey gold, stained to the color of wine. Bits of shredded draperies and tapestries clinging to the walls. Broken furniture. The rank smell of fear and false hope. And a sound—not heard, but felt—as if the screams of the victims have somehow been caught in the rafters.

But this is not what I see. This is not what I smell or hear.

There are hundreds of lit candles in the room. The Hall is bathed in light until it no longer looks like a meeting hall. It looks like a chapel. The shadows hanging over the place are retreating, curling back from the light, as if burned.

The room has been cleared and cleaned and scrubbed, and it smells of food eaten in peace and the deep sleep of a warrior unconcerned by my existence.

And there is Beowulf standing in the center of the Hall, looking at me. He is not armed, but the light surrounding him pierces me more sharply than any sword.

He isn't quite smiling, but his face is full of anticipation. He is not afraid; he is excited.

And then he speaks.

"No more, Grendel. Prepare to be judged by the Maker of all."

My heart shrivels, but then the storm remembers me and defends me once more.

At Beowulf's words, the heavens open and the storm finally breaks.

A burst of thunder and rain shoots down to the ground, carried by a wild and savage gust of wind that blows sideways across the courtyard, slamming into my back, streaming past my shoulders and straight into the Hall.

All but the furthest candles are snuffed out, plunging us into darkness that is barely pierced by a single candelabrum and the now dying embers in a brazier.

Safe once more in the dark, I leap forward, and the monster and storm blow into the Hall as if they are one.

I open my mouth and let loose the inhuman roar that has terrified every man that has ever tried to face me—warning Beowulf off.

But Beowulf rushes towards me, pressing into the driving rain and wind, unarmed and unafraid.

I shudder. Or perhaps it is only the roof, trembling under the sudden gust of savage wind that curls around the Hall.

I catch up a stool at my feet and fling it at Beowulf, and I feel I am flinging away my dignity with it, for I have never before used furniture to defend myself. I have always gotten in close, used my claws.

But as Beowulf bats aside the stool with his forearm, smiling with exultation, I do not close in. I do not dare.

I throw myself sideways towards the wall, scuttling across it like a spider, rushing past Beowulf with a rattle of claws, trying to dart behind him. I can slice his back open, if I am quick.

But Beowulf is quicker.

He turns with me and lunges for my head, seizing me by my covering and yanking with a ferocity that pulls me to a stop.

White glare fills the room once more, illuminating ten silver talons as I slash at Beowulf's throat.

Beowulf ducks to avoid the blow. I pull back too . . . and a howl escapes me when Beowulf refuses to loosen his grasp on my hood.

I thrash and scream and flail, but I cannot shake him off. Terror makes me weak. Lightning flashes in the doorway and sears the room. My claws gleam red in the sudden brilliance. Is it his blood or mine? I am not sure. I only feel as if I am dying.

Thunder follows the light and rumbles above the corners of Trollhattan, caught in the gables and echoing down into the empty spaces of the Hall, echoing in my frantic feet as I start to run. Beowulf is dragged across a floor slick with rainwater, pulled after me the way he might be pulled by a wayward pony's reins.

Beowulf springs forward and wraps his arms around me, reaching for my throat. My snarl turns into a gag as we stumble backwards.

I spin in his arms, as supple as a snake because of the slimy tatters of my robe, and reach for his face. Beowulf's elbows fly out, knocking my arms away long enough for his hands to shoot up and grip me by the wrists.

Our faces are almost touching. He meets what I know is a yellow animal gaze and he smiles, determined and sure. As for his eyes, I cannot bear the sight of them.

I don't breathe. I am so weak before his resolve! The nimbus around him is like nothing I have ever known or seen. It is as bright as wheat, as strong as death—and it makes me shrink back.

Beowulf uses that moment to lever my feet out from under me for a mere instant, letting go of my wrists and reaching for my throat a second time.

My head shoots to one side on instinct, and Beowulf's fingers slide across my jaw and tangle once more in my hood.

I leap away just as Beowulf pulls—and a scream like nothing I have ever heard, not even in my darkest moments, bubbles out of my throat and fills the Hall.

Beowulf keeps pulling. He isn't just pulling at cloth—it is my skin, my covering, my very life, the source of my strength, and I am helpless to wrest myself free. All of my dark power is as nothing in his grasp, and I scream in agony as I flail. I do not even try to fight now. I only want to escape.

One last agonizing rip. The pain is unbearable.

But it is nothing compared to the feeling when my hood is finally torn away.

I screech and clap my hands to my naked head—but it is not naked. My claws tangle in hair—long human hair—and tear at soft, human skin.

What is happening to me? What is happening to me?

My mind is coming apart, unwinding. I am coming awake, dashed into hideous consciousness by ice water and opening my eyes to a terrible reality that I cannot understand.

I am sobbing, almost slobbering, face down on the floor. I push away from it and look up at him, waiting for him to kill me, for surely this is the beginning of the end.

And for the first time in years, I hope it is.

I want to die.

We stare at one another, unmoving, our rapid panting strangely alike. There is no other sound save for the storm outside that whirls into the room and rages inside my heart.

No—it is the lack of the storm inside of me that keeps me pinned to the floor. For years, the thunder of anger and hatred has made me live, has kept me going, kept me killing.

But now the crushing weight about my head is gone, leaving an acute awareness of the emptiness in its absence.

I feel my throat working, but I don't recognize the voice that comes out of me. It is harsh, broken at the edges, as if it could barely form words in a human throat anymore. I can only gasp a single word.

"*No.*"

6

There is silence for one tortured breath of time—a single heartbeat that seems to go on for an eternity. Shock has shattered our battle.

My covering dangles in Beowulf's hand. His breath pulls in as he stares at me.

He can see me—without my hood.

The realization explodes in my mind, shriveling my thoughts under its blast.

I was not born a monster. I was born a girl.

I am a thing caught between two identities. And now my greatest enemy can see that. He can see me—stretched between woman and monster like a moth on a page.

A wail bursts from my throat, as shocking and sudden as the bursts of lightning that illuminate the room once more . . . and make my face even clearer to Beowulf.

"Do not"—I choke, hardly able to form words in a human throat—"look at me!"

I turn and run towards the door, frightening even myself with the keen that pours out of me.

I race out into the night, pausing for a moment on the doorstep of Trollhattan, shocked and frozen by the furious onslaught of cold rain that strikes a human head and human skin that is unbearably sensitive.

I throw my arms up to shield myself and realize I am sobbing as I struggle down the wet steps.

He is following me. I know it, and all I can do is flee. The confident, savage monster has turned into some pathetic creature that is a half-girl who wants nothing more than to escape.

The rain sheets off the gables of the Hall and the buildings in great waves. The torches on the walls have been doused, plunging the courtyard into darkness, and hiding me from view except for when lightning flashes send long curling claws of light raking across the sky.

I half fall down the steps of Trollhattan and into the sloppy mud of the earthen courtyard. Dirt has turned to mud beneath the sky's downpour, and the cold, wet muck pulls at my ankles, slowing me down.

The Watcher on the Cliffs—Auschere—pierces the night: his thin, reedy cry sounds the alarm between claps of thunder.

Lights appear in the windows of the bothies as I pass, so quickly it seems that many of the Frisians had not been in their beds but instead had been watching and waiting, praying for victory.

The Almighty has clearly heard them, for now I am the one running for my life.

Beowulf must be following me, he must. I do not dare to turn around and look, for he might see me again, and that would be like death itself.

Why doesn't he catch me? I am moving so slowly: I can barely move. He must be taunting me. He could easily catch me. He will catch me at any moment, and then what will I do?

I do not go towards the tunnel. It is too late to double back and head towards it, for that would mean I would have to turn and face him.

I run instead towards the wall. I am up the ladder in two

great leaps as the sky speaks again with a shriek of storm and sound.

I am aware of men fleeing from me as I crest the wall, but out of the gloom and storm there is a cry, and a single sentry races towards me along the battlement.

It is Auschere.

I freeze, unable to move as his blade falls.

But some great force has pity upon me at last, for the one man brave enough to attack me is either too frail to aim true, or his eyes are too weak to see clearly in the storm.

He should have aimed for my head—my vulnerable, utterly human skull.

Instead his sword glances off my shoulder, leaving me unharmed but jarring me to movement once more, as the rain suddenly turns from downpour to deluge and the darkness between lightning bolts turns to blinding grey.

I leap off the wall. My body takes the impact of the rocky ground without any pain at all. The rest of my covering is still strong: it protects me.

I dart into the night, slipping on the tall grass beaten flat by the storm.

It is only then that I look over my shoulder.

My heart stutters.

Beowulf is on the wall, looking right at me. And in his hand is my hood, thick and sinuous, the face of a monster ripped clean away.

LIGHTNING LACES its fingers across the sky, like claws trying to tear the darkness apart—trying to pull apart the last thing that protects me.

Except it no longer protects me.

I run into the night, but the dark no longer hides me from the truth.

I have slipped and fallen in the slush and the dirt more times than I can count. I cannot run fast enough. He is chasing me—I know he is. The walls of Trollhattan are far behind, but I can still feel his gaze, always right behind me. He must be following me—that is the only explanation for the terror that still hounds me.

Oh, what if he catches me?

What if he looks at me again?

That face is worse than all the light in all the world. Those eyes are more blinding than the sun.

For that gaze, full of whatever relentless, awful power or presence that keeps the sun rising every morning . . . that power judged me and pitied me.

And I knew it was right to do so.

I feel naked, exposed. I am as weak as a child. I feel like a newborn—as if I had been born five minutes ago, launched kicking and screaming straight into hell.

Help me, help me. Let me escape.

I don't even know who I am praying to. Some instinct leads me to appeal to that gaze itself, to the power behind it.

But this god does not hear me.

There will be no escape.

No matter how fast I run, nothing will change.

Lord Beowulf has seen me.

Trees whip past me, falling across my face and shoulders like the lashes of a whip. It feels like a flogging that has been owed to me for years.

I tumble down into my valley. Its dark folds of grass close about me, and then I race across the ravine of gravel and into the cave, calling her name.

But there is no one there. I am alone.

For a moment, I am too stunned to move.

Mother is gone once more.

How can she be gone? For the second time in two days, in the two times I have needed her the most, more than I have needed her for years, she is gone.

I shriek in frustration and shock, circling the cavern in endless circles.

I want her to come back and cover me once more with words and images and dark dreams so thick they weave a covering over my body and my mind. But she is gone, gone, gone.

I throw myself into the pool, trying to sink, trying to hide in its murky depths, clinging to the loose stones at the bottom of it.

Again and again, I rise to the surface, sobbing as my uncovered head is exposed once more.

The bats fluttering in the shadows, the walls themselves—they all see me as I have never allowed them to see me.

My hood is gone.

Mother placed these garments on me years ago. I could not remember a time when I had not worn their impenetrable woven breadths.

I now know I had been lucky to forget what it was like without them, for this sudden, nightmare exposure is beyond all bearing.

How could Mother leave me alone like this? How could she send me to face him in the first place, perhaps knowing this could happen?

I chop at the water of the pool, turning it into a raging sea, and I rage along with it, screaming out all my pain and frustration. But the feelings never end—they simply keep on unwinding, a never-ending spiral of agony.

And still Mother does not come.

There is no relief.

7

All of my pent-up horror seems to pour from the sky. It's as if the heavens are in their death throes, a frenzied storm that pulls the air to pieces. And then, as the air turns deathly cold, lashing rain shifts into furious flakes of snow. The valley outside the cavern entrance is frozen, the bracken about its rim heavy with drifts, bent double, like mourners.

For whom does the land mourn? The monster that the warrior injured? The half-girl that ran because of sheer terror?

I lie like one dead, sprawled where I first fell. I have barely moved since I returned, too sick and stricken to even writhe, and some part of me drains away, like pus oozing from a wound.

On the outside, I do not bleed, but my mind is shredded.

I no longer attack the Frisians. Instead, I am attacking myself. My thoughts are claws, my emotions curse me, rage at me, judge me, doubt me.

He tore off my hood, the thing protecting my mind, and now my mind is crumbling to pieces. My robe is the only thing keeping the rest of me from falling apart.

I shudder to think what would happen if he disrobed the rest of me—if he could see me wholly.

He doesn't have to kill me. He could simply strip me and then let me live . . . exposed.

Such a fate would be worse than any death. It already is.

Air touches my cheeks. It is sharp. I feel as if it could slice through me. My face and my ears are cold. I wrap my arms around my head, trying to let my robe shield my mind, but it doesn't work. I want to tear my head off, cast it into the shadows, but I know from experience that my claws can do little to hurt me. They are enchanted to kill only others, not me.

I am in the deepest shadows of the cave, but still I feel light tracing me, knowing me, exposing me.

I look towards the pool, but I do not dare look at my reflection. If I did, I would fill the pool with so many tears I would make its levels rise.

The pool is deep. A human or a monster could drown in it. Why do I want to live so much? Why can I not simply let go? What is the purpose in my living any longer?

Part of me waits for Mother. I know she will be back; she must come back. I know she will not let me die; she wants me to live.

But there is something else . . . someone else . . . that also insists that I live. And that hidden power that controls me when I thought it had rejected me long ago makes my misery all the deeper.

I have no idea what time it is when Mother finally returns, sweeping in with shadows trailing in her wake.

In the moments of doubt before today, her dark presence was enough to calm me once more, to settle my crawling uncertainties and to remind me of my dark purpose.

But I do not feel reassurance when I look at her now.

She stops short and stares at me.

Just like Beowulf, just like the moon and the sun, she sees me without my hood.

She is shocked.

I shut my eyes so I can't see it, but I'm too late.

She judges me, though it is a different kind of judgment. Beowulf—I think—judged me because I am a monster. Mother judges me because I am half girl. Because I am weak, and I have failed.

In the end, it is all the same. I am lacking—and I am exposed in my lacking.

Mother speaks at last. "What . . . happened?"

A sob gurgles in my throat. "He did this to me—Beowulf."

She hisses a little, examining me. "So. This warrior is powerful after all, as the stories have said. But it is only a wound, Grendel. Easily mended. You shall simply go back and retrieve what he tried to take from you."

I shudder at the thought of facing that pair of eyes again, and I shake my head, vehemently. "I cannot go back. He . . . saw me."

Mother scoffs. "When Beowulf is killed, what then will it matter if he saw you without the covering I placed on you?" Her eyes narrow. "Never before have you feared the gaze of mortals, nor have you feared the opinion of fools."

"He took something from me," I whisper. "He took something . . . off me."

"So I can see," Mother snaps. "But all is not lost. Get up, Grendel." Exasperation rings the edges of her voice, making it as sharp as a sword loosened in its sheath.

My voice sounds dead in my own ears. Am I dead? Did I die years ago when Mother first found and shaped me? Have I actually been living in hell all this time? I no longer know. "I can't."

Mother's voice drips with the disdain that I have only ever heard her use towards humans before. But now, for the first time, it is directed at me. "So, the human warrior tore off your hood. And because of this you lie here sniveling and crying? Are you a child?"

"I am not a child," I rasp. "I am not a woman. I'm a monster."

She hits me—right on my exposed face.

I am so shocked I lurch to my feet, staring up at her.

"So, that got you up now, did it?" Mother hisses.

She pushes and pokes at me, making me sway and stumble and grip the wall. She tweaks my hair, pinches my hands, prods at my feet, hissing and spitting in her rage.

I stumble on the pebbles that skid beneath my feet, throw out a hand to prop myself against the cavern wall. My vision spins and my mind tangles. She is a hair's breadth away from killing me.

If I push her any further, she would kill me as gladly as the Frisians would.

Tears run down my face, and she slaps them away as she raves at me.

"You deserve this. You've brought this upon yourself. You hesitated, you doubted all I have taught you, and so you failed!"

"No," I rasp. "It is the hood that failed. It was not strong enough to hide the truth." I press against the wall, away from the thing I thought I trusted. "You lied to me. I am a monster!"

There is a brief pause.

No sound but the ripple of water and my own moans.

"Look up, Grendel."

It feels impossible: my head is like a boulder. But I cannot disobey that command, even though, to my shock, something inside me wants to.

Slowly, painfully, I raise my chin and meet her gaze.

Mother looks back at me calmly. "From the neck down, anyway, you look like me."

Her words split me in half—as if they are lightning and I am a rotten tree. They echo in my mind like thunder.

And suddenly, I understand with a brutal clarity. The lack of my hood doesn't just expose me to the scrutiny of others—it exposes me to thoughts that now seem painfully, horrifically obvious.

This was why she needed me. This is why she wants me. Not for my own sake, but for herself.

Because for a monster to feel safe, to not feel alone, to not feel judged, they need other monsters. I know that full well.

She never cared about me; she only used me to justify herself.

And most surprising of all, she admits it.

She reaches for my chin. "You are whatever I call you. You are whatever you declare yourself to be."

"No," I whisper, jerking my head away. "I'm not."

It is as if the sky has been green all these years, and I did not know it, or the sea has been dry and stones wet.

I cover my raw face with my hands, tears leaking between my fingers, trying to hold in the horror that pours out of me, and a name rushes to my lips, unbidden. "I'm a monster. Oh, Almighty, help me, help me—I'm a monster!"

Suddenly I am flying through the air. My unprotected head feels like it might shatter in half from the single blow that she lands at the base of my skull, and then she has mercy and beats the rest of me—the part that is still protected by my cursed covering.

If a beating could be called a mercy.

Mother uses one of the weapons from her hidden hoard to attack me: the great pile of weapons and precious items she has stolen from the bodies of those she has killed. She uses a giant's blade on me now, just the flat of it, striking me again and again.

She is screaming at me, spitting, livid, as if she will explode into pieces with a fury I have never seen in her before.

Her voice trembles when she can finally form words again. "Now, *that* is pain to snivel over, not that foolish idea you've allowed the mortals to put into your head." She puts the blade down. I hear it scrape against the rock, and I flinch. "Say that name again in my cave, and you'll wish you'd never lived."

But I already wish that.

I raise my aching head and look at her.

I speak without thinking. "You haven't held me."

Mother abruptly stops walking, as if she has slammed into a wall that I built with my words. "What do you mean?" Her voice twitches.

"Before, when I have doubted, you have always wrapped me in your power. But you won't now. It's because you can smell him on me, can't you?" I look at her with a growing realization. "It burns you too."

I did not hit back when she was hitting me—but I think I have hit her with my words, for she steps away and turns white with something that I think might be fear.

She punches out her words between her clenched teeth. "You will retrieve your hood, and I will put it back upon your head before another day has passed, and then you'll forget all about this Beowulf, all about this idea that you are in the wrong. And since you are too afraid to return to the Frisians' hall, I shall lure Beowulf out of Trollhattan. And then you shall kill Beowulf."

I try to imagine him dead. I try to imagine tearing him apart with my claws.

But I already tried to kill him, and I failed.

I am incapable of defeating him—such a task can only be achieved by the one that calls herself my mother. Perhaps she might toss me some piece of him afterwards to gloat over and then shred.

My stomach lurches. I loathed him before, and now I fear him, but despite that, I do not wish him dead. This realization is almost as shocking as the acknowledgement of my true identity.

I flinch as Mother comes closer, but her mood has suddenly changed. She coos and, with only the smallest hesitation, she reaches out to touch me with her gnarled hands. But her claws scrape my wounds, hurting instead of comforting. She is trying to soothe me, but at the same time, there is something on me—or perhaps inside me—that she wants to tear.

"Grendel, Grendel. Be calm. So your first encounter with this golden warrior did not end as it should have. You are young—the mistake can be undone. You have been bewitched—dazzled by their worshipful regard for this foreign killer. Once you see him here, in your own home, you'll see him for what he really is—full of hate and dark prejudices, a destroyer of anything that does not adhere to his fanatical beliefs. Here, in the shadows, you'll see the truth."

Our eyes meet, and her gaze burns into mine as she finally lets her hands drop away from my face. I can feel something wet on my cheeks: blood mixed with tears.

"You will fight him, Grendel, because you do not have a choice." She starts to turn away and then flings one final command over her shoulder. "You will stay here until I say you can leave."

With a rush that stirs the water into a frenzied froth, blowing grit from the pebbled shore into my eyes, she is gone, blocking the light shining in the cave entrance for one merciful second.

And then the light seeps in once more, and there is no voice to counter the accusations in my head, no presence to fill the yawning emptiness pressing around me.

I sink slowly to my knees, then stretch out like one dead again. I roll onto my side, sand shifting beneath me and then molding to me once more, like an embrace. Like the death I wish would come and claim me.

Instead I live in this hideous, horrible clarity.

I live, and Beowulf will die.

I look towards the entrance of the cave and I wonder—and dread—what Mother is about to do.

8

I am miles from Trollhattan, but I hear her roar, even in the cave.

The sound is as dark and powerful as thunder. It rushes across the land, and the ground seems to heave beneath me, a ripple of horror.

It isn't a mere roar; it is far worse than that. It is a laugh—a long hideous scream of maniacal glee, a kind of rejoicing in the dark.

The earth trembles once more, as if something that has been making it strong has suddenly been wrested out of it, leaving it hollow.

And then—silence.

9

Mother is exultant when she returns.

I can smell blood on her. She is covered in it.

Vomit pushes at the back of my throat and I look away.

"It is done!" Mother proclaims. "The Watcher on the Cliffs has been torn and scattered before the eyes of all Trollhattan!"

She smiles, showing all her fangs, but I do not smile back.

Just like that—the Watcher is dead. How strange that the infernal presence that has angered and plagued me for so long is gone.

"That foreigner—Beowulf—was on the wall when I brought the Watcher's body to the settlement. I saw him cry out." Mother speaks with satisfaction. "And I saw him trying to gather what was left of the Watcher's body before I returned to you." She laughs.

I shut my eyes, shocked by a sudden rush of emotion I can't understand. It is almost as if I am standing there by the wall, listening, and I can hear Beowulf's grief ringing in my head as clearly as if I had witnessed it.

Mother does not notice my silence. She is sorting through something she has brought back with her—whether it is armor or bones, I do not know, for I do not look—I only see her brooding over it with wild delight.

Mother finally finishes crooning over whatever grisly thing it is and congratulates herself over another trophy. "It was a good night's work. That interfering Watcher was not the only trouble I dealt with. I had a gift to bestow on an ally."

I follow the triumphant gesture of one claw and look towards the far corner of the cave. Her hoard has been disrupted, as if someone has rooted through it. I had been so disturbed these past few hours that I had not noticed till now that one of the swords is missing, one I know well.

The sheath was ink black leather, but the hilt was a strange translucent crystal—clear as glass and eerily beautiful. Mother told me that it was forged from a star by an ancient race of giants that pounded a curse, as well as an edge, out of the sky's brightness. The curse was this: that while the sword would dazzle the beholder, it would always fail the one who bore it. It is a sheathed death trap.

"You wonder how you will defeat Beowulf?" Mother crows. "It is simple. The sword he will be using is one of my swords. He will put his trust in the very thing that will bring about his downfall."

She laughs again: a long cruel note of sound. "That stupid, trusting Beowulf will of course accept a sword from Unferth if it is given as an apology. The fool! He will fall for anything if he thinks he is showing mercy. Unferth will play his part, and Beowulf will believe in a false power that will fail him at the last second. One moment is all you need to end it. And you will end it, Grendel."

My thoughts collide and tangle together—too many thoughts. The thought of facing Beowulf again, the thought of Auschere dead, the thought of Unferth giving Beowulf a cursed sword.

It is this last thought that rises to the surface so that a question bubbles from my mouth. "Why would Unferth do this?"

Mother almost sighs at my question, as if I am stupid, and

seems to make a decision. "He has long been my ally within Trollhattan."

"What?" I try to form the word but no sound comes out. *Why had she not told me this?* I have wondered for so long if Unferth was an ally. What is Mother hiding from me? My mind spins: a wheel without a cog.

Mother paces back and forth. "The Dragon Below has spoken to me."

Her words jolt my tongue awake, and I blurt out, "You mean our Dark Father."

She stops walking with a look that is almost stupefied, as if shocked that I dared interrupt her, let alone correct her. I shrink inside my robe.

"The Dragon Below," Mother says coldly, putting me in my place with a look that makes me step away. "Remember, Grendel, you are not just his offspring, but his servant. And he requires your service, Grendel. The destruction of Trollhattan will be a worthy sacrifice."

I stand still, confused. Mother has always told me before that it is the crimes against me that the people of Trollhattan must pay for. She never said she was sending me to spill their blood on someone else's orders.

My thoughts dart back and forth—a scuttling lizard caught between two boulders.

When Mother first called me into her fold, she promised me freedom from all masters. These new words make no sense. Am I really free if I am serving the Dragon Below?

Mother is still speaking. "The time is coming, growing closer. Our darkness, our great covering, is growing stronger. Our hold upon this land is increasing. But in order to claim it forever, to replace the Enemy's lies with the Dragon's truth, we need more soldiers, more children like you. You are no longer enough."

I nearly reel. I cannot pull in air. I cannot breathe.

I am not enough.

I am nearly choking in my effort to speak.

"What are you saying?" I whisper.

She does not seem to see how her words have damaged me. Or she does not care.

"My poor dear creature, why do you think they have been so helpless in repelling you? It is because of the groundwork I laid when I whispered to a far traveler to erect an altar to the Dragon Below outside Trollhattan's walls."

"Unferth," I repeat, my voice curling around his name in a rising growl.

What secrets has she shared with him—what help has she offered to him instead of to me? How long have I thought I was the only one? Her special one, her daughter, her heir?

I have been robbed by the one person I thought I could trust.

I choke on the horrible thing she is implying: I am not enough, and all the carnage I have brought, all the nightmares I have endured to see Trollhattan brought down, would not have happened without some foreign priest.

"You are angry," Mother says simply.

The wind screams outside, covering the tense silence between us.

Mother turns towards me, and I see the glint of her eyes, echoing the sharpness in her voice. "Good. Be angry. But not at me, and not at Unferth."

I look at her, unspeaking.

That sharp gaze grows even sharper; I could cut myself on it. "Prove that you are powerful. Prove that I underestimated you. Prove that I don't need Unferth. Prove that Beowulf is a puny upstart and no match for a daughter of mine and a servant of the Dragon Below. After all, there is nothing stopping you from killing him yourself."

Her challenge lingers in the air, as thick and vile as poison.

She drifts closer, her voice soft, coaxing once more.

"Do it, Grendel—and I will weave you a new hood. Everything will go back to the way it was. It will be better than the way it was before, for with Beowulf dead Trollhattan will be ready for the plucking. We will sit on that throne."

I look to the dripping wall beside me, searching the pattern the water makes, looking for words.

In one evening, Mother has done what I either could not do or would not do: she has killed Auschere and entrapped Beowulf.

"You don't need me," I whisper, with a bitterness that shocks me. "I'm not enough; you said so yourself. You have Unferth now. Or you could destroy the Frisians yourself. Why should I help?"

Mother enlarges before my eyes, her eyes blazing scarlet with a rush of maddened color that I have never seen before. She pins me to the wall, stealing my breath as I stare up at her.

"Do you not yet understand, you stupid piece of filth? You are an outcast. Only I was willing to take you in. No one else ever will. I am your one ally, your only protection in this whole wretched world. If you turn your back on me now, you will be defenseless. You will belong to nothing and no one. You are right: I could kill Beowulf myself. I don't need you. But I own you. You belong to me. I want you to be hooded once more. Do you think I can really endure looking at you like this forever?"

She thrusts me away from her. I stumble into the wall and pain blossoms at the back of my human skull.

She fills my vision, and I look up at her and see in her face . . . revulsion.

And I finally understand.

When Beowulf pulled off my hood, he thrust me into a horrible in-between place where I repulsed everyone. If I do not regain my power by killing Beowulf, Mother will reject me. And if that happened . . . what would I become? A ghost. A thing belonging neither to the Almighty nor the Dragon Below, forced to wander, rejected once and for all by everything that walks this earth.

"You see at last what must be done," Mother whispers,

placing a claw on my shoulder. "You must kill Beowulf. Tonight, while he is mourning his ally and armed with a false sword. *Kill Beowulf.*"

10

K*ill Beowulf. Kill Beowulf.*

My mother's command echoes in my mind as I walk into the night, my feet as heavy as stone.

I try to reassure myself that this fight will be easy. He has seen the full power of my mother—he now knows what kind of dark power we wield. His one ally has been destroyed. Never has the time been riper, never would a kill be easier.

I am Grendel, servant of the Dragon Below, full of anger and power. I have killed mortal warriors before, and I will do so again. I have even confronted Beowulf in that hall and survived the encounter, despite my grievous wound.

But as I wander across the moonlit moors, none of these thoughts can belie the terror that flutters through me in a thousand shadows of panic.

The earth under me is soft beneath a blanket of slush. The ground was not cold enough for the snow to remain pure, and so the sky-fall has become only mud. The ground that churns beneath me, cold and sticky, echoes my mood as accurately as if it were a reflection.

My mind is in such turmoil that my vision is blurred, and I

am only half aware that my feet lead me not to Trollhattan but north, into the hills.

I climb the crest of a bluff and look down into a hidden piece of world. A small silver lake is nestled between the two folds of land, like a mirror tucked in a drawer.

There is a scent—sweet and sickening—that has been drawing me further into the wild, away from the Schrawynghop. I realize now that it is the smell of Beowulf.

I look down into the valley and see the dark outline of a figure crouched beside the lake.

Relief bursts inside of me. I cannot believe my good fortune. Some great force in this universe favors me at last and has led my enemy out into the open. Beowulf had an unfair advantage in the Hall. But here, in these desolate fells and empty heaths, where only shadows lurk, the advantage is mine.

Kill Beowulf. Kill Beowulf.

I slip silently down the hill, moving cautiously through the tall grass that alternates between black and silver in the ever-changing light.

The figure by the lake does not move. My heartbeat quickens. I am sick with anticipation and something else I do not want to name.

Fear crouches, fetid and foul, at the back of my throat as I draw closer to the beast hunter.

It is all right. He does not know I am here. This will be quick. It will be easy. It has to be.

I am only a few spear-lengths away. I extend my claws, staring at his shoulders. The smell of him is almost overwhelming. I must put out that smell, I must.

My heart seems to stop beating when he suddenly moves.

Beowulf turns and faces me, and I see his face clearly in the moonlight.

He has been weeping.

His tears bring my feet to a halt. There might as well be a stone wall between us.

I look at him, hating and fearing, bewildered and riveted all at once, in a welter of emotions that pull me in every direction and set me adrift.

Even his tears are beautiful—they have more weight and worth to them than other men's tears. They are like diamonds.

I look at him and I know—suddenly and sharply—that he is crying for the Watcher on the Cliffs.

His hands rest easily at his sides. He does not draw his sword.

I know he doesn't have to. I felt those hands at my throat. I felt the power inside him that comes from something stronger than muscle and bone.

I stand my ground, though I want to run. If Mother could see me tremble, she would despise me.

I look at Beowulf and I despise myself.

Beowulf rises slowly to his feet, unhurried, unafraid, and he looks at me and speaks, not in the terrible thunder of last night, but with a voice as soft as rain.

"I'm glad you've come to me."

His words pull me from my frozen reverie. Fire shoots through my veins. At first I think I misheard him; words sound different, strange, after losing my hood. How can he be glad to see me?

He is mocking me! He is gloating, just as he did in the Hall. That must be it.

But I am still confused. His words are the boast of a warrior challenging an enemy, but his voice is gentle, like the tiny ripples in the lake behind him.

"Soon you won't be glad," I snarl, but my voice does not sound as it used to, fierce and horrible; it sounds like any other woman's voice, like one of the pathetic, sniffling women of Trollhattan. I want to rage and scream as I used to, but the sounds tangle and diminish in my throat.

All that I can force out is a harsh whisper. "Even you should fear walking in these parts. These hills are our territory and belong to us, just as Trollhattan will soon belong to us."

I wait for him to charge me, my heart thundering, but he doesn't move.

He is waiting for me to come to him—but it is all I can do to remain upright.

A shudder escapes me before I can stop it, and I lurch forward. I sneer at him, but still that quiet face never changes. "What are you doing outside your walls? Have you come to find me?"

"I came to pray—and to understand something." His head tilts slightly, and in the sudden play of shadows caused by the cloud-mass above, I cannot read his expression.

He can't read mine either, but he steps forward, as if he suddenly wants to.

Alarmed, I step back. I do not want him to see me wounded, uncovered, exposed. I cannot let him.

But it doesn't matter if he sees me, because I have come to kill him.

Rush in fast before he looks too long. Kill him, and then it won't matter if he has seen me.

The sky itself is against me, for it unrolls the cloak of clouds that shroud the moon and lets light shine upon our faces, and I see him as clearly as if we are standing in full sun.

He is exhausted—there are lines around his mouth, grooves of fatigue. It is not just sadness, but something like resignation, as if he has lost a battle.

Why then do I not feel victorious?

I step closer, curiosity overwhelming my instinct to attack.

He looks as if he has been fighting all night—but I do not know how that is possible, since I have only just come. The only one he could have been fighting is himself.

He is weakened.

This is my chance. I could attack him now.

I am trembling, caught between the temptation of charging him and ending this and the terror of what he might do to me if I dare, for the fear that he is still more powerful than me, even when he is weak, lingers.

I cannot let him see how fragile I am. I must taunt him into attacking. We must fight—before I lose my nerve and run away into the night. I want to run away so badly.

"Go ahead, beast hunter—attack me! What's stopping you? You wanted to kill me! Go on, hero, fight me! You hate me—I made you fail in your boast to kill me last night. You should hate me. I killed your friend."

"It wasn't you," Beowulf says, looking down at the ground. "I could see it from the wall. It was like a troll, only bigger. It is stronger than you, blacker."

He pauses and lifts his head to meet my gaze.

He says it again. "It wasn't you."

I try to lick my lips, but my face feels numb.

A human is looking me right in the eye . . . and not blaming me. Not judging me.

It has never happened.

"The thing that killed Auschere . . . it . . . laughed when it brought his body to the wall." He forms the words carefully, as if trying to make us both understand something impossible. "You never did—when you came. They say they heard you screaming, others heard cursing, some thought they heard you weeping. But you never laughed. The creature last night was fully monster."

I don't breathe.

"You are not," says Beowulf.

I shut my eyes, suddenly sick.

"There was a reason why you didn't kill Auschere, wasn't there? You should have, but you couldn't."

The world around me is spinning.

"Why didn't you, Grendel?"

He says my name differently than Mother does, or even the men of Schrawynghop. I have never heard anyone speak to me so, even before . . . was there a before? Memories push at the darkness

I try to wrap around myself, a distant past in a place not unlike Trollhattan.

I don't want to remember; I can't remember.

A branch cracks under a foot as Beowulf moves closer.

My eyes fly open again and I jump back a pace.

He stops. "I won't hurt you."

I laugh. It is more like a shriek: a screech of disbelief and frustration. "What do you call what you did to me in the Hall?"

"Necessary." Beowulf says, with such firmness I stop laughing. "The Almighty stayed my hand and let me only wound you, so that I could see the truth. Because I did not know what you truly were, then."

I am speechless. How can he speak of knowing what I am?

I don't even know what I am.

I am frozen, unable to move back. A few more steps and he will see me: my disparate pieces. Was I made by him or undone by him? Or both? I don't know. I can't think, I can't think.

Beowulf steps ever so slightly closer.

"I did hate you last night, Grendel, because I thought you were the enemy. I thought I was sent here to kill you."

My voice is the size of a pebble, an ant, a speck of dust. "Weren't you?"

Beowulf shakes his head.

He is still speaking, but I can hardly hear him. My pulse is hammering in my ears; my breath is loud—so loud. A gust of wind stirs the water. It lifts Beowulf's hair away from his eyes, pushes my covering against my flesh, and makes me shudder.

"Before you attacked—I dreamed about you," says Beowulf. "A girl asking me for help. I thought she was one of the Frisians, but when I saw your face, I realized that you were the one in my dream. The Almighty showed mercy to us both and stayed my hand from destroying you, because He never meant for me to kill you. . . ."

The wind dies down.

"I was sent to save you."

I spring away from him. Something inside me snaps.

I do not wish to be saved. I do not need to be saved. What does being saved even mean? There is nothing wrong with me; I am what I am meant to be. I am enough.

It is some new trap, meant to lure me into letting down my defenses. It is merely some new, torturous way to destroy me. If he cannot kill me, he will take away what I am.

I reach up with a shaking hand to touch my face, whimpering when my claws cut soft skin. The sudden pain brings me to my senses. With a shock, I realize that we have both been moving, circling one another.

He has backed me towards the lake. Does he mean to drown me?

A movement out of the corner of my eye makes my heart leap into my throat. Something terrible is behind me, coming out of the lake.

I whirl with a startled cry, and then I freeze, staring down into the silver glare of the pool and into the eyes of my own reflection.

I have not looked at myself since Beowulf wounded me.

"Oh no, no," I whisper, holding my hand to my throat and realizing, once more, that my voice is different without my hood. It is a girl's voice—and horrifically incongruous with my appearance.

I am disgustingly disproportionate—my human head looks grotesque on my massive and misshapen body, clad in the slimy, dark raiment of my mother's design—like moss wrapped around an ugly boulder.

There is no hiding from the truth I have been running from for years. There is no avoiding this fact I have been trying to kill.

I am disgusting, vile, unnatural: a base creation. Even the people of Trollhattan—with all of the falsities wrapped around their weak hearts and souls—are still normal. They are weak, but they are simply human.

I am the monster.

I stare, though I want nothing more than to be able to look

away. I am half woman, half creature. I am something that was never meant to be.

When Beowulf removed my hood, what was beneath—not just thoughts, but features—was revealed.

The face looking back at me is an old face I have all but forgotten. I think it is the face of who I used to be—a frightened, unhappy girl with dark hollow eyes who cannot believe what she is seeing or what she has become.

I sink to my knees, wrap my arms around myself, and dip my head until it nearly touches the surface of the pool.

"What have you done to me?" My moan leaks out of me, like blood seeping from a wound. "Give me back my hood."

What is he trying to do to me? What does he want from me? I don't understand.

Beowulf's voice is soft. "It is gone, Grendel. I threw it into the sea."

I reach out a hand and dash the surface of the pool, scattering my reflection, and leap to my feet, turning on him in a flurry of helpless rage. I can barely speak through my sobs. "I wish you had killed me."

"The Almighty has willed that you will live again."

I try to laugh, but the sound tangles in a sob. "My mother will destroy you, even if I cannot, and then she will replace my hood and I will be stronger than ever—and no beast hunter will ever be able to touch me again."

Beowulf's eyes are troubled. "Do not let her, Grendel. You mustn't. You can be free of all of this. You can be human again. I won't rest until you are."

He steps closer—he could almost touch me.

I can't breathe, can't move, can't look away.

"Don't be afraid," he says.

We are both as still as the night around us, looking into one another's faces—our eyes wet.

I look at him . . . and I realize that he is telling the truth. How can it be possible?

He doesn't hate me anymore. And that, more than ever, makes me want to despise him.

I do not understand. I have always been able to hate before. But I cannot hate him now.

He is everything I am not, and now, without the hood shielding my shame, I finally know that it is not his fault—it is all mine.

I turn and flee into the night, sobbing, a scream growing in my throat.

This time, Beowulf does not follow.

11

Mother again orders me to leave the cave and strike Beowulf down.

I try to convince her, with sobs that I am unable to control, that I cannot.

So she punishes me once more—with a fury that shocks me as much as the pain.

It is strange . . . she weakens me even as she urges me to get up and hunt. But no matter how I plead and reason and ask for more time, she refuses to give me anything but more torment.

I am unsure how long the torture lasts, or at what moment I passed from screaming wakefulness to murmuring dreams. In that terrible night, I remember only one thing clearly.

Mother is so angry with me that she turns briefly away to pace, tearing at the water with her claws while she curses me. And, hidden by the noise of her fury, I hear myself whisper three words past swollen lips.

"Beowulf—help me."

I must be feverish, for they make no sense. But still, I speak them, before I slip once more into tormented darkness.

When I wake, dawn is not far off and Mother has mercifully gone.

Sometime during the night, she grew so frustrated with me that she left to go hunting, anxious to kill something that she did not need for her own purposes.

I lie in my own dried blood for some time, listening to my rough breathing, and then, following some urge I do not pause to examine, I crawl slowly to my feet and move to the mouth of the cave to step out into what I have never willingly stepped into before—the coming light.

Mist drifts in great swathes from the surface of the stream that runs from the cave, blurring the crest of the valley walls into a blurred smear of hoary shadows. The boulders lining the ravine are mere impressions of dark, humped shapes—like the backs of bent monsters—and the bracken and gorse nestled at their feet stretch away in skeletal outlines, black against stark grey.

My pulse flutters, for as I stare, a new shape silhouettes itself on the rim of the ravine, picking its way between the great boulders to find the hidden path that leads down to my hidden lair.

Beowulf is making his way down the steep slope, the tall grasses bending and whispering about his knees as he pushes through the bracken. Behind him, the sky is twisted in a stormy cloud-wrack, sharp shards of grey and black tinged at the edges with lightning. The storm is still far away, but coming nearer, and it warns of its coming with a low growl that ripples across the top of the valley and slithers down its slopes behind Beowulf, as if to announce his coming.

I stumble backwards into the cave, staring at its entrance, waiting, unable to draw a full breath.

I listen to the sound of dripping water and then, beneath the dripping, I hear footsteps.

I gasp and tumble backwards into the lake, thrashing across it until I am on the shelf at the far side, pressed up against the rock, searching for a shadow in which to hide myself as I look back towards the entrance.

Beowulf stands silhouetted in the mouth of the cave, one hand braced on the earthen wall above him as he looks in.

It's as if the sun bent to look into hell. His eyes seek me out, with a fierce compassion that tears me apart.

I shake my head over and over. He should not waste his goodness on me. He should not throw away his life to try and help a monster.

I cannot speak, but my lips form the words silently. *You should not have come.*

And then a darker and bigger shadow emerges from the back of the cave behind me. Mother has returned to our lair through another entrance, just as Beowulf arrives.

"So you have come!" Mother cries, her voice as bright and as harsh as the heat lightning in the clouds beyond the valley. "Fool. You stupid, stupid fool. You have come to your death!"

Beowulf barely looks at her. I can feel his focus on me from across the cavern pool as clearly as if he has laid a hand upon me. "Then so be it," he says. "Death may be your greatest fear, and the threatening of it your greatest weapon, but it is not mine. I have come to break the chains you have placed over Grendel and the people of this land."

"You presume much, Lord Beowulf!" Mother sneers.

"I presume nothing," Beowulf answers. "When I saw you last night, I realized it was you I was meant to defeat, not Grendel. You will keep her hostage no longer. I am here on the Almighty's orders."

Mother shudders and cringes away, and in that brief moment when she is silent, Beowulf smiles at me.

"Oh." The sound escapes me before I can stop myself.

I only saw him smile once before. On the beach with Auschere, but at a distance, and not directed at me. It is like a benediction, an invitation. It is a smile that invites me to let go, to belong. His smile is unbearable.

I begin to weep. A slow silent trickle.

"It's all right, Grendel. It will be all right." Beowulf comes closer, slithering a little over the loose rock, but still as upright and steady as a forged blade, never losing his footing.

"Stay back," Mother warns. "She's a killer and she'll slice you in half just as easily as she did those Frisians."

Beowulf is at the far side of the pool now, and he steps into the water, never taking his eyes off me.

My heart hammers in my chest. I could dive into the pool. There is another way out of this cavern, the underwater tunnel Mother just came through. A place so tight, so narrow, I do not like to use it.

But it is there—and I could escape through it if I wanted to.

Do I want to?

Mother has thought of the tunnel too. Her voice is tense. "Grendel, if you will not deal with him, then leave the cavern until I have."

Beowulf holds my gaze, pinning me in place as gently as a blanket. "Are you really going to run away from me again, Grendel?"

I blink. I can't see past the tears on my lashes.

I take a step towards him.

"Grendel!" There is something like panic in Mother's voice.

I ignore her. I stumble a little closer to Beowulf, nearly falling. Beowulf holds out a hand, as if he can catch me.

Mother is screaming now. "He will destroy you!"

I do not know the name for the thing in his eyes, but when I see it, I begin to sob.

It is not pity. If it were, I would have turned away.

I saw this expression once in the face of a healer when he set the leg of a village mongrel that was crying all the while. It is a gift that Mother has never given me.

It is more than sorrow, more than kindness. I don't even know its name—I have forgotten it—but it pulls me towards him. And, amidst the hideous and vague weightiness of wishing for my own death, something crystallizes amidst the haze—an absolute certainty that I want Beowulf to live.

I speak in a voice I don't recognize, the words coming from some long-buried place. "I am dying already. And I would rather he destroy me than anyone else."

She stares at me, dumbfounded. "He will expose you to all I have tried to protect you from! He will undo everything I have tried to give you. If you value yourself at all you will slay him!"

Beowulf is up to his waist in the water now, his eyes still upon me with that unwavering look in his eyes. How could I strike the one person who has ever looked at me like this?

"You can't make me, Mother . . ." I say softly, my voice lingering on the shocking corners of my words, tasting them, astonished by them. "It is up to me. It is my choice. You can't make me."

Mother is screaming again—in a voice that rivals storms and thunder. She hits me. I am on the ground and she strikes me again and again, using her claws, tearing and scraping.

She can make me suffer; she can beat me and scream at me; she can even kill me.

But she cannot make me kill him.

The blows suddenly stop. I raise my battered head and see Mother flying through the air, flung across the length of the pool like a rat, and Beowulf is standing over me. With one savage charge, one blow from his powerful arm and one quick leverage of his weight, he has thrown Mother bodily across the cave.

His voice is like steel. "You will not touch her again, creature."

Mother staggers to her feet, throws back her head, and laughs on a long savage note. "You wish to fight? Then come and face me, hero."

She charges and Beowulf draws his sword.

The glittering crystal blade blinds me and I remember a moment too late.

"Beowulf!" I scream. "It's a trap!"

Beowulf sends his gifted blade plummeting towards Mother's head, slicing down hard as if to cut her face open.

It makes a sound like iron against stone, and there is a strange silver flash, like lightning, as the sword breaks in half.

Mother shrieks, not in pain, but in anger. She bats the cursed sword away as if it is a toy. The two pieces fall into the pool and drift down into darkness.

I see one glimpse of Beowulf's face as the realization strikes.

The sword had failed the one who bore it. Unferth had tricked him.

Mother seizes him by the neck and, before he can defend himself, pulls him underwater.

I pull in a breath and dive in after them. Fear bubbles up inside of me like the froth foaming around my eyes. I plunge downwards, searching the dark water frantically for a glimpse of what is happening.

Mother is pulling him further back into the cave, where it is harder for human eyes to see, hoping to gain the advantage.

Beowulf will not go quietly. He reaches up with those powerful hands and rams his thumbs into Mother's sensitive eyes.

She howls, and the sound splits the water. She lunges for his face, and Beowulf flings himself backwards. He kicks his legs and windmills his arms until he shoots away, just out of reach, and swims for the surface. No matter how strong he is, the foreign prince is running out of air.

I must do something, I must.

I kick forward, and my fingers grasp at some of the tall waving weeds along the bottom of the pool—plants as twisted and tight as rope—to hold me in place underwater.

Beowulf heads for the surface and Mother starts to follow. Their combined efforts churn the pool until it turns into a violent sea. I dart forward long enough to loop an entangling coil of weeds around Mother's foot.

The weeds hold her tight, suspending her helplessly between the bottom of the pool and the surface, trapped underwater, as Beowulf climbs out of the pool.

Mother whirls in a vortex of bubbles, snarling in disbelief.

But I have already darted away, behind a rocky obstruction that juts upward from the bottom of the pool, hiding behind it so that she does not see or suspect me. I hear her struggling to free herself as I head to the surface.

I gasp for air and blink water from my eyes as I scrabble onto the rocky shelf and look anxiously over my shoulder.

There is an explosion of white as Beowulf dives back into the pool to confront Mother once more, just as she uses her claws to free herself from the weeds. She heads to the surface for air and Beowulf follows, wrapping his arms around her, ignoring her claws.

They are locked around one another, slamming into first one wall and then another, two tidal waves intent on destroying one another.

I press back into my corner, trying to scrape up the courage to intervene.

I am flirting with death. But I do not fear dying: I only fear the thing that has always known me, claimed me, embraced me . . . I fear that it will turn around to destroy me.

I have always found my semblance of peace and identity in what Mother said about me. If I betray her, I also betray myself: the last claim I have to my identity, my rights, my innocence, will be stripped away.

If I help him, I will lose everything—forever.

But Beowulf cannot die.

I clamber onto a pile of rubble and stretch towards the bit of cave roof that is not rock, but earth.

I jam my claws into the crust of packed dirt and yank, wresting the rock and earth apart, searching for the sky.

The battle rages behind me—two forces determined to kill one another. I pull frantically at the ceiling until a miniature landslide pours down into the cave. A burst of illumination shoots downward, streaming past me like a blade of pure light.

I look over my shoulder in time to see Beowulf's fist collide with Mother's skull. She tumbles away . . . and steps into the beam of light.

Mother twists around in the water, her mouth half open in a snarl of shock and rage. As the radiance falls clearly across her, she flinches back, raising her hands as if to fend off blows. The light that is poison to monsters like us sweeps over her.

Mother's wide eyes turn on me—as red as blood, as bright as fire—and shock bubbles from her throat, first in a gasp, then in a single strangled word.

"You."

I chop at the ceiling again, my claws scraping against rock, trying frantically to enlarge the hole, not stopping or caring when it burns me too. If it kills me as well, so be it.

Mother lunges towards me, her claws outstretched.

And I know that, at long last, I am truly expendable, for I see in her eyes that she means to kill me.

I fling a shard of rock at her and spring away, half falling as the pile of rubble beneath me crumbles under my sudden shift of weight. The impact of my fall causes more of the roof to collapse, and Mother surges into a new beam of light.

She halts, hissing and clutching her eyes.

Shielding my own damaged eyes, I look around frantically for Beowulf.

But I cannot see him anywhere in the cavern.

Fear blossoms inside of me, and I dive into the pool to search underwater.

Relief floods me when I see him floating a few yards away—still alive. Golden shafts from the ceiling above pierce the churning dark, and our eyes meet, for one brief moment, beneath the water. Then I see his gaze fall upon the glitter of silver.

It is one of Mother's treasure hoards, the booty she and I have taken from our enemies.

Beowulf's eyes rest on the tangle of swords, unrusted and still silver-bright even beneath the water.

Then Mother dives beneath the surface.

Mother turns to face him, guided by scent now more than sound, and at last I see it in her face.

She fears him. She has always feared him, but the terror hid behind her hatred.

She lunges, and Beowulf turns to meet her head-on. They lock together in a titanic crash once more, and a new color floods the water—crimson.

A displaced wave rushes towards me, pushing me up and away from the battle, even as I try to swim against the current. I break the surface and slam against a rock pillar, my vision spinning, as a figure darts past, diving towards the bottom of the pool and the dark glitter in the depths.

Beowulf swims deeper down into the pool, scarlet wrapping him as if in a cloak. Is it his blood? If it is, he doesn't stop or slow. His eyes are upon a sword thrust hilt-deep into the silt at the bottom of the pool, its broad cross-guard as glitter-bright as the sun.

He seizes the hilt and pulls.

The sword comes free of the tangle in a rising billow of dirt mingled with small pieces of treasure that fills the pool with a strange glittering cloud. He pulls the sword towards him through the dark water. I see, as if in slow motion, everything that follows as clearly as if it is happening to me.

He breaks the surface near me and pulls air into his lungs. One breath. Two. Then the water moves and billows beneath him. A great movement displaces the water and sends him upwards on a sudden violent swell. Beowulf draws his legs up, bends at the waist, and dives again, sword first, to meet the oncoming creature.

Mother, driven by a wave of her own making, cannot stop or slow her speed.

Beowulf thrusts the blade downwards as she rises towards him.

And Mother jerks to a halt. Her arms and legs shoot forward, wrapping around the blade that sinks into her chest.

Beowulf tears the blade from her heart and then plunges it home again, this time into her throat, cutting off her final venomous scream, twisting her curse into what it really is—a final hopeless and helpless protest.

He jerks the blade free. Mother sinks, slowly, towards the bottom of the pool in a cloud of scarlet, and Beowulf takes hold of her throat and raises his sword once more, intent on bringing back some part of her body to Trollhattan. Proof to all Frisia that the monster is truly dead.

And at that, I turn away and swim for the shale-slick shelf at the far side of the pool.

Mother is dead, and I helped Beowulf kill her.

I try to suck air into my lungs as I crawl out of the water. Suddenly, I can't breathe—I am smothering in this cavern now. I get to my feet and stumble towards the entrance.

I have never willingly gone into the sunlight before, but I cannot stop myself.

I walk out of the cave and into the day.

I stagger in the brilliant light and collapse face down on the rocky soil that surrounds the stream trickling from the cave mouth. The storm that was brewing earlier has been blown away. The sun beats down upon my uncovered head. I cannot remember the last time I felt its rays.

Slowly, I roll over and look up into the sky, startled by the sight of blue and clouds whiter than the snow melting on the upper-most edges of the ravine. It is a world I do not recognize.

My mother was right. I do not belong in this world, but I no longer belong in the cave.

I am more trapped than ever.

Beowulf steps out of the cave, dripping, panting, exultant.

I look at him without fear, without longing, without anything. I am numb. Why did he do it? Why did I let him do it?

Beowulf is carrying a bag heavy with a bloody burden. I shut my eyes.

He half sits, half falls, beside me, and we both lie there side by side for some time, silent in the sun.

At last I hear the sound of mail scraping against the sharp pebbles of the little rocky bank. Beowulf sits up, slowly—as if checking himself for wounds.

I do not move. I listen to the sound of the water in the grotto behind us lapping against the cavern walls, a hungry monster no more. It is more echo than sound now. It is the noise of something lost.

Mother is dead. Beowulf is alive.

Where does this leave me? Stuck between the two, neither dead nor living. Only frozen.

Beowulf is reaching for me. He lays a hand on my arm.

Unlike Mother, he is not afraid to touch me. I look down at his fingers dispassionately. This is the hand that killed the only thing I have ever known.

Then he starts pulling at my collar.

"No!" I pull away from him, and my robe shreds. A wave of pain thrusts through me and I scream—the short, shrill cry of an animal at bay—as my head reels.

Beowulf's hand retreats. "It's already half off. It will only take one more try. I can pull it off of you."

I whimper and lean out of his reach as he extends his hand once more.

He stops and watches me with those steady eyes. "Let me take it off of you. I cannot take it off unless you let me, but I will not force you."

I shake my head and wrap my arms around myself. Beneath this covering, I know I am small. I shall be exposed. I shall be seen. I shrink inside my covering, pulling it tight across the throat that cannot hide a whimper. These are the coverings of a monster now, but better to be a monster than to be nothing.

He has given me so much—I am worse than a beggar before him. This golden warrior has reached down from his lofty height to extend a hand to the cursed girl.

I clutch at my robe while inside I clutch at my shattered pride. I may be wrong, but I am not weak. I am not helpless. I am not pitiful.

Beowulf moves closer to me. He does not touch me, but his voice reaches softly out to me. "When the Almighty first revealed to me that it was *you* I came to save, and not only Trollhattan, He showed me your true self. I had a vision of you—the person without the cursed robe. It was beautiful. You were beautiful."

I shake my head, panic bubbling in my throat. "I will be nothing."

"Perhaps at first," Beowulf concedes, and my heart sinks to hear him confirm my fear, instead of disprove it. "But you must be resolved that you will be nothing. I was nothing once, until I was filled." He lays a hand once more on my arm. "You can begin again. But you must begin with nothing. You cannot take this with you."

I want to run away. I want to tell him to leave. I want to return to the cavern and hide.

But to do that, I would have to go into the pool, which means I would see my reflection. I would see what is left, and I am not sure I could bear the sight again. For, now more than ever, I am half human, half creature—torn to shreds.

And beneath the fear of what Beowulf will take from me . . . I realize I do not want to return to the cave. I can't. It is no longer a refuge.

There is no refuge at all—there is only the hideous choice before me.

Remain a beast without peace, or become a human without hope or dignity.

True death would be preferable to what I feel. This is a living death, a hideous, inescapable torment. I am fighting for my very survival.

But *what* is fighting for survival?

What am I?

Beowulf watches me. "I promise you I will not let you face the world alone. I will be beside you all the way. You are halfway there already, Grendel. You have already reached out to the Almighty, else you would not be free of that foul creature. You have already helped to destroy her. Be entirely free. Come out of the thing you hide behind."

He is asking me—Grendel—to die.

But what is beyond Grendel? I do not know.

He says that if my enchantment is removed, I will become nothing.

And yet, lying here in all my disparate pieces, I realize with a moan that I am already nothing—not fully girl, not fully monster.

And I can't go on this way.

I meet his eyes. "Take it off."

I lie down on the shale, like a body being prepared for burial, and I surrender.

Beowulf looks down at me. "This will hurt you."

He doesn't have to tell me that.

Very gently, Beowulf does his worst, and the uncovering begins.

I do not know what happens next, except that it is worse than when he removed my hood, for it is like death, except that I do not die.

I scream, all four limbs thrashing in a frenzy of panic and horror. I cry and cry and cry and cannot stop. Once, the robe snags in a place near my heart, and one last scream gurgles out of my throat. This time Beowulf is not gentle—it is the final pull, and he does it with a brutal yank, for the monster hangs on with its claws till the last second.

I think I lose consciousness, or perhaps I really do die for a moment, though it is more like a fevered sleep.

I am plunged into a strange splintered darkness. In the blink of an eye, I see my life, sailing past me in dim images. And then, even dimmer, I see a life that I might have lived, but did not, for I turned my back on it years ago.

All my thoughts, all my past, all my hopes, all my could-havebeens, seep from me like blood from a gushing wound until I am empty.

There is nothing left, no pride, no dignity, no hope, no dreams—I only exist—small and alone in the darkness.

Then suddenly, there is Someone beyond the emptiness.

This Someone has a name, and Beowulf spoke it often.

There is no one to stand between me and this Light. No Mother. No Beowulf. It is only Him and me.

For all these years, I have cringed away from Him, but now, surrounded by darkness but no longer a part of it, I find myself reaching for Him, choking, helpless, hoping, yet not daring to expect anything except destruction.

And then He reaches back.

The darkness is gone, replaced by a light so blinding it threatens to disintegrate me faster than the darkness crushes me. I am consumed, on fire, burning to pieces, and yet the hole in my chest seems to be filling. I am going to fly apart. It is too much.

In an instant, the monster, and all my past before, is blasted away, like a stone bursting from the face of a cliff under the point of a chisel.

Beyond this blinding light, there is a future.

Then another presence pierces the dream.

Beowulf leans over me and shouts into my face.

"*Live.*"

Something moves in my chest.

A heartbeat.

My eyes open.

PART II

While the gold-friend of Geatmen gracious saluted
His fireside-companions: woe was his spirit
Death-boding, wav'ring; Weird very near him,
Who must seize the old hero, his soul-treasure look for,
Dragging aloof his life from his body

— LESSLIE HALL, *BEOWULF: AN ANGLO-SAXON EPIC POEM*

12

I open my eyes.

Beowulf leans over me. He is smiling.

I wince, feeling sore, and reach up an absent hand—real fingers without claws—to rub my chest. It feels strangely hollow, but I can feel my heartbeat: harder and faster and clearer than I can ever remember.

Beowulf slips an arm around me and helps me sit up, causing pebbles to crunch and shift beneath me.

"Praise the Almighty," Beowulf murmurs. He pulls away and I wobble, nearly falling over backwards.

Beowulf's hand is on my elbow in an instant, holding me up.

I shiver and look down, bewildered, realizing that I am clad only in the thinnest of tunics. Slowly, I recognize it.

It is the tunic I wore when the beast I called Mother first found me years ago on a hot summer day. It is shorter and thinner than it had been then, but I was still wearing it, all this time, beneath the monster's skin.

Beowulf bends down and plucks up a bundle of cloth from the ground—a cloak that he must have discarded before coming into the cavern. He wraps it around me, pressing it tight against my shoulders, covering my cold and sense of exposure that runs far deeper than an outgrown tunic.

"Thank you," I whisper, the words unfamiliar on my tongue.

I look around. The ravine is cool and green beneath an overturned shell of blue sky. The pool flows softly out of the cavern in a stream that breaks into rivulets at the foot of the rocky walls that make up the gully, lining the base of the gulch in silver. Out of a crevice in the ravine's wall, a butterfly appears, as pale and bright as a leaf. I have never seen one here before. Or maybe I only did not notice them before—for already those years in the cave feel like a dark and disturbing dream. Or, perhaps, I did notice the butterflies, and I hated them, as I hated everything that was beautiful.

I turn to Beowulf, who looks back at me, covered in blood that is his and not his, with eyes that are so kind, so good, I don't know how I can bear to gaze back into them. And yet I can.

"I was a monster before," I whisper as I search his face, and I feel a lostness inside of me as wide and as barren as the sky. "What am I now?"

"You are free," Beowulf answers, very gently.

I try to understand, but I do not yet know what that means. I am sane once more, that I know for certain, and when I try to reach for the hot burning coal of hatred I once carried inside me, I cannot find it. It has been burned clear away, leaving only ashy shame behind.

I am not angry. I can control myself. I am ashamed. These are all new, and it is a blessed and terrible beginning. But what now?

Beowulf breaks apart my thoughts with five words that land like a pebble in a pool. "Do you remember your name? The name your family gave you?"

Memory explodes inside my mind. I suck in a breath and squeeze my eyes shut. Old offenses and old pains etch themselves across my mind as clearly as the markings of a map. "I am not sure I want the name they gave me." I raise my eyes to his, swallowing back the enormous emptiness that sweeps over me. "Will you rename me?"

Beowulf rests his hand, very carefully, over mine, where it clutches at the lichen-covered boulder beside us. "It would be better if you could reclaim the name you were given as a gift at birth."

"A gift," I repeat, and I am dismayed by the old familiar taste of bitterness. "To be alive, to remember two people . . . my parents . . . who failed me? Is that a gift? They did not understand me. They rejected me. I was alone for so long. And then . . . it came . . . and drew me into the wood and—" I break off and look away, my voice suddenly hoarse. "It was easy to be renamed by the monster in the cave. I hated that first life—that life failed me."

Beowulf's voice is low. "Do you blame your enchantment on your parents?"

I shut my eyes, sorting through the broken shards of the past, wrestling with the flood of resentment and sorrow that washes over me. The truth pierces it all, unpleasant on my tongue, unwilling to escape my lips.

But at last it does. "I cannot," I whisper. "It was my choice. I chose to become a monster."

"It is good that you know that," he says simply. He raises his head to the dawn, as one would turn their face towards a healing touch, and then pulls in a deep breath. "Come, it is time to go."

I recoil, staring at him. "Go? Where?"

Beowulf's brows knit together. "To Trollhattan, of course."

I nearly run back into the cave at those simple words.

"I can't." My heart is beating frantically, winging up into my throat. "They will kill me."

Beowulf holds out a hand to me. "I won't let them."

"Everyone hates me," I say desperately, trying to explain. Does he not understand that not all men are like him? I am still barely awake in this form that is both old and new, but one thing I know beyond a doubt is that Beowulf, and only Beowulf, has a heart that could pity a monster.

His gaze is unwavering as he looks at me. “I don’t hate you.”

I shake my head. He still does not understand that he is unlike the others. He doesn’t give evil what it deserves—but I know the men of Trollhattan will. They would be right to do so.

And at last I acknowledge that the thing that angered me for so long—that they were right to judge me—is true.

I start to cry: the silent, trembling tears of a child about to receive a dreaded punishment.

Beowulf stands so close I can feel his strength holding me up. His voice is the only thing that can pierce the wave of panic. “It will be all right. I won’t leave you, I promise. I will protect you. Don’t be afraid.”

I wipe my face and try to stop crying, but I can’t seem to stop.

I flinch as Beowulf brushes away the next tear with his thumb.

I look up at him, my agony brushed away by a startled wonder.

“You must understand,” says Beowulf, “That what has happened here this day is not about you or me. It is a testimony of the Almighty that must be shared. He has delivered us both. It must be made known to Trollhattan so that they might turn back to the one true God and be saved. The king must be told, Grendel.” He speaks my cursed name without revulsion, without anger. “But no matter his decision, no matter their reaction, I’ll stand by you. I swear you won’t be harmed while I am living.”

My pulse steadies and I am able to squint through the wet that tangles my eyelashes together. Beowulf looks back at me, as steady and sure as a rock.

Where else can I go other than where he leads? I am as lost and weak as a child. And besides that, he is my savior. There is no real choice before me. I followed him out of the dark, and now I must follow him into the light—there is simply no other option.

So when Beowulf holds out his hand, I take it, and we walk together across the narrow valley and up the soft and slippery rocks to the world above.

13

This journey to Trollhattan is different from the journeys I have made before. Though I walk through the same grass, climb the same hills, move around the same rocks, it feels like a place I have never seen until now.

The sky is once more familiar. The brief shine of blue and sun is gone, replaced by foul weather again: clouds roiling and racing in grey breakers across heaven's sea. And yet while the sky is recognizable, the earth beneath it has somehow changed.

I might look like a young woman again, but my eyes are those of a newborn. I look around with wondering eyes, half frightened by the world around me. I even walk carefully, somehow feeling that the grass could cut me if it wished.

The whole time, Beowulf holds my hand, never once slackening his grip.

I cannot remember the last time I held someone's hand. Perhaps when I was a child. I have a vague unpleasant memory of the woman that was my real mother grabbing me by the fingers and dragging me along beside her, disapproving, scolding, uncaring. Not like Beowulf at all. Unlike that half-remembered woman, he isn't angry when I keep tugging him to a stop to look at everything around me. Walking beside him makes me feel safe in a world that seems on the verge of swallowing me whole with its awful beauty.

I stare at a tiny purple flower resting amidst a clump of grass, mesmerized. How the seed came here is a mystery, for it is the only bloom of its kind for as far as I can see.

Beowulf bends down and picks it, holding it out for me to take.

I accept it cautiously, as if it might crumble, feeling once more that strange sensation of being a newcomer to the world. I cannot look away from the perfect purple petals.

"It's so beautiful," I whisper. "It's all so good . . . and I once hated it." I look up at Beowulf. He is watching me, and I quickly lower my head again. "I . . . resented everyone for being able to enjoy the world, when I could not." I don't know what to do with the flower in my hands, so I give it back to Beowulf, unwilling to drop it on the ground. "All I could see was that they had all that I wanted and never got. I hated them for judging me." My words falter. "And they will judge me still."

"You know Hrothgar only as an enemy," Beowulf reminds me, "but I knew him as a friend, as a young king who, in his youth, saved a wolf-hound thought by others to be so wild they called for it to be drowned—taming it until it became his companion. He was once more than what you see now." Beowulf tucks the flower into the cowl of the cloak he placed on me an hour ago—his own cloak. "The people must be given the chance to receive the truth. How can we expect the Almighty to extend mercy to us and not to them?"

His comment drives home like a nail and I hang my head, unwilling to reveal my fresh shame and confusion.

Beowulf dips his head so that he can look up into my face. "Even if you do not share my faith in the Almighty yet —trust me."

I lick my lips and whisper, "I am afraid."

Beowulf takes my arm and squeezes it lightly. "It will not be for long. I ask for no reward for my services from Hrothgar except this: that your freedom be guaranteed. Then I will take you home." He pauses and looks at me. "Do you remember where you came from?"

The word 'home' strikes me like a fist, slapping away the overwhelming gratitude of his promise of protection.

It has been coming back to me in bits and pieces. There was a village, perhaps fifty miles north of here. Parents who hadn't cared and were glad when I left their home for the lonely independence of a hovel. A hovel on the edge of a settlement that I had never liked, full of people who had never liked me.

I remember years of loneliness and bitterness, festering behind the walls of a cottage surrounded by dark trees that seemed to carry whispers—echoes of someone calling for me to come out of my shadow and into my power.

I flinch away from those memories and swallow back sudden bile. "I don't want to go back."

"Then you can go anywhere," Beowulf promises.

I look at him and the words are at the tip of my mind, but freeze on my tongue. *Could I not go anywhere with you?*

I do not know why I think it, except that the thought of being without my savior in this strange world, a world that loves me no better than when I was a monster, terrifies me.

I hold on to him as we crest the next rise, and my breath drops from my lungs as Schrawynghop appears, spread out below us. It no longer looks like a curse to me. It looks like a child's toy. It's just wood and stone. It is no longer a fortress keeping me locked outside. It's just a settlement.

I stare at it, my lower lip caught in my teeth. "It looks . . . different."

"That's because you are different now." Beowulf starts to tug me forward.

For the first time, I pull away, everything inside me urging me to run.

Beowulf places his free hand over my fingers, clasping my fist between two rough palms, and waits until I finally drag my gaze away from those distant walls and look at him.

"Trust me," he says.

My breath stutters in my ears, but I jerk out a shaky nod, and we start down the slope.

Slowly, we walk across the expanse of grass, towards the shadow of the wall, towards the gate where I was never allowed to pass through, into full view of the guards that only a few nights before had fled at the sight of me or thrown their spears at me—intent on avoiding or killing me, hating me either way.

I am shivering uncontrollably, and Beowulf lets go of my hand only to slip his arm around my shoulders and draw me to his side.

"No one will hurt you," he whispers. "I promise."

I press close to him. I have no reason to doubt that he will fail in what he has promised. He has already done the unthinkable and impossible, simply because he has sworn it.

We walk into a courtyard that seems strangely deserted, save for the sentries who shout for a messenger to be sent to King Hrothgar. The call goes out across Schrawynghop: Beowulf has returned alive.

Gripping Beowulf's hand, I move up the steps of the Hall that never welcomed me, that always loathed me. I stand on the threshold of a building I never dared to enter without the protection of my monstrous form, and I walk into the inner room, with no defense but the man beside me.

Just as when I walked out of the cave, once more I go willingly to my end, because I can see no other path.

I half shut my eyes as the warmth of candles floods my face and body, as if the room wishes to burn me alive. The name that I cling to is the first thing I hear in the Hall.

"Beowulf!"

The cry bursts from the center of the room and ripples to the edges as a sea of faces turns to the warrior beside me.

Their greetings are a clamor of warring speech. "Beowulf! You've come back! What happened?"

Beowulf's great, glad voice reaches the farthest edges of the room, and I cling to the sound of it, even though his words make me tremble.

"The monster that has plagued this hall is dead at my hand."

Shock and joy races through the room, dozens of exclamations running together in one dizzying outcry, until one question penetrates the clamor.

"Who is this?" a man asks, and I suddenly, horribly, feel their gaze upon me. I drop my chin so that my hair falls forward to hide my face: a pathetic shield.

Beowulf puts an arm through mine so that I can lean on him once more. If he had not, I might have fallen. My legs felt like water beneath me.

"This is . . . one of the monster's prisoners," Beowulf says carefully. "She has been a slave for many years, but I freed her from the cave when I killed her mistress."

A compassionate murmur fills the room, and it makes me writhe. I feel that I might break to pieces with dread, knowing how that sound will change in the next few moments.

A skeptic pierces the sympathy directed towards me. "What proof do you offer of the monster's death, Lord Beowulf?"

Beowulf frowns as he turns towards the speaker, and he casts the bloody bag he carries onto the floor. "There is your evidence."

A few men come forward and cast a grisly look into the bag before they recoil. I shut my eyes, not wanting to see.

A whisper runs through the room and turns into a gasp.

Beowulf raises his voice again. "Schrawynghop is free, by the power of the Almighty."

Beowulf lets go of me then and presses through the onlookers, moving towards the back of the Hall. Men part before him like water, and I, afraid to let him out of my sight, move to the nearest wall, away from the crush of people. I slide along it, following Beowulf at a distance, keeping in the shadows and away from the glare of the candles.

Beowulf stops before a man with a white face above a blood red robe.

Unferth.

The dragon priest stands his ground, clearly not because of courage—his red robes tremble like an autumn leaf—but purely because some last shred of the bravado he carried as court challenger makes him stand his ground.

Beowulf looks at him for a long moment before he speaks, so softly the entire hall goes quiet to listen.

"You did not expect to see me again, did you Unferth?"

Unferth lets out a kind of panicked snarl—the sound of an animal at bay. "You are a fool, Beowulf."

"It is true I wish to believe the best in people." Beowulf does not look towards me, but I feel his voice reach out to me, and I shiver. "Sometimes that results in good and other times it leads to error." His voice sharpens. "But I would rather be a fool than a liar and a murderer." He turns to the onlookers and pulls a fragment of giant's blade from his belt, holding it aloft. "This man you have welcomed into your court is more than a demon worshiper. You know the stories, that he murdered his own kinsman—well, now I have evidence that he has not given up his old ways. He gave me a cursed blade with the hand of friendship, swearing to me that it would not fail. It did fail me, and because of it I nearly perished when I battled the monster."

"Lies!" Unferth screeches above the sudden outcry from the onlookers. "This man is using this monster to sow dissension in our community and to make himself indispensable to you. He wants my position—he wants power—and he will spread lies to achieve it! It is only his word against mine!" Despite his bold words, Unferth's eyes dilate, and they dart around to take in the suspicious looks cast his way.

"Auschere would know if this was a cursed blade," a man built like a blacksmith says, and a moment of sober silence pushes the whispers to the corners of the room.

"But Auschere is not here," Unferth says with brutal satisfaction, rallying himself a little. "I am not denying the blade is cursed—perhaps it is. I only maintain that I did not give it to Lord Beowulf. Perhaps he brought it back from the monster's lair to entrap me. Beowulf cannot prove his accusations. He could have broken it himself. What witness do you bring?"

"Me."

Everyone in the Hall turns to look at the strange girl in their midst, and I feel myself sway under their collective gaze, but I never look up. My hair hides my face, and my voice is barely audible, even in my own ears.

"I saw it. I saw the blade fail him. There was a flash like—like poison. I have been enchanted these ten years: I know curses when I see them. The blade was cursed to fail any who wielded it."

A man raises his fist as if to hit Unferth. "That's all the testimony I need! It is you who crave power, Unferth, and that is why Beowulf is a threat to you!"

Unferth is backing away towards the corner of the room, searching for an escape, sensing the mood of the room turn ugly. "You all know this can't be true. I have proved myself to you."

"How so?" someone shouts from the back of the room. "What have you done for us? This only proves what many of us have suspected for years: that you brought the curse of the Dragon with you into Trollhattan! We have tolerated you because of your royal favor, Unferth. I, for one, no longer care who holds you up. It is time you were brought down."

The men surge forward, sweeping Beowulf to one side as they rush heedlessly forward. Their shout rings to the rafters.

"Cast Unferth out! Cast him out!"

And Unferth is lost in the crush of the crowd.

I stand frozen and terrified against the wall, foreseeing my own fate in the heedless judgment of the Hall and Unferth's helpless scream.

"Hold!" Beowulf yells over the roar. "Do not take this matter into your own hands!" He springs into the mob, pushing them apart as he cuts through them like a drawn sword.

"Hold! If you tear him apart like dogs, are you any better than the monster you've just been freed from?"

The crowd subsides at that, murmuring with a mixture of reluctance and shame.

Unferth's head reemerges when he is yanked up from where he had been pressed into the floor. His eyes meet Beowulf's, wild with fear and hatred, hating that it is Beowulf's words that had saved him and yet trembling to be saved.

Beowulf looks back at him. "The king must decide his fate."

I do not dare move, for fear of drawing attention to myself. I only wait and watch and dread along with Unferth.

"Let him be held somewhere, unharmed, until Hrothgar decides his punishment," Beowulf continues. "But keep a hold of him," he adds, as the challenger tries to twist out of the grip of two of the biggest men.

Despite Unferth's efforts to free himself and plead his case, the crowd is implacable, and he is borne out of the Hall with the energy of long-repressed dislike, dragged out the door to some unseen prison.

I watch with sickened eyes, my chest heaving, as the man who was once an ally, but who was really another pawn of the monster I had called Mother, is carried away, cursing and spitting and utterly powerless.

I feel as if I am in a fevered dream, somehow seeing my own future playing out before me. This is what the people of Trollhattan would do to me—if they knew the truth.

My mind goes blank, my thoughts snapping apart at last under the unyielding pressure of anxiety, wiped clean by dread and confusion and the chaos of the room.

I am only half aware that Beowulf has been swept off his feet and onto shoulders. He is twirled to the center of the room as scorn turns to triumph. My savior is swallowed up by a roar of such energy that I stumble backwards, seeking some alcove in which to hide myself. Instead, I stumble into someone on the Hall's doorstep.

I leap back, terrified, and look up into the gentle face of a woman perhaps a decade older than me, with a wan face and fair hair, both touched prematurely with age. She seems familiar to me, but I know her only as a kinswoman of Hrothgar of some kind, perhaps a cousin.

I am half aware of a young boy peeling himself away from the cheering audience and approaching us, bowing to the woman that has only now entered the Hall. "My lady Yrsa!"

"What has happened?" Her voice is husky and her eyes surprised as she studies me.

"Lord Beowulf has returned!" the boy says. "He has killed the monster and accused the court challenger of attempting to destroy him."

Yrsa does not look any more displeased by this than the crowd did, and she dismisses Unferth's fate with a disinterest that chills me.

Her eyes move from the boy back to me. "And who is this?"

The boy takes my arm. I flinch at his touch, though it is kind. "Lord Beowulf said this girl was a prisoner in the monster's cave for ten years, my lady! He begged that she be treated kindly."

Yrsa looks at me with a sympathy she would not have possessed if she really knew who I was. "Why, you poor child." Without warning, she draws me close to her.

I stiffen, almost choking on the sudden fragrance of blossoms. Yesterday, the scent of such a human would have enraged me. Now, it only overwhelms—the sharp femininity pricking me with the needling reminder that I am still so far away, and so far beneath, this gracious lady.

"You have shelter here, my dear. I welcome you into my own household. You shall serve me as my handmaiden, and I will train you myself."

My stomach shrivels within me, and I cast a wild look over my shoulder at Beowulf.

He looks back at me, and his brows knit as he watches Yrsa bearing me away. He is unable to break free of the men crowding around him, but he offers me a quick smile of reassurance, reminding me with his eyes that he promised on his life to save me.

I might as well be a leaf on a wave. I am whisked away from him, swept away to an unknown future.

14

I bathe for the first time in years and am clad in a gown of pale gold that someone gladly lent, but the warm bath and bright gown do little to melt my nerves. Sitting rigidly in Yrsa's private quarters, surrounded by her maids and feeling as if I am trapped in a dovecote, I do not know where to look. I am a monster hidden amidst clucking birds.

I wonder if I killed anyone they knew—a father or brother or sweetheart. I do not dare meet their eyes. I merely wait for the messenger that must surely arrive at any moment telling me that Hrothgar demands my immediate execution.

I will, at least, die presentable.

Yrsa kindly offers to comb my hair, a terrible tangle that only the greatest patience could unravel. Rather like my life.

I accept meekly and sit in front of a hammered bronze mirror, my hands twisting uncontrollably in my lap as she works.

"You have beautiful hair," Yrsa says kindly.

I do not answer as I look once more at my reflection: this time into a mirror, instead of a pool, to observe a girl, and not a monster.

I can recognize, with utter dispassion—as if making note of someone else—that I do have pretty hair: straight and dark. It is strange to see long flowing hair after years of looking at a reflection in which so many of my features were distorted by the enchanted hood Mother had placed upon me, and the little that could be seen of my face was all fangs and hideous skin.

I am a girl again. Pale and startled and a little lost-looking, but a girl. When did I last wear a dress like this? When was I last clean and groomed? I can't remember. The frenzy of whirling thoughts that I had grown so accustomed to are gone. My thoughts are slower here, individual threads that I can sort into patterns, but the memories are still slow in returning. I know it is partially because I do not want to remember. There is nothing good to recall except a lifetime of shame and sin.

I cannot remember. I can only focus on the present, though that is little better, for the alarm I feel surrounded by these once-hated strangers crowds out the hoard of hope that Beowulf gave to me.

I look away from the mirror. If these people really knew who I am, the banquet planned for tonight would turn into a mob. All their joy would be dashed, turned to betrayal and anger. In between the mutton and the venison, they would serve up Grendel the monster, torn limb from limb, to be devoured by their hatred.

Yrsa does not press me to talk and soon falls silent herself. I find my ears catching the giggles of two of the handmaids at the end of the room, who gossip as they prepare their lady's finery.

"Hrothgar is still so weak the healers only dared to rouse him long enough for Lord Beowulf to tell him that the monster is finally dead."

My pulse quickens. So this is why a messenger has not yet come. Hrothgar has not yet been told.

I am safe. But for how long?

"I heard that Beowulf wished to entreat Hrothgar for some great boon, but he did not have the opportunity to ask for it before he was made to leave by the healers."

"Did I hurt you?" Yrsa murmurs, her comb suddenly stilling. I had just jumped as if bitten.

I shake my head, still too afraid to speak to her, and turn my head a little towards the girls.

" . . . what of the shrine? Will it be torn down, do you think? Now that Unferth. . . ."

"I do not know. I heard Lord Beowulf urging some men to do so, but without the king's orders. . . "

"He can barely speak, I hear. Not since his breakdown at the death of Auschere."

Yrsa's hands stiffen on my head, and I cast her a startled glance in the mirror. So this explains the delay in Beowulf telling Hrothgar who I really am—and it explains the strained look on Yrsa's face.

"Perhaps he will be better tomorrow," one maid says hopefully. "At least the monster is dead and there will be the great feast—in our old Trollhattan!—to celebrate Lord Beowulf. We are free."

"And free to feast our eyes on Lord Beowulf tonight."

They burst into peals of laughter that gurgle to a stop as Yrsa turns sharply towards them. "Enough of your gossip. Fetch my gems."

The girls scuttle away and I watch them, troubled by their words—not just because of what it means for me, but because of their comments about Beowulf. They do not understand him or what he has done. He is more than just a face to be admired; the feast is more than just a party. How is it that I can see that, and they cannot?

I finally dare to speak to Yrsa as I rise quickly from my stool.

"My lady, I . . . I would like to be alone, if I may."

"Of course—" Yrsa begins, and I do not wait for her to say more. I offer an awkward and belated curtsey and hurry out of the room, thinking bitterly that only the day before I would have never dreamed of offering her such respect. Now it is all I can do not to drop at her feet and beg forgiveness.

It is strange to wander freely through Schrawynghop. Not one person stops me—in truth, few even notice me. The entire court is gripped with excitement as they prepare for a grand feast and speculate on what will become of the unfortunate Unferth.

I do not stop to hear the rumors, for I know it will only be fuel upon my own fevered imagination of what might be in store for me.

I do not ask anyone where Beowulf might be. Somehow I already know.

I find him on the beach, at the point where he first met Auschere only a few days ago. Now it is only he who watches in the place where land, sea, and sky meet. Alone.

I hang back in the shadow of the sea cliffs, unsure of how to approach him, telling myself I am content merely to observe him, even though I am not. Shame holds me back. The creature I had pledged my service to murdered his friend—how can I go to him as if nothing is wrong?

He must have sensed eyes upon him, for he turns and sees me. And, to my astonishment, he invites me to come closer with a wave of his hand.

I creep across the sand, unable to even meet his gaze as I stop before him.

Beowulf sees the look on my face. "Are you all right?" He takes in my dress and hair. "You look well, but your face is still pale."

My hands move nervously to pluck the folds of my dress and the ends of my hair as I try to form my fear into tangible words, while Beowulf waits patiently, as kind and strong as the nearby boulder shielding us from the brunt of the wind.

"What is it?" he prompts gently.

The words sound like a death knell in my own ears. "They don't know yet."

He knows what I mean without needing further explanation. "No, they don't."

Beowulf rises to his feet with a little shower of sand. "I will not throw you to the wolves, Grendel. I intend to tell Hrothgar and then see you safe away—he cannot refuse me that. And then I shall come back, alone, long enough to tell them of the Almighty's mercy." He smiles. "I shall be able to tell them that you have begun again in a good place."

I look at the sand, watching the wind make patterns in it that are as meaningless as the future he describes for me. "How do you begin again after you have died? You killed me in that cave, Lord Beowulf."

"No," says Beowulf. "You laid down your own life—you chose to do so."

I wrap my arms around myself, suddenly cold. "However it was done, I died in that cave and . . . and I don't know what I am now except that I do not yet feel what these people feel or you feel. Something inside me is still dead. How can I be sure that I was really meant to be saved?"

"The Almighty wishes that all might be saved." Beowulf takes my hand and I try not to cringe. "You surrendered the sword in your heart, but now you must choose to take up arms again under a new master."

Slowly, I withdraw my hand. "I cannot begin again. No one will let me. The people of Schrawynghop will kill me, or at least cast me out, when they discover who I am. The story will spread, and no matter where I go, all anyone will ever see is Grendel."

I try in vain to hold back tears, but I cannot contain a long ugly sniffle, and finally I give up with a pathetic snort, rubbing my nose on the back of my hand.

"My mother—the thing I once called Mother—once told me that death was my destiny. She was right, in a way, wasn't she? Except the death of others was not my destiny—only my own."

Beowulf steps closer. "I told you I won't let any harm come to you. But before I go"—my heart sinks at that—"I hope you come to understand that the fear that once enslaved you is not as unbearable as it would seem. All of us live only to die, so it seems to me that the greatest goal in life is that we die well. We are all moving towards the end, Grendel. But the fortunate die twice. The second time is at the end of life, but before that, some die to self—putting their pride, their ideas, their desires on the altar and slaying them as an offering."

I feel my brow furrow. "Like the little altar at the hawthorn tree?"

Beowulf tips his head to look up at the sky. "Far holier than that. That altar is only a brazen imitation, an insult, to the one altar that matters: the Almighty's."

I glance up at the sky too, remembering that Someone who spoke to me out of the storm of my first ending. "You speak of Him as if He were so close, so real."

"He is real, and He is close."

There is a brief pause, and his assurance that someone watches me, even now, reminds me of another sentry.

I look back up at the cliff top, and Beowulf looks with me towards the window in the rock where an old man once watched, and might have watched us still, if the worst had not happened.

My voice cracks. "How can you not loathe me?"

There is no blame in Beowulf's words, no reproach. "Because the Almighty loves you."

I am blinded by a rush of tears. "I don't see how. Can He forgive me for what I've done?"

"He could forgive even more." Beowulf's voice is soft, but it carries easily over the sound of the waves, for we are standing close together, so close I am in his shadow. "The other night, in the valley, when He showed me that you were not my enemy, I begged Him for your salvation and asked Him that He might forgive you. And look how He has brought you out of the dark! But now you must ask Him yourself to bring you into the light."

My voice is strangled. "I'm not sure He hears me."

Beowulf smiles. "I know He does. If you had not cried out to Him in your heart, I would not have been able to come so far. If you had not wanted Him, we wouldn't have removed your curse."

I bite my lip, trying to wrap my mind around it—wanting to —but struggling to surrender the fear of the future.

Beowulf suddenly drops to the beach and leans back on his elbows, cocking his head to look up at me and patting the beach with one hand.

"Come, sit with me. Look at the sea. Do not worry now. He has brought you into peace. Taste it. Learn its name."

I sink slowly onto the sand and for the first time look around at something other than the man beside me.

The sun is beginning to set, staining the sky with soft smears of purple and pink, as soothing as the waves rolling over one another, again and again. The wind has calmed, so that the sand no longer stings, and as I slowly relax, it enfolds me like soft arms, revealing a modicum of this morning's warmth, still stored beneath the surface.

The silence deepens and my heartbeat calms for a moment as I look out across the seemingly endless horizon, where the fading sun has begun to pour like molten gold into the crucible of a sun-streaked sea.

I can look clearly at the light now—a miracle in and of itself. I cling to that, and, for an instant, do not think of what lies beyond this moment.

I point my chin at the expanse before us and ask shyly, "Heofon is beyond all that?"

Beowulf tilts his head in a nod. "Yes."

The necklace around my throat suddenly chokes me. "You must be eager to go home."

There is a strange silence beside me, and I look around to see Beowulf drawing in the sand. But he does not draw homes and hearths, only swords and ships.

"Soon, I will take my leave of this place, though I will not be going home—my path lies wherever the Almighty leads me next. The only home that concerns me now is yours. I can take you back to your village. Would you like that?"

I wouldn't.

Beowulf looks over when I make a whimper of protest in the back of my throat, sand sliding between his fingers. "What is it?"

I do not tell him the resistance that is raging inside of me. Instead I ask, "What is your home like, my lord?"

Beowulf stops drawing and gives me a strange glance. "It is a beautiful place, a land far richer and more peaceful than these shores. But I am rarely there."

I feel a stirring of longing at the tenderness in his voice and speak to the translucent wave nibbling at the edges of my shoes. "If it is so good, how can you stand not to be there always?"

Beowulf wipes the pictures out of the sand, and it is just a beach once more, and no longer a glimpse into his mind. "I cannot enjoy my peace when I know there are people in this world who have never tasted it."

I dig my hands into the sand until the grit scrapes my palms. He means me.

It is so very wrong, that Beowulf must spend his life saving wretches and friends, and so unfair that I want more from him. I am ashamed that I cannot leave him in peace, even now. And yet . . . and yet, I cannot bear to leave him. . . .

Beowulf tosses a sliver of shell into a wave, like an offering, and we watch the sea swallow it.

"Since I was a boy, I knew I had been given a gift and an unusual strength to war against the Almighty's enemies. A fighter cannot be resting by a hearth; he must go into the world, searching for the enemy."

I try to nod, though I am not sure I can imagine giving up a place of belonging and peace for a lifetime of wandering and hardships. It is too great a mystery for my already swollen mind, and besides, all I can think of is the implication behind his words.

He is not returning home. If Beowulf does not return to Heofon, where will he go?

And how can I go on without him?

Something moves in the waves before us, a flash of paler silver, startling me from my thoughts.

Beowulf jumps to his feet, sand kicking up beneath his feet.

"Sea wolves!" he exclaims, his voice as bright as his eyes. "Are they not beautiful?"

The waves shatter as one of the creatures flings its great, shining body free of the water. It hangs for a moment, sleek and silver, suspended in glistening fountains of spray, before plunging into the sea again with a great slap.

I jump up too, and we stand there watching, shoulders almost touching.

Beowulf moves forward, until he is up to his ankles in foam, and turns towards me with a quick smile. "It is in my heart to take a swim. Stay on the beach—you'll be safe." Then he turns and dives into the sea.

I stare as Beowulf swims towards the beasts with strong and steady strokes just as a sea wolf breaches the surface with another joyous burst. The light of the sunset catches on the shining skin and the shining water with a sudden searing beauty that makes my heart ache.

My pulse stutters as the bright eye of the nearest creature rolls back to look at me, its curved muzzle seemingly upturned in a smile, before it slips beneath the waves again.

Hardly realizing what I am doing, I kick off my shoes, slough forward through the surf, and plunge into the sea after Beowulf.

The water is cold enough to slice through me, and I can feel every nerve, every heartbeat, every movement, painfully heavy and real.

A kind of strange exultation seizes my heart as I break the surface with a gasp and find that a receding wave has borne me quickly out into the depths and nearly alongside Beowulf.

Beowulf meets my gaze with a look that is only briefly startled before it transforms into a grin of delight. Understanding flashes between us so intensely I am nearly breathless—or perhaps it is only the chill of the water—and then we both turn to swim on together—into the glorious dance of the sea beasts.

Beowulf's powerful strokes cause him to shoot ahead of me. I squint through the splash and murk to see him catch the fin of one of the creatures. It turns briefly to snap at him, but he twists out of the way and holds on until the sea beast finally accepts him and begins to pull him along behind it.

Heart hammering, but determined, I kick towards a sea beast slipping past me and catch at its fin.

This one does not snap at me as Beowulf's creature did, but it races forward at such a speed my arm is nearly pulled from its socket.

I hold on, fighting for breath, exhilarated as I stream through the water, my heart rising with my head as the creature springs towards the surface in a spray of glistening water.

I open my mouth to breathe and laugh, and then we plunge down into the depths again.

I turn my head and glimpse Beowulf riding his own creature, laughing underwater, exultant and happy, and I suddenly realize, with a strange yet clear knowing, that at least in this moment, I am happy too.

We heave ourselves, wet and panting and coated in sand, onto the beach.

Beowulf rolls over on one elbow and looks down at me, surprise lingering at the edges of his face. "Weren't you frightened? Most would be."

I shake my head, making a little nest in the sand for my head.

"You did not stay where it was safe," Beowulf points out.

I gulp and stop smiling, fearing his reproach. "I'm sorry. I did not mean to ignore you. I just . . . I could not stay out of the sea when I saw them."

Beowulf looks at me with the slow dawning of a smile. "I understand," he says simply and looks out to sea, his expression lost in memory.

I do not speak, wary of disturbing him or ruining the

moment of peace, but after a pause I can no longer hold the words back. "I wish to tell you my name."

Beowulf turns quickly to me with a look of such pure gladness I cannot meet his eye, so I glance at the sky for safety.

It tastes foreign on my tongue, and unfitting. "It was—it is —Wynnhild."

"Wynnhild," Beowulf repeats. "A good name. You know its meaning?"

I feel myself flush. "Joyous battle. It does not suit me."

"Does it not?" Beowulf rumbles, his voice even more soft.

My brief happiness disappears—blown away like the wind sloughing away the grit on my skin. "I was born with a sword in my soul, but I have never known joy in wielding it."

"You fought amiss, but your heart did seek a higher truth, and now you have found it. There is nothing stopping you from finding the joy in your name now." His eyes crinkle down at me. "I am pleased to meet you at last, Wynnhild."

I smile, the salt of both tears and ocean clinging to my lashes, and then I laugh and Beowulf laughs with me, his voice ringing out so loud and clear across the beach that we do not hear the shouts until the servant is nearly on top of us.

"Lord Beowulf!"

Beowulf gets to his feet, and I scramble after him. We turn to the young man in servant's livery stumbling across the dunes to speak to us.

He bows to Beowulf and darts a quick glance at the ocean, as if he cannot believe what he has just seen. "The feast in your honor is about to begin, my lord, and the Lady Yrsa requests your presence. And you, little maid! My lady was worried by your absence and sent a girl to fetch you—she is waiting now for you at the top of the cliff."

I realize, with a rush of mild mortification, that I have just ruined the new dress I had been lent and filled my clean hair with sea salt. I look guiltily up at the small figure on the cliff top who will have to do her kind work all over again.

But . . . I cannot be entirely sorry for what I have done.

The servant is laughing as he looks at Beowulf. "Riding sea beasts once more, Lord Beowulf! And not alone. When the serving girl said that the lass had jumped in right after you, I did not believe her at first." The servant is clearly delighted, and some of that delight blossoms inside of me as he adds, "She is certainly the right companion for you, my lord."

"Yes," Beowulf says, with a swift, searching look at me, "she is."

15

Cleaned and dressed once more by the two servant girls, who do not giggle as much the second time around, I scuttle shamefacedly out of the women's quarters to make my way to Trollhattan. I struggle with the surprise of being invited to join them, and the surprise of hearing laughter and song coming from its doors, instead of sorrow. I no longer resent the sound of joy. This change rustles at my mind the way my skirts rustle at my ankles, but all my marveling grinds to a halt as I step into an inner courtyard and see what has been placed in its center.

Unferth is in a wooden cage in the middle of the compound, on full display for all to see and mock.

The pride that he always held closely about him is as tattered as his robe—his self-importance and his clothes shredded by the crowd that bore him from the Hall.

The people must have had their fill in tormenting him, or else they are distracted by the fresh pleasure of preparing for the celebration, for Unferth is alone save for the three guards ringed about his cage, and even they ignore him now.

Unferth—the court challenger, whose every word used to hold the people spellbound—is completely forgotten.

I press back against the shadow cast by the eave of the nearest building and watch him, trying to recognize this beaten man.

For a brief time, I hated him—a man I thought was coming to replace me in my master's estimation—but I feel no resentment now. I only feel unease, for I know, looking at him, that it could just as easily be me in that cage, and, by all rights, it ought to be. Unferth wasn't the only one who tried to kill Beowulf.

His shoulders are slumped in defeat. He tried to challenge Beowulf, and he failed. I know, a little, what that is like, and in this we are the same.

I must have stepped forward unconsciously, for Unferth's head jerks up, as if sensing movement, and I realize I have moved forward into the faint glimmer of torchlight.

We look at one another, and then he wraps his hands around the bars and leans forward, pushing his face between the bars as far as he can. His amber eyes are nearly yellow—as wide and wild as an animal at bay—and they rest right upon me.

He is shocked at first, then his face turns hungry, and he devours me with his gaze.

He looks at me as if I am an answer.

I back away, unnerved, as Unferth smiles—a slow curve of triumph—and I hurry away, heart pounding.

My uneasy feelings follow me into the Hall and do not loosen their hold, even though I am surrounded by high spirits.

The feasting around me only adds to my discomfort. I cannot remember the last time I saw people celebrate, and I cannot shake the sensation that there is something hollow beneath the singing. Surely that must only be me—I am the hollow core at the center of this unwitting crowd that laughs and eats believing that the monster is dead, not knowing that the monster sits amongst them in an uneasy knot.

I would prefer to be seated beside Beowulf, but he is on the dais at the end of the Hall with Yrsa, while I am seated some spear-lengths away at the table that lines the right-hand side of the room.

No one seems to notice that Beowulf himself is far quieter than a man who has won a great victory. Despite the many toasts offered to him, Beowulf looks distant and unhappy, mirroring my own feelings.

It is strange to be sitting in this hall as a welcomed guest when, seven nights ago, I spilled blood here. I should be satisfied. At long last I am one of them—accepted with warmth. But the feeling of Unferth's eyes upon me in the courtyard, the sight of Beowulf's somber face, and my own burgeoning secret is a three-pronged prod of discomfort that keeps me from enjoying the feast.

I wonder at the unease in Beowulf's face, as if he also senses something wrong in the room, or does not fully approve of the celebration. And suddenly I remember: the shrine in the copse. Has it not yet been torn down, as Beowulf so deeply wished?

I look at him and guess that it hasn't—and I wonder if the emotion I feel lingering at the corners of the room might be defiance.

"More wine, little maid?"

I timidly hold out my glass for the man beside me to fill it. I am too shy to look him in the face, so my gaze slides towards his forehead instead. I freeze when I see the ugly wound at his hairline, only half healed.

My hand tenses, and when I look down at the puddle of wine I spilled on the floor, I see his outstretched arm, with the five scarlet lines caused by my claw marks.

I shrink back, avoiding his gaze, as he turns to speak to a more talkative companion, leaving me to my churning thoughts.

Trollhattan's bard paces before the roaring hearth and begins to sing of the beautiful and brave captive who aided Beowulf in defeating the great monster.

I squirm: it is fitting that they should sing of Beowulf. Every bit of praise for him that rings under the rafters is fully deserved. But such praise I do not deserve—and every line of the bard's song strikes me with a knife-wound of guilt.

The merriment continues, but I am only feverishly aware of it, and I cannot eat another bite. The celebration goes on, unabated, until the windows begin to reveal that the night is stained with dawn.

King Hrothgar was not with us when the feast began. While his people rejoiced through the night, he was resting in the care of healers. But he comes at dawn, mounting the dais to join Beowulf and Yrsa as a chorus of happy cries greets him from the rest of the Hall.

I am the only one who makes no noise. I grip the arms of my chair and look towards the door.

Hrothgar does not smile as he greets his people. There is a grim purpose in the set of his face and shoulders as he turns to face the crowd that has grown restless with the coming day, looking for some fresh interest and entertainment to revive their flagging energies. Hrothgar provides it with three words that cut through my exhaustion like a fist through glass.

"Bring in Unferth."

The Hall greets this order with a low murmur of interest and approval, but Beowulf frowns, and I feel an echo of his discomfiture.

I knew Unferth would be put on trial for his crime against Beowulf, but I did not know it would be now—like this. Justice for the trap laid for Beowulf now feels more like a spectacle. Just as bones are thrown to the dogs on the hearth, Unferth will be thrown to the people of Trollhattan. And that is not what Beowulf wants.

There is a commotion at the doors, and then the former court challenger is brought into our midst.

To my shock, Unferth is no longer dragged between two men: he walks of his own volition. He almost seems eager to be brought before the king. The animal-like panic and the fervor of shame have fallen from him like a cast-off robe, and he walks up the aisle wrapped from head to foot in self-assurance.

My heart twists into a knot and rises slowly, sickeningly, into my throat.

He looks at me and smiles—the slow, calculated smile of a hunter about to strike.

I know what is coming, but I am unable to move.

Run. The old instinct whisks through my mind, but I stay in my chair, gripping the arms to keep myself from automatically fleeing. Whatever is coming is more than just inevitable—it is deserved.

I am done running.

Hrothgar leans forward on his throne as Unferth and his guards approach his dais. The jeers that started at the appearance of Unferth die down as the king raises his hand for silence. His voice is hoarse, but it still carries to the edges of the room, strengthened by his displeasure.

"Unferth, you stand before our court accused of treachery. We accuse you of willfully aiding and abetting the monster that plagued us and of attempting to murder our friend, Beowulf, prince of Heofon—the one man able to free us of the curse of Grendel."

Unferth does not speak, but he fairly gleams with gratification. An angry mutter runs through the crowd at his implacable calm.

Hrothgar's face darkens. "Do you have nothing to say for yourself? No defense at all?"

"I must confess, Your Highness," Unferth smiles, "I am shocked by this erroneous judgment. There is a monster in your midst, and yet you waste time and words accusing me."

Someone laughs, another person snorts, but the court challenger's persuasiveness still carries a mystical weight, for everyone begins to look at one another with questioning eyes.

Fear, along with my meal, rises inside me to sit hot and fetid in my throat.

"You ask me to defend myself, but I think it is Lord Beowulf who should be preparing his defense." Unferth looks around, enjoying himself. He is the only one who is. "Perhaps customs are different here, but I did not think the people of Trollhattan would hold a feast to honor a traitor and his monster."

All the air seems to leave the room, inhaled on a silent question as gazes swing, befuddled, towards the foreign warrior sitting beside King Hrothgar.

"It is true I gave Beowulf a cursed blade," Unferth purrs, "but I did it out of concern for all present. For I now know the secret that he hides from all of you."

Hrothgar slams a fist onto the arm of his throne despite the visible tremors that rack his body. "Enough of your games, Unferth. What is it you hint at?"

"I hint at nothing," Unferth retorts. "I accuse Lord Beowulf of lying to all those in Schrawynghop. I accuse Lord Beowulf of letting your most feared enemy live." His eyes are on Beowulf now, not Hrothgar. Venom twists his words into a snarl. "I accuse him of not only failing to kill Grendel, but bringing her here, to this very hall."

Unferth turns slowly, pretending to scan the room, but his gaze goes straight to me, his words striking like a knife. "That girl and Grendel are one and the same."

My stomach drops into my shoes.

Through the sudden pounding in my ears, I hear Hrothgar laugh. "You are mad, Unferth. You really believe that this girl was the thing that killed our warriors? How could you even conceive such an impossible story?"

"I will tell you how," Unferth snarls. "Because the night Grendel attacked Beowulf, I stood at the window as Beowulf made ready to face the beast, and I was watching when Grendel came through the door."

I can't stop shaking. No one moves in the Hall.

"The two of them fought, and during the struggle, Beowulf tore the thing like a covering off its head—a foul hood. And beneath it was the face of a human." Unferth's eyes find me and his voice rises to a near shriek. "Her face!"

All eyes turn to me, staring, staring, staring, and there is nowhere for me to hide.

16

I could not run even if I wanted to.

Unferth paces towards me, and his guards do not stop him; they are slack with shock. Only Unferth is crackling with life, like lightning about to burn something to the ground.

"Until less than an hour ago, I assumed with you all that when Beowulf claimed he killed a monster, he meant the thing attacking our hall. I had not realized there was more than one monster. The beast that killed Auschere must have been something other than Grendel—for Grendel still lives. She is sitting there, eating our food and drinking our wine and laughing at us. Just waiting to turn on us!"

Those on either side of me get up from their chairs and move away from me. I shut my eyes against Unferth's fresh lies, feeling the absence of the people's approval, as well as their growing fear, with a coldness that strikes at my very core.

"Impossible!" someone whispers, the single word carrying clearly in the stricken silence.

Unferth laughs, a cruel sound, a knife twisted into the pain enveloping the room. "Is it impossible, Lord Beowulf? Notice how he does not defend himself—because it is true! I testify to all of you that I saw the girl-beast he held at arm's length, and I saw his eyes when he beheld her. He was enchanted. Mesmerized."

Beowulf's hands curl on the arms of his chair, but he does not move, nor does he speak.

"He came here, preaching at us, calling us sinners," Unferth continues, his eyes glittering, "when he was the one embracing perversion. Bringing this creature not only to your midst but to his side. Shame upon him!"

I gasp aloud. I cannot believe what he has done to the truth. I cannot believe how he has tainted the purity of what Beowulf did for me. I was there too, and much closer than Unferth, and I now know what was in Beowulf's eyes. Pity. Kindness. Not desire.

Unferth has taken what happened and twisted it to sound sordid: his suggestive tone implies that Beowulf was motivated by lust. The very idea is absurd.

I want to cry and scream and pound at Unferth with my fists for daring to suggest such a thing, but I sit, uselessly, where I am.

Hrothgar breaks the awful pause. "Lord Beowulf, deny these wild accusations! Or you, child? Say something! Deny it!"

I cannot look at Beowulf; I can only stare at my hands. He says nothing, so I follow his example and do not speak, even though my mind is screaming.

"Is this true, Beowulf?" Hrothgar demands in a voice like growing thunder.

The room is silent. It is as if the Hall has become what it was under my wretched attacks once more: it has died. All of the festivity and joy has been sucked from the place, broken into shards that nothing can repair.

"It is true that Wynnhild was once Grendel," Beowulf says at last.

All the air seems to leave the lungs of the people in a strangled gasp.

Despite his illness, Hrothgar rises to his feet in a surge of cold and terrible fury. "You know what the Dragon Below has done to our people—to me!—and yet you brought its spawn into our midst."

Beowulf bows his head. "It was not my intent to insult or grieve you, Your Majesty."

"And yet you have"—Hrothgar's voice is like ice—"beyond all forgiving."

All is silent and frozen as Hrothgar pulls his sword from his sheath and lays it on the table before him with a clang that grates against my pulse.

"Beowulf." Something has died in his voice, and he doesn't sound like a human at all. "Give me one good reason why I should spare her life."

I look up at that and lurch unsteadily off the chair and onto my feet. Beowulf has risen too. Our gazes slam into one another before his eyes skid away to snag on the implacable Hrothgar. He spreads his hands, and my heart twists as I see him implore.

"Because you gave your word that you would give me anything I asked for as my payment for restoring Trollhattan. Your hall has been restored, and I ask now for my prize—that Wynnhild's life might be spared and that she would be allowed to go in peace. It is true that she was once Grendel. But she was only a Frisian, like all of you, under a terrible curse. The Almighty has broken her enchantment and restored her to her true form. Your prayers have been answered. You have been freed from Grendel's attacks—simply not in the way you expected. Will you really resent the Almighty for choosing to have mercy upon your enemy when He has shown mercy to you?"

"*Was* it a god's choice," Unferth interjects, "or was it yours?"

Beowulf looks at him coldly before turning to face the rest of the room. "You all know I go only where the Almighty commands and seek to do only what He says. From the moment I set sail for these shores, I sensed that this mission would be different, although I did not know how. I was sure I had been sent to kill Grendel. I was so certain of it that the Almighty had to speak to me in a dream before I would listen. He did not just send me to destroy the monster—but to free the prisoner trapped within the beast.

"When Wynnhild was freed from her enchantment, she was too vulnerable to be sent on her way, too weak to fend for herself, so I brought her here. It was not by choice or by plan that I did not reveal her identity to you as soon as I returned, King Hrothgar. I wished to speak with you privately, to arrange for her clemency and then help her on her way. Your ill health and great hospitality delayed me in achieving that."

Unferth strikes again, as quick and poisonous as a snake. "So you did not plan on telling the rest of us? Did you think our king was the *only* one who would want to know that you brought a monster into our midst?"

Beowulf keeps his gaze upon Hrothgar. "Forgive me for not informing you sooner. I sought only to extend the great mercy the Almighty has shown to all of us to someone else in greater need of it."

"Someone else? Or *something* else?" Unferth sneers.

At that, the room explodes.

A great cry rises to the rafters. It sounds like a pack of wolves giving tongue. There is a shocking hiss of steel being drawn as daggers and swords spring into hands and point towards me.

Beowulf jumps down from the dais, holding out his hands to placate the crowd.

"Stand aside, Lord Beowulf, or be cut down along with that monster you are sheltering," a man snarls.

Beowulf is shoved aside. Hands seize me. It is like being dragged into the dark undertow of the sea, drowned by thundering waves.

I am borne forcibly to the front of the Hall, hair and limbs yanked and pulled mercilessly, just as they were when I was attacked by the creature I once called Mother not three days ago.

And then suddenly I am free of them, thrown up onto the dais like a piece of meat, breathless and staring into the crowd—seeing nothing but frenzied fingers like claws, teeth like fangs.

My gaze drops to the long scratches on my arms. With a sick recognition of its rightness, I recognize the marks I made on others upon my own skin.

This is what you knew was coming all along. This is what you deserve.

I raise my head, swallowing back vomit, and cast a glance into the crowd, looking for some shred of hope.

Hrothgar looks at me with a face white with fury: there will be no mercy there. Yrsa stares, her eyes huge, as if her worst nightmare has come to life before her. I was right—all the sympathy that had been in that gaze before is gone now.

Then Beowulf is there, forcing his way through the seething crowd.

"Leave her be!" Beowulf leaps onto the dais beside me and bats away a tankard that someone throws at my head, with a savage glare for the perpetrator. "Wynnhild is under my protection. Anyone who harms her shall have to deal with me."

The chorus of outrage subsides into a chorus of angry muttering as the men hesitate to outright attack a renowned hero and, in that pause, I find the courage to speak.

I keep my eyes on Beowulf, and I find the words that have been growing inside of me since the moment my enchantment was broken, pushing at the edges of my heart and mind and now, finally, spilling freely from my lips.

"I have sinned against you all."

The crowd hisses, and I have to raise my voice to be heard. "I know I cannot expect your forgiveness—I dare not even ask for it." I lick my lips and press on. "Cowardice kept me from confessing to you who I was, and I accepted your kindness under false pretenses. But none of that blame can be laid upon Lord Beowulf. If his plan had been carried out, the truth would have been made known to King Hrothgar immediately, and Beowulf would have sent me away. Due to your king's illness, this was delayed."

"Yes!" someone shouts from the back of the room. "An illness *you* brought upon him!"

"That's a lie!" Beowulf snaps. "This girl is not the creature she once was. She has been under a curse for many years, but she chose to be free of it. She helped me kill the monster that enchanted her. I would not have escaped that lair without her, and she would not be a woman again if she had not chosen to become one."

"Then why didn't she choose it before and spare us all our grief?" a man shouts.

I shut my eyes, and the justice of the question pulls me apart.

Beowulf's voice lowers. "I know the sins against you are grievous. All I ask is that you spare her life and allow her to walk out of this hall free and whole."

"Why should she be allowed to walk away free and whole when threescore of our own lie buried beneath the waves, never to walk again, because of her?" the man demands with a snarl.

A chant rises from the crowd—so loud and so prolonged Beowulf can no longer make himself heard.

"Kill her! *Kill her*!"

There is the flash of silver, and I freeze as it plunges towards my chest.

Beowulf kicks at the man's wrist, and the blade swings wide, while I simply stand there, staring at my attacker's twisted face.

"You have no fear of our weapons, monster?" the man spits, and the spittle runs down my face. "Is it because you still have those cursed powers? You might at least cower before us. Have you no shame?"

"I have no powers," I whisper, and the Hall goes reluctantly quiet to hear me. "And I do have shame. But it is my lord Beowulf who saved me. It is up to him whether I live or die."

All eyes turn to Beowulf, waiting to see what he will say to that.

Beowulf draws in a long breath and meets the gaze of each man in the Hall in turn. "Only the night before last, you offered me a boon for delivering your country from death. I took no advantage and asked no favors until now. This is the boon I ask: that Wynnhild will be allowed to live. Vengeance has already been wrought—there is no need of further recompense."

"Perhaps no need for you, Lord Beowulf!" someone shouts. "You are not a Frisian, and it is not the blood of your brothers and fathers and cousins that has been spilled these past months."

"I did not bring this girl out of that cave to be killed here," Beowulf retorts.

"We would sooner die ourselves than have the creature that has haunted us sleep in peace in this hall!"

I swallow and hear myself speak again. More than hear it—I see myself—as if I have stepped out of my own body and am merely watching from some corner. "What you say about me is true. I deny nothing. Treat me as you will."

"Wynnhild—" Beowulf says under his breath.

I ignore him and raise my voice and, for a moment, the girl on the dais almost sounds like the golden warrior beside her. "All I know is that you do my lord Beowulf a terrible injustice. He left his home to help you when no one else would. He risked his life over and over again to free your hall and faced what no one else would. You owe him your lives."

The man with the blade explodes. "You, who have spilled blood in this hall, have the gall to stand there and tell us our blood runs cold? You, who have murdered our brothers, tell us we are unjust? Why should we listen to you? Your claws and fangs may be gone, but you're still a monster—no matter what Beowulf claims! How dare you criticize us? You, of all people. You, who last week crawled about on the earth in filthy rags, as senseless as a mad dog?"

Hrothgar raises a hand, silencing the man, and as all eyes turn to him, I expect him to fall over. It is as if the argument raging around him has been battering away at his resolve: he is unutterably weary. "I have heard all I wish to hear. It is an ugly story indeed, and now I shall make an end of it."

The silence in Trollhattan stretches to the breaking point.

Beowulf looks at Hrothgar with hope, and I realize it is not hope for himself or even for me—it is hope for Hrothgar. He wants the king of the Frisians to make a stand, to come to his own decision, to make a sound judgment at last.

But Hrothgar meets his look with something almost like cruelty, his next words crushing.

"Since you are so concerned with mercy, Lord Beowulf, you should be content with this decision. To show that you do not have the monopoly on magnanimity, we shall extend clemency ourselves. Let you both live with the shame of what you have done. Beowulf of Heofon, Unferth Far-Traveler, and you, girl-beast." He looks me in the eye, and my insides shrivel. "Leave our midst—and do not come back."

Unferth's smile has disappeared from his face, brushed off the way one of the men brushed the bones off his plate and onto the rush-laid floor for the hounds only moments before.

I blink away tears. I do not look at Beowulf—I cannot bear to, but I can feel Hrothgar's words strike him as clearly as if they had been fists.

"Great king," Beowulf speaks softly and swiftly. "Will you not sort the lies from the truth?"

Hrothgar does not even look at him. "I am not sure that is possible. And even if it were, my command stands. You will not speak again in this hall. Be gone, and do not return."

Beowulf holds his tongue at that, but Unferth does not.

"I have unveiled the traitor and saved you from the creature in your midst! I am your hero—not Beowulf. I have done nothing to warrant your judgment! I demand sanctuary!"

As he speaks, he draws unconsciously towards Beowulf and me. The three of us stand in a row, surrounded by the people of Trollhattan, who watch us like a pack of dogs waiting for the signal to ravage, their eyes on us, their ears straining to hear Hrothgar's final word.

Hrothgar's voice is dull as he turns and steps off the dais, away from the disaster, retreating to his own quarters to nurse his own thoughts.

"Cast them out."

His bowed shoulders disappear behind the sudden crush as the people of Trollhattan descend with a howl of approval.

Surrounded by the din, I realize with a sudden clarity that the people have gotten what they most wanted.

By casting us out, they will be free not only of the shadow of Grendel, but of the two men that wished them to change their ways and commit to one way or another. Worshiping Beowulf's God or Unferth's idol was all the same to them—an inconvenience.

They couldn't be more pleased right now.

Unferth tries to follow Hrothgar, but he is seized and borne away. Beowulf and I are jerked down from the dais and ushered down the long hall, to the great double doors that Beowulf had ordered to be restored.

Yesterday, they applauded Beowulf. I know. I was there. They hung on his every word.

Today they no longer give him their ear—only their spittle, long streams of it, falling at his feet, on his clothes, upon his face.

I begin to cry hot tears of fury at their inconstancy. I want to fly at them, but how can I? Only a few days ago, I tried to kill Beowulf in this very place, and I did not raise a claw to stop the killing of his best friend.

I have no right to judge them, and I look at Beowulf's face and see that, even though he has such a right to do so, he does not despise them. So I try to imitate him, wrestling with loathing for them and for myself, as I follow him through the sneering crowd.

The crowd presses us into the dawn, and we stumble in the sudden blinding glare of flaming color that sweeps across the sky. We do not pause for long before we are driven forward again, through the bothies, in one long, miserable procession straight to the gate.

I shake under the onslaught of their hatred as memories pour over me. All the old feelings and fears threaten to overwhelm me again: I can never belong, I will never be welcome, I will always be cast out.

Then I look at Beowulf's face, and my heart casts aside my own hurt as I think of his own rejection that he bears so silently. I fix my mind on him, and I can bear the pain.

No one touches us—even in all their fury they still do not dare to touch Beowulf or the one he advocates for—but Unferth is given no such wide berth. He is man-handled through the gate and physically thrown to the ground where he is kicked and spat upon, before the crowd turns to simply glare at us as we walk past them.

The difference is marked—as is the reason. The people wished to punish someone, but they did not dare insult the son of a foreign king. Happily, no one was afraid to physically eject a wandering court challenger without a court to call home.

I see one final glimpse of Unferth's furious face as he stumbles to his feet. He is incapable of believing that his schemes against Beowulf have failed him catastrophically once more.

I have one small moment of wicked satisfaction at seeing Unferth's jealousy erupt again as he fully and finally understands that Beowulf is the superior man.

"Come away, Wynnhild," Beowulf says softly, and I turn my gloating face from the sight of Unferth, avoiding Beowulf's gaze as I fall into step beside him.

We pass through the gate with the curses of the people of Schrawynghop pelting our backs like stones, and then we strike out across the moor. We do not stop until we are out of sight of the wall. It is only then that Beowulf halts and turns to face the settlement he can no longer see.

"I'm sorry," I whisper. "I'm so sorry."

Beowulf keeps looking back, towards his former allies. "It's not your fault."

"But they think—" I break off, humiliated for him.

Beowulf turns around at that. "It doesn't matter what they

think. This is not a new trial to me, Wynnhild. There were rumors about me before I ever came here. There will always be rumors about those who seek the Almighty's path, spread by those who do not understand."

I remember Beowulf's first confrontation with Unferth, and all the accusations made against him then, and I realize he is right. And yet, I feel this time is still worse. Those other places and people that might have treated Beowulf badly were strange to him. Trollhattan is different. Here he had been happy as a child, accepted as a friend and even as a son. Those memories made this betrayal bite far more deeply.

I wish I could offer some comfort, but I do not know what to say. I walk with him to the coast, gripped by the feeling that we are in some bizarre and uneasy dream.

A few men of Trollhattan follow us at a distance, clearly to ensure that we leave Frisia's shores immediately. Their presence lurks at our heels like a shadow and makes me hurry, aware of little save for Beowulf's silent, solid presence.

We arrive at the coast and make our way down the steep, sandy path that leads from the cliff tops to the natural harbor where, only a few hours ago, Beowulf and I had played.

The men remain on the cliff top, watching us. No one offers us a boat, and we have to swim for Beowulf's small ship anchored in the bay. This swim holds nothing of the joy of yesterday evening—we are silent as we cut through the waves.

I tread water while Beowulf lets a swell lift him high enough to clutch at the bowsprit and clamber aboard, where he throws a rope ladder down to me.

I struggle up it until he can reach me and pull me onto the deck. I stand there, shivering, and look around at the vessel that brought Beowulf here to kill me. How strange that it will now be my sanctuary.

I have never been on a boat before. I fumble to obey Beowulf's soft instructions as he pulls up the anchor, and we leave this small harbor of Frisia's coastline and turn the vessel out to sea.

"Where will you go?" I ask, keeping my hand on the tiller as he has instructed.

A stiff breeze fills the sails, and Beowulf raises his face to let it brush his frown away. I can see his mood lifting to meet the rising wind. "Wherever the next monster is. Wherever the Almighty leads me. It could be anywhere."

Anywhere. I taste the word on my tongue. Never before have I been free to go anywhere. Before the cave, I was trapped in my village, too poor to leave, and then when the creature I called Mother enchanted me, I was trapped in my own body—strong enough to go anywhere but too afraid to wander far from that dark cave.

It doesn't seem fair that Beowulf's humiliation and expulsion should be yet another gift to me, but it is.

Beowulf glances at me, and suddenly he smiles. It is a sad, sober smile, yet edged by that unshakable peace that reaches out and touches me, and I realize that he has not been ruined by what happened, and neither have I.

I look back towards the beach and see a few figures lingering on the sand, as if making sure Beowulf truly leaves.

I was right. Even in my terrible enchantment, I wasn't wrong about these people. Many of them are weak—as fickle as the wind, as changeable as the sky.

But, looking back at them now, I don't despise them for it, because I know I could just as easily be them and, indeed, I have been something much worse.

For the first time in my memory, I do not crave their approval. It does not destroy me to not possess it. I only want one person's approval now.

I turn my back to the shore and look at Beowulf's profile fixed steadily on the horizon.

I do not know if I am free—but I think I am beginning to be.

PART III

"Joy over all this
I'm able to have, though ill with my death-wounds."

— LESSLIE HALL, *BEOWULF: AN ANGLO-SAXON EPIC POEM*

17

I remember much in the next week: how to cook food—I had never eaten when I was in that bewitched cave—how to lie down and sleep at night without waking every other moment in a hot rage, and how to care for myself and for someone else.

I learn many new things as well: how to sail, how to clean armor, how to read a chart.

But, mostly, I learn about Beowulf and his God.

I learn that Beowulf likes his food well-seasoned and enjoys a cold plunge in the sea every morning. He raises his left eyebrow when he is thinking and smiles a little when he prays, as if over some great secret—though he does not make his faith secret in any way to me. He talks freely of his God with me, opening a door to a world I have never known.

In that village that I first came from, the Almighty—if He was spoken of at all—was viewed in one of two ways. Some viewed Him as a cold and distant God—a merciless and relentless judge, not a father. Others viewed Him as a kind of lucky coin, to be pulled from one's pocket and rubbed when one needed a favor. He was a vaguely powerful spectator of men's doings who might be cajoled into favors—He was not the source of life.

Not so with Beowulf. He does indeed call the Almighty the

judge of all, but he also calls Him Father, and sometimes I can see the love between Beowulf and the Almighty, as if there were another presence with us on the ship: a vibrant, powerful feeling that wraps itself—or Himself—around Beowulf in a sparkling yet invisible cloud.

Beowulf is the greatest person I have ever known, but he makes himself sound so small before this Almighty. The Almighty that Beowulf speaks of is not a God to fit in one's pocket. He is a God that holds you in His hand, and yet He does not close His hand into a fist to crush his followers. Instead, He holds them to His heart.

This Almighty is a God that is with Beowulf when he eats, when he sleeps, and when he wakes. Beowulf seeks His help and opinion on everything, whether he is praying for a wind or looking over a map and waiting to hear a word on where our ship should head next.

Our ship is not the only thing at sea. I have been pushed under the surface of an unknown pool, submerged in a strange and wondrous life entirely different from every other life that I have known, and I have not yet come up for air.

The future is as blank as an endless horizon, and my past weighs upon me as darkly as the waves around us, but something I cannot explain begins to flicker in me as clearly and surely as the lamp Beowulf keeps lit night and day on the prow. I didn't know life could be like this—a life full of purpose and peace, in which even the simplest and humblest things are full of joy and covered in a holy sheen.

And I am happy—in a small, guilty way—that I am finally alone with Beowulf, learning to live again in this curious new world, taught by him as if I am a child. I soak up all I can like a sponge: from sailing, to cooking, to listening to stories of the Almighty.

I want to learn it all, for I don't know how much longer I have.

How can these days last? Beowulf has hinted several times

that my days with him are numbered, pointing at different places inland on his charts, speaking of various hamlets he knows of that he claims are full of good people.

He wants to find me somewhere safe to start over, and I am too ashamed to tell him that I wish to start my life anew as his servant.

After a week of sailing, we find shelter in a small bay. I wake up the next morning in the small ship's cabin to find that Beowulf has already left his bunk. The ship is moving beneath me. Beowulf must have set sail from our anchorage.

I kick aside my blankets and dart up the ladder, twisting my wild hair into a knot and straightening my skirt with a jerk as I step out onto the deck and into a tossing wind.

Beowulf is at the helm and he greets me with a grin. "Are you ready to walk on land again?"

My eyes sweep past him, across the sea and to the horizon that is no longer horizon, where a great looming headland of rocky beach and tall cliffs overlooks a wide, roughly circular bay, as if a giant sea-beast had taken a bite out of the coast.

My heart sinks a little.

This is it—it has to be. I had known it was coming, the inevitable landfall, but I woke every morning and went to my berth every night hoping that it might not be quite yet. The longer as we remain at sea, the longer I can delay the inevitable parting with Beowulf.

But now he feels it is time to come ashore and let me begin again on my own. He has kept me with him a little longer because he pities me—because he would feel like he is releasing a newborn babe into the world. This is the only reason—he feels obliged to instruct me, but he does not need my companionship the way I do his. How can he? Like King Hrothgar said, I am a girl-beast. And, very soon, I will be someone else's burden. Or worse, left alone.

"Wynnhild." My name in his mouth makes me jump back to the moment at hand, both tense and eager.

But all he says is, "Will you take the tiller and steer for the bay?"

I hurry meekly to obey, my attention divided between attending to my task and watching him trim the sail, before he returns to the tiller and bids me to stand by the anchor.

"It is easier to handle with another pair of hands," Beowulf remarks, smiling kindly at me when I remember to tie off the anchor before I drop it over the side.

My heart swells with hope. Does this mean he doesn't wish to leave me after all? Perhaps I *am* helpful and not just a burden. But he doesn't say any more, besides the occasional gentle instruction, and I do not ask.

"Look." Beowulf points to the cliff face, and I squint and see a man making his way down the cliff tops to greet us, carrying a fishing spear.

He could be armed with an axe and I wouldn't be afraid, not when I am with Beowulf. My hesitancy in jumping over the side has nothing to do with the stranger waiting for us.

Beowulf smiles as he goes to the ship's side and sees me as I look down at the waves and hesitate. "You've swum in far worse, Wynnhild! Do you wish me to catch you?"

Confusion and hope collide inside of me. He is teasing me! He has never teased me before. Teasing is for friends. Are we friends? Of course we aren't. But his eyes are laughing at me, inviting me to laugh with him, and I am not sure. . . .

My frustration propels me over the side and into the sharp and salty sea.

The cold pain of the water is almost a relief, pulling me out of my torturous thoughts and into my body and the task at hand: getting ashore and out of this miserable cold.

I thrash forward, carried on a breaker, as the sea swells around me, pushing me forward until my feet strike hard silt. I straighten, and water sluices from the top of my head and slips down my neck and arms.

A few feet ahead of me, Beowulf laughs on a note of exhilaration, as if he revels in the ocean's cold bite, and then I too feel the shiver of the untamed ocean and the wild land before us, the whisper of the danger to come. Beowulf must sense it too: the thrill of the threat, the tenuous reality of being alive, and the wild risk of defying and daring death by hunting monsters.

It all sweeps over me in one breathless rush that makes my heart leap in my chest. Is this what Beowulf feels? Is this what glory tastes like?

It is like wine—sweet and intoxicating—and I want more.

We splash forward until the waves lap at our knees, sucking at the edge of my tunic like a nursing babe. The man with the spear moves forward through the rough, knobby boulders at the foot of the cliff to greet us, a tall, proud figure in simple robes.

A strange sensation moves through me, as if I have stepped out of my own skin and I am watching another person swish through the surf.

Was it only two weeks ago that I hid on a cliff top and watched someone else greet a stranger named Beowulf on a beach? Now, in the strangest twist of fate or in a deliberate weaving of destiny, I am no longer hiding in terror from this beast hunter and cliff watcher—I am walking beside one and greeting the other, a part of them.

We stagger a little as the hard-packed sand gives way to soft, shifting dunes. The man bows as he stops before us, looking at Beowulf with bright, eager eyes beneath thick, salt-filled brows.

"Lord Beowulf, we have heard many stories of you. We are glad you are here."

The man is a fisherman, living in a house built partially into the cliffs with his wife and three children.

The family is being plagued by a sea salamander that lives in the clefts of the seaside.

Beowulf kills it all by himself, in the space of an hour.

I had asked—begged—to come along, but Beowulf gently reminded me that I did not have the sword knowledge for such a task.

Of course I don't. I am not a warrior like him.

I sit on the beach and brood, throwing shells helplessly into the sea and wondering why he didn't let me come, wishing that he had. I try to write out speeches in the sand, practicing what I will say to convince him to let me come with him when next he slays a monster, but the wind and the water wash my words away.

Beowulf returns an hour later, glowing with victory and the secret glory he seems to share with the Almighty.

I had not doubted for an instant that he would return safe and sound, but the fisherman and his family are astounded.

Beowulf declares that it is the Almighty's provision that we arrived when the beast was asleep—it gave him the opportunity to trap it in its lair, rather than meet it on the open sea.

The fisherman and his son go to retrieve the corpse and butcher the salamander on the beach while Beowulf and I unload what supplies we will need to venture inland—for Beowulf felt the Almighty leading him to land at this point and to travel east across the northern part of Frisia.

East or west, inland or sea, it would all be the same to me as long as I could go with him. The wish burns in my chest, desperate and unspoken.

The family invites us to dinner and we feast on sea salamander meat, tough yet flavorful, but it seems to lodge in my throat.

When the meal is done, Beowulf wanders out of the cave to sit upon the little rock ledge outside the home that enables the family to observe the sea.

I awkwardly help the fisherman's wife clean up. If I am to be returned to my village, I had best get used to these simple tasks. I scour a pot, hating it and everything around me. I am still trying to keep down the little I've eaten as I wonder if this will be my last meal with Beowulf.

When I am done, I go to the mouth of the cave. The fisherman's son, a lad of ten years or so who answers to Geralt, has not taken his eyes from Beowulf since the moment he first saw him, and he has joined Beowulf on the ledge ahead of me. As I approach, I hear them talking.

"I wish I could be a monster hunter, instead of just a fisherman," the boy declares, a little guilty over his disloyalty to his father but obviously anxious to impress Beowulf.

Beowulf looks down at the boy with a curious expression.

"When you are older, you will have the right to choose your future. If the Almighty has called you to hunt monsters, then He will make it clear to you. But you have time to decide—and much to learn first. Being a monster hunter isn't all excitement and honor. When the Almighty made my path clear to me years ago, He asked that I surrender all that would tie me to any land, that I would make no plans for earthly security."

Beowulf rests his elbows on his knees and glances over his shoulder, noticing me, and then he looks past my shoulder to the warm, cozy cave beyond—looking back to the place of homes and hearths while Geralt looks out to the sea and sky.

"You wish to be like me, Geralt? There have been times when I wished I could be like you."

Geralt whips around to stare at him, his eyebrows flying up in disbelief and surprise, and Beowulf laughs a little. "Truly. It is a good thing to have a place waiting for you, a land to call your own, and people to care for. I wander the world with no place and no one to call my own. But we all have different parts to play in life's story."

Beowulf reaches between his knees and tears at a bit of moss that grows determinedly on the ledge. Some of the earth clings to the moss, and Beowulf brings it to his nose, smelling it as if it is precious.

"Some are called to harvest from the earth or sea, others are called to fight. I knew when I was young that I was meant to destroy monsters, not plant seeds or feed a family."

The boy frowns, his lower lip caught between his teeth, considering Beowulf's words.

"You have an opportunity to try something I never have, before you make up your mind," Beowulf continues. He rests a hand on Geralt's shoulder. Then he turns and looks at me, as if inviting me to join them.

I lick my lips. "Lord Beowulf, may I speak to you . . . on the beach?"

Geralt returns reluctantly to the cave and Beowulf follows me down the narrow path that winds down the cliff face. He joins me amongst the dunes.

"What is it?" he asks, and I turn to him, pushing back my hair as the wind tosses it into my face.

I take my courage in my hands and dare to ask, "Has the Almighty said anything to you about what to do with me?"

Beowulf studies me. "He told me that He would make your path clear to you."

I stare at him, stunned. It never occurred to me that the Almighty might speak to me directly. In my wildest dreams I had only dared hope that He might speak to Beowulf on my behalf.

"I . . . I don't know anything," I stammer, blown off course by this sudden revelation. "I haven't—I haven't heard anything. There's so much I don't understand."

Beowulf looks up at the cliff dwelling and then back at me. "Children like Geralt have the benefit and blessing of being raised from youth to know the difference between right and wrong. I have watched you, Wynnhild, and you have come so far in so short a time. You who, I gather, were never taught, have more courage and loyalty than all the men of Trollhattan put together. That is why a demon came for you and wished to make you its servant. Zeal is an easier thing to mold than cowardice, and she manipulated your strength into hate. But your strength remains, Wynnhild."

My insides quiver, curling up in equal measures of mortification and gratitude as I wonder if what he says could possibly be true. I want it to be true.

I shut my eyes, push down the fear and the shame, and blurt out, "Will you teach me how to use a sword?"

There is no answer for a moment but the cry of a gull.

"Why?" Beowulf asks.

"I would be a beast hunter with you if—if you would let me." I open my eyes and meet his gaze—it cuts through me as sharply as the wind.

Beowulf studies me. "Why do you want to hunt monsters, Wynnhild? To make up for past sins? We can never make up for our past mistakes: they can only be forgiven. Are you hunting monsters in the hope of atonement?"

"No." I can barely choke out the word. I am unable to look into his face, fearing that I insult him, and yet I cannot remain silent, so I plunge on. "I just know, I always knew, that the hearth was not for me. I thought my place was in a great hall, but in that I was also wrong. I want you to train me because I know that the one true thing within my curse is that I was born to fight. And I want you to train me—because I wish to be with you. I know I am not worthy of it, but I would bear your shield, if you would let me."

Beowulf is silent for so long I writhe, but still I do not look up.

It is only when his hand suddenly touches mine that I raise my head, startled, and see, to my utter shock, that he is smiling.

"If you are going to be a beast hunter, you will need a sword."

WE USE the fisherman's boat to go back to the ship, and Beowulf unlocks a little chest in the main cabin that he has never opened before.

I pull in a breath as I see the gleam of an armor I know well. I had seen it for years upon the thin shoulders of the Watcher on the Cliffs.

Beowulf steps out of the cabin long enough for me to dress in men's tunic and breeks, and then he returns to help me with the armor.

I stand stiff as stone as Beowulf fits me out with Auschere's mail shirt and helmet—a little too big for me, but not by much, for Auschere was a small man.

I shift unhappily as Beowulf cinches my sword belt, and he looks up into my face. "Did I hurt you?"

I shake my head and mutter, "It only seems wrong that I should be wearing a righteous man's armor." I flush in shame.

Beowulf smiles, a little sadly, and shakes his head. "He would be pleased that you bear it. Unlike Unferth's false gifts, these, I think, will not fail you." He gives my belt a little wiggle with his finger, making me stumble and causing me to look up into his grinning face. "And if it does fail, I shall warn you, as you warned me."

He holds out a hand, in the way he might offer it to an equal.

The ship creaks around us as I hesitate.

Very slowly, I clasp the hand of the beast hunter and, in my heart, pledge my fealty.

THE FISHERMAN and his family watch as we set off across the high fells, walking into the wind as we set our faces eastward, our armor jingling and our swords banging against our hips in a shared rhythm.

I look back at the family as they wave goodbye. The parents look bewildered, a little awed, as they watch us march towards certain disaster. They will return to their hearth, their good and simple life. I look beyond them to the sea and think of Trollhattan and the men of the Hall who will go back to their drinks and their shallow peace.

Then I turn my back on it all and do not look anywhere but forward, at the back of Beowulf's head and shoulders, leading the way.

There is nothing but death before us, nothing but misunderstanding and ingratitude behind—but I feel only a kind of odd exultation. There is a strange exhilaration in being completely free from trying to win men's understanding, in being bound to no one's hearth. There is nothing left but the battle, nothing but the glory of the fight.

I laugh and, ahead of me, I hear Beowulf's laugh drifting back on the wind to meet me, echoing the sound of hope that escapes my mouth.

18

By day, we travel across hard country, gathering and hunting as we go. Beowulf teaches me songs from his country and poems about the Almighty. Meanwhile, I work through more than rough terrain as more memories of my past resurface. They exhaust me, but Beowulf pries them from me, one by one, and bathes each one the way he would a wound, only with wisdom and kindness instead of ointments, teaching me to accept what is behind me.

At night, my sore muscles and tired mind are strained even further as Beowulf trains me with a sword.

Beowulf says that I am a quick learner. I am not sure if he is just being kind or if it is true, but as the weeks go by, I do notice that I become less sore. I grow quicker to block his blows and get in a few of my own.

With every practice session, my confidence grows and—though I did not understand how such a blessed thing could possibly be—so does the sense of rightness. I think, perhaps, that the Almighty may be guiding me after all. Not as he guides Beowulf, for that would be impossible, but perhaps in some small way . . .

We travel until the moors change to marshy wetlands. The

weather turns foul, catching us in a sudden squall just as we reach open country and blinding us so that we stumble straight into a bog. Beowulf sticks fast in the middle of it and I nearly bury myself in muck trying to help heave him free. In the end, I do little good except to swallow enough mud to feel sick afterwards, but strangely, I enjoy the entire thing, reveling in the dirt and the cold and the strain as we help one another through the miserable little spot that turned us into a matched pair of muddy travelers, laughing together as if we had always been doing so.

Days pass, and bogs turn into thickets, full of rocky ravines that yawn wide beneath unsuspecting feet as we journey deeper into a place full of warrens half hidden in briars.

It is there that we encounter our next monster, near midday. Thoughts of a meal turn to battle.

I spot my first basilisk out of the corner of my eye and throw myself off the path to slide down into the ravine before Beowulf can even give me a command. Without thinking, I leave the real monster killer behind and plunge into the monster's pit with Auschere's sword in my hand. As Beowulf has promised, this blade does not fail me—nor does Beowulf's training. As I duck the lashing tail and sidestep the snarling beak, my hands remember what a beast hunter has taught me, and my sword finds its mark in the monster's neck.

Beowulf laughs when he pulls me away from the dead beast after he jumps in to help me deliver the killing blow. He looks at me with something that I think—I hope—might be admiration. Even respect.

I felt no fear at all plunging into that ravine, not even when I could feel the basilisk's spittle on my face, burning my skin and covering me in welts, not even when I heard its teeth snap beside my head. Not once did I hesitate. My heart was pounding not with fear but with a kind of wild thrill.

Perhaps it is because I have been a monster myself—and I know for a fact monsters can be defeated.

No, I am not afraid of monsters.

I am afraid of disappointing Beowulf.

After traveling for over a week through open fells and then another few days through thickets and bogs, we come at last to forest country, mercifully free of underbrush, making traveling easy at last as our boots pass over soft moss and earth. There is no brush or thorns for our packs to be snared upon, amongst a forest full of tall and smooth trees set far apart, a deep ferny world that shelters without stifling.

We camp that evening in a copse of white-barked trees.

The birches gleam silver in the moonlight, a pale and gleaming hall. The forest is carpeted in the softest moss I have ever felt, or perhaps it only feels unusually soft because I am tired from walking and fighting all day and am ready to rest.

I lie back on the moss and tilt my chin to look up at the irregular circle of star-flecked sky framed by the feathery shadows of treetops, and I fall into a kind of happy doze, letting myself do what I have not willingly done in years. I relive the day.

We are both in high spirits—almost giddy. Our last job was an easy one—the easiest yet. A hamlet of no more than a dozen families was suffering because beasts were killing their already tiny flocks. The enemy was only a small pack of wolves, but there were few men in the hamlet young enough and strong enough to hunt them down or to harry them out of the unpleasant thicket where they hid.

But a beast hunter and his servant had all the time in the world to thrash through thickets and stalk leery prey, and before the day was done we had killed the wolves and brought their corpses back so the villagers could keep their pelts.

Beowulf had refused any payment, but when the villagers proved insistent, he admitted that he would covet a small basket of nuts from their chestnut tree.

The villagers had given us two, one for Beowulf and one for me.

We roast Beowulf's chestnuts and split the treat between us, saving my basket for another day.

I am glad to save my reward. I cannot remember the last time someone gave me a gift, and I am afraid that when I roast the nuts, the memory of the gratitude given with them will somehow be burnt up too. I want to hold on to the memory of the villagers' faces, their thanks, the way their eyes looked at me with friendliness and gratitude, the way they gave me a gift and I accepted it, as if I were just like them and they were just like me, as if I would be welcomed again as a friend if ever I went through their hamlet again.

I hold the feeling to me, letting it warm me like the blazing fire at my feet.

"I haven't roasted chestnuts since I was a boy," Beowulf remarks, pulling me from my thoughts just before he tosses me a chestnut without warning.

Startled, I only just catch it, but I squeeze it so hard the soft treat squishes between my fingers, smearing my hands.

I fish another chestnut out of the fire with a stick and throw it at him, and of course Beowulf catches it in his mouth like an expert. I throw a pinecone at him after that, almost shocking myself that I dare to tease him in such a familiar way, but I don't stop to think about it. I am too busy basking in the sound of his laughter as he ducks away from my missile.

I lick my palms and wrists clean, reveling in the sweet and buttery taste and the feeling of flames on my face. I push my feet closer to the fire and wiggle my toes, glad to be free of my heavy boots.

For a moment, all is quiet. There is no sound but the contented crackling of the fire.

I am happy. The wild bursts of exhilaration and battle, the hideously hard journeying, cushioned between moments of peace and friendliness and quiet. It is all I want.

Was I meant for this? If so, why has it been such a circuitous route to this point? Why did I go through hell to get to this heaven?

Beowulf counsels me every day, trying to pull me away from

the guilt and shame that haunts every step, but I still cannot understand how a life as stained as mine could ever be enjoyed again.

But for now, at least, in this present moment, I am happy without worrying.

Beowulf rolls onto his knees and looks up at the sky, and his hands clasp in his lap. "Time to say good night, I think."

I get hastily to my knees too and bow my head, though the sign of respect still makes me feel like an imposter.

Beowulf closes his eyes, and so do I, listening to the bright ringing of his voice.

Every night Beowulf prays aloud, his words always short and strong—like the thrusts of a sword. I barely dare to move when he does, knowing that he is allowing me to hear something sacred and private solely out of kindness.

"Almighty, thank You for this night and for the soul with me. Protect her and show her Your love. Guide us in the path before us. May we be quick to strike at every enemy that rises up against You and quicker to help those that suffer from the Dragon's curse. Make our souls as bright as our swords and as true as Your name. We honor You."

His words surround me, and I drink in the peace that he shares with his heavenly lord, basking in the reflection of their love.

Before tonight, I have tried to pray with him silently, following his lead like a child stumbling in the footsteps of a parent, but I never dared to pray aloud. I had the vague anxiety that if I dared to address the Almighty audibly, I might somehow be struck dead.

And yet, tonight, I hear myself speaking audibly, without opening my eyes.

"Almighty, help Beowulf, Your servant. He carries much. Please lighten his load." I pause and add in a rush. "And help me to do whatever it is You intended for me when Beowulf removed my curse."

I open my eyes, a little sheepishly, and find Beowulf gazing at me with a strange expression that makes me think at first I have said something wrong.

"It has been a long time since anyone has prayed with me," Beowulf says softly. "Not since—" He pauses.

Now I understand the look on his face: he is startled and also sad.

I silently finish the thought. Not since Breca died . . .

Only a few days before, I would have never asked, but the question slips from me now, quietly but calmly, and I know I will be answered. "What was Breca like?"

Beowulf is quiet for a moment, thinking, looking into the fire, and the dancing embers are reflected in his eyes, making his gaze starry.

"He was my echo," he says simply. And that is all.

I had hoped for more, but as I reflect on those four simple words, it dawns upon me how much they entail.

An echo is always with you, as true as a reflection, as present as a heartbeat, as steady as time. To say such a thing about a person summons up a truer picture of the friend Breca must have been, more clearly than I had first thought.

I look at Beowulf, and I see the firelight reflected in wet eyes. Those four words have cost him so much, for they have released a flood of memories so precious, so painful, he seems frozen in place, as if he might break if he moves. His face is far away, reliving something he will never truly live again: for his echo has gone away.

"Thank you," I whisper, and I find my own eyes suddenly misting.

Beowulf shakes himself a little, and he smiles at me, though he offers no more memories. "I think it is time you and I got some rest."

He suddenly tosses me a blanket—without warning, the way he did the chestnut—and it hits me in the face. It jostles a startled laugh from my throat, and as I yank the blanket away, the former high spirits return, darting between us in warmth we share as happily as the fire that Beowulf carefully banks.

I watch him and think what a grand and wonderful thing it would be to be his echo. Breca was a fortunate soul.

The coals will keep me warm all night, and so do Beowulf's words. "Good night, Wynnhild!"

And it is a good night.

19

The forest bleeds into open country, and we leave the shadow of the wood behind by the afternoon of the next day, making camp on a narrow band of meadow before venturing with the dawn into higher country, where great peaks of green hills plunge down into hidden pockets of silver and blue lakes.

Beowulf and I spend that day watching reflected clouds in the still pools as we walk and, later, we stop to catch fish. The moments of peace are beginning to blur together in my mind in a haze of pleasure and peace and something that I am almost afraid to name—but that I suspect is belonging.

But Beowulf's calling, and his heart for monster-killing, ensures that the serenity is punctuated by sudden action.

It is not long before we get another taste of battle.

Just after noon on the next day, we come upon the small house of a hermit who welcomes us for a midday meal—and his welcome warms considerably when he learns of Beowulf's skills. A troll has been stalking him when he goes out to gather food. Beowulf promises to make an end of that.

We destroy the troll's nest later that day. I have to go over it in my mind afterwards, for it all happened so quickly, I barely knew what was happening in the moment. There was a long crawl into the ravine as Beowulf and I snuck up on the troll's burrow. Then we lit our torches and Beowulf smiled at me and went plunging into the dark, and I followed right after him. And then after that, all was clamor. There was a roar that sent my torch streaming back, burning my hand. Then a rush of massive feet and the flash of Beowulf's sword. I faintly remember swinging my torch at a smaller troll and stabbing until my sword was stiff and sticky with troll's blood. Just as suddenly as it began, it was over, and Beowulf pulled me to his chest and laughed. That, too, I remember in perfect, shining detail. Beowulf clapped me on the back and told me I had done well, and I smiled happily into his sweaty and bloody shoulder as our hearts beat against one another's, and I felt, for the first time, that maybe I could pay him back for all that he had done for me.

I find myself smiling uncontrollably as I think of it again during the morning march. My spirits soar, in stark contrast to the lowland we descend into. My heart lifts even higher when I spot smoke, and I find myself wondering—without truly stopping to study why—when did the sight of other people last excite me?

It is a small hamlet of perhaps twenty or so bothies nestled in a valley, surrounded by rough-hewn pens enclosing bleating sheep, their bright, woolly coats brightening the otherwise grey landscape.

The village well sits some distance from these pens, and three figures stand about it. Two women draw water while a man leans against a staff to speak to them.

My stride lengthens. It has been nearly three weeks since we left Trollhattan. Hope for the hospitality of a warm hearth and a soft pallet rises inside me, and eagerness gives me renewed energy.

As we near, my mouth turns up and a cheery "good morning" perches on the tip of my tongue, and I marvel a little at myself. Only a few weeks with Beowulf, and already it feels natural to hail people with a smile and good wishes.

But my optimistic feelings do not last.

The moment the people at the well turn to look at us, I feel the smile slide from my face.

They know.

I stop walking, rooted to the ground in fear.

How could they possibly have heard Unferth's false testimony —all the way out here—so far away from Trollhattan?

But they do. The resentment and dislike is there in their faces, as strongly felt as a blow.

All of Beowulf's reassurances, all of my careful work to forget the past, come unwound in an instant. For one panicked moment, I feel the beast's hood on my head once more, smothering me.

They know that I used to be one of the things they most fear, and it nearly makes me sick.

But Unferth's lies must have been altered in the telling and twisted in the traveling, for somehow, it is only Beowulf's name that is tarnished.

After only the briefest glance, they do not glare at me . . . only at Beowulf.

The oldest of the group, the man holding the shepherd's crook, steps forward.

"You are Beowulf," he says flatly.

Beowulf smiles at him, willfully ignoring their hostile looks. "I am."

The shepherd examines Beowulf the way he might look at a piece of refuse. "We heard tales of a great blond foreigner. Some say that he really saves the lives of monsters he was paid to kill."

Beowulf only looks mildly surprised at this statement. It is as if the accusation flies right past him and slaps me.

I was thinking only of my own fear of being exposed—what would have been my rightful punishment for past sins. That was my first thought, not the slander against Beowulf caused by Unferth's lies.

Shame erupts in my chest and loosens my tongue. I lurch forward, shaking but determined.

"Beowulf is never paid anything for beast hunting!" The

words explode from my lips. "How dare you say such a thing? You don't know anything—"

"Wynnhild." Beowulf rests a hand on my arm, and I deflate like sails suddenly bereft of wind.

Beowulf steps past me, still holding on to me as if he thinks I might fly at the man. There is no resentment in his face or voice, only quietness.

"It is true that I am Beowulf, the beast hunter. I heard there was a troll tormenting these parts. I would see you free of it, if you would let me free you."

The man raises his crook. "We do not want your so-called services, foreigner. Rather a beast we know than a traitor fashioning himself as a friend! We will defend our own selves from this troll!"

Before the man even finishes speaking, Beowulf turns and walks away, his head bowed in sorrow.

"Good fortune with that!" I yell nastily over my shoulder as I hurry to follow him. "If you think you can survive fighting a troll better than the warrior Beowulf, you deserve to be—"

Beowulf rumbles a warning low in his throat. "Wynnhild."

I swallow back additional words. Beowulf has worked so hard with me these past few weeks, but in an instant all of his examples slipped away from me like a cast-off cloak. Beowulf does not taunt and sneer like an evil child: I am not like him at all.

The eyes of the villagers bore into our backs as we take a wide path around the rest of the village, heading for the far hill.

"Unferth has been here before us, it seems," Beowulf murmurs at last, with a hint of ironic laughter that astonishes me.

I look at his ever-calm face and wonder—how can he bear the uncertainty of how he will be received from one place to another? One moment he is welcomed, the next he is cast out. One day he is lauded, the next insulted. Despite his placidity, I know it must hurt him, deep down, where no mortal can see it.

I want to touch him, put an arm around him, the way Auschere did on the beach, all those weeks ago, but I do not dare.

In the troll-nest, it was Beowulf who initiated the embrace, not me, so I keep my hands at my sides.

"I am sorry," I say miserably—three choked words to try to encompass everything: my brief flash of cowardice, my harsh words that Beowulf did not sanction, my sorrow for how he has been rejected, my compassion for how his name has been slandered. Three words trying to wrap themselves around so much.

"Thank you," says Beowulf. "It is not necessary for you to be sorry—but I thank you, anyway."

The wind twists around us as we climb a rise, hissing at our ankles, doing nothing to fill the yawning emptiness of the world as we walk away from the cold welcome at the well.

"Is this how it has always been for you?" I whisper. "How it will always be?"

"It is," Beowulf replies, and I am puzzled and strangely exasperated once more by the glint of humor in his voice. "It is people's nature to cheer one moment and then jeer the next. You cannot look to the world for security, Wynnhild—only the Almighty."

"But still," I persist, almost desperately. "Have you never had any security from men? No friends at all?"

Beowulf pauses for a fraction of an instant before answering softly, "You know I have been blessed with a few."

Of course—Breca and Auschere.

I wish I could bite off my own tongue.

As we walk across the moor, away from the angry villagers, I look at the man beside me and wonder, is that really all? When he said "a few," were those the only two he meant?

Could I ever be counted as one of those precious few?

But of course I cannot, for in a way, I have taken both away from him. The beast I had served killed Auschere, and now here I am, a former monster myself, walking beside Beowulf where Breca rightfully ought to be, just as if he had not been killed by another monster like me.

I am a fool.

I do not speak again for a long, long time.

THE DARKNESS around me is broken by a face. It is a man, staring at me as if I am the most hideous thing he has ever seen or that has ever lived.

Then I realize where we are standing. It is the great Hall of Trollhattan, and it is night.

Oh no. I try to scream it, but I cannot speak. The only sound that escapes me is something like an animal's snarl, and the sound terrifies me as much as it does the man. I want it to stop, but it doesn't stop, any more than my feet do, for I am rushing to seize the man by the throat.

My hands are stretched out before me, but they are not hands —they are claws.

No, no, NO!

The man tries to ward me off with a sword, but it has no effect—it never did.

I do not want to, but I break it in half. I try to stop myself, but I cannot keep my claws off of him.

He looks into my face and, with a hideous shock, I recognize him.

It is Auschere, his stern face transformed by fear.

"Please—have mercy!"

Auschere screams as I dig my fangs into his throat. I feel his flesh tear and his spirit splinter as his blood envelops me.

I try to let him go, but it is as if he is smelted to my hands until the moment he dies, and then he slips away, collapsing into the pile of bodies that surrounds me. As I look at it, the pile grows, higher and higher. I am up to my waist in dead men, and when I try to run away, there is yet another man in my grasp begging me to spare him.

"Wynnhild!"

I jerk awake, plunging out of the dark memories, and I look up into Beowulf's face.

His hand is on my arm, anchoring me to the ground and to reality, pulling me out of my nightmare and back into a moonlit clearing far, far away from Trollhattan.

"You were crying," Beowulf says softly.

I lay there rigidly, not answering, and only half aware that he is looking at me, waiting for me to say something, but I am too sick to speak. Guilt and horror choke me, keep me silent. I just murdered his dearest friend in my sleep.

It was just a dream.

I look at Beowulf, and while I know my dream twisted reality, it still revealed the truth: Auschere's death is on my head. His life and the lives of a dozen others.

Beowulf sits back on his heels. "Would you like to tell me about it?"

I shake my head and roll over in answer, turning my back on him.

Beowulf moves slowly back to his side of the dead fire, but neither of us goes back to sleep. I know because I hear him murmuring under his breath. I think he is praying for me.

It only makes me more miserable. I do not deserve his prayers. The Almighty will not listen, even for Beowulf's sake, because I do not deserve it.

I am a fraud. I don't deserve to fight by Beowulf's side, and I don't deserve the mercy of men or God.

I stare up into the bristling shadows of the treetops and think of the memories of my past few weeks with Beowulf. I try to bind the feelings to me, but they feel as vague and as distant as the dark clouds above me.

My hands form into knots where they rest on the ground, and I tear fistfuls of grass from the earth as the dream slithers through my mind once more. I cannot believe that Auschere ever screamed for mercy or fled in terror in his life. It seems that even in my dreams, I dishonor good men.

I try to scrub the image of Auschere from my mind, but his face is replaced with others, and these are no nightmares. They are reality.

The men of Trollhattan rush through my mind, as clearly as when I first saw them. Souls lost forever, their lives squeezed out of them by my cursed claws. The images overwhelm me until I long to vomit. My thudding heartbeat counts off their lives. Too many. Far too many. Those faces that I tried so hard to forget parade through my mind, open mouths begging me to let them live.

But I did not let them live.

The awful truth makes itself known to me at last. My foolish dream that I could become a beast hunter is as silly and fragile as a child's wish.

I am here on borrowed time and borrowed honor.

I try not to move—I do not want Beowulf speaking to me or looking at me with those deep, knowing eyes again—but I writhe inwardly as unforgiving clarity floods my mind.

Beowulf's accusation on the beach was right: I thought that by killing enough monsters I could somehow make recompense for what I had done as a beast.

But it will never be enough. I can stab and slice and skewer every second for the rest of my life and it will not be enough.

That moment in the troll-nest comes back to me in vivid detail, mocking me, sneering at me. A brief moment of hope that made me drunk with delight. What a stupid, deluded creature. How could I ever believe that I was worthy to fight beside Beowulf? I don't deserve to touch the ground he walks on, let alone hold his shield.

I am more than just a monster: I am a fool.

I turn my face towards the pine needles under me. Silently, I sob and sob until I have no more tears left to shed.

20

Morning comes, but it is grey and heavy with clouds that spit mizzle, as if the sky is crying. It matches my mood as I fumble into the straps of my pack.

For the first time since joining Beowulf, I feel aggravation with Beowulf's Almighty, and the dark stream of resentment running through my mind scares me. The silent accusations flow so quickly and easily it makes me wonder if I have truly begun to follow the Almighty or not. I don't see how I can be following Him when I feel this way—angry and confused—when I know I have no right to either feeling.

The torment that attacked me last night lingers in my mind and mood today. We move forward, but I feel as if I am moving backwards, mired once more in endless questions.

I want to ask Beowulf so many questions and hear him preach to me in the way that somehow sets the world straight again, but my questions tangle in my throat.

I do not think I was utterly wrong in thinking I was—or at least could be—a good shield bearer, or a minor beast hunter. I like this life that Beowulf leads, perhaps even love it, albeit with a cautious love, because I have always known it could be taken away from me.

I bite my lip until it bleeds. Why did the Almighty torture me with a future? Why did I start on a path that stained me so deeply and horribly that I could not possess the gift of a future?

I do not understand.

Beowulf is quiet, as if sensing that I wish to be locked away in my own thoughts. As the hours pass, he tries several times to speak to me, but each time, the words fall to the ground with the rain, leaving puddles of awkward silence behind.

The temperature plunges and snow spits in our faces. The hills begin to fall away and the land grows flat, with no protection from the wind or the skies that grow darker with every step.

It is late afternoon when Beowulf jostles my elbow, pulling me from my dark reflections. “Look.”

I raise my head: it feels like lead. I squint into the snow flurry, peering into the white haze, and see on the horizon the low, dark outline of bothies.

Beowulf’s hand is still on my elbow. “Shelter from this wind for a little while would not be amiss, would it, Wynnhild?”

I grunt in response, and when Beowulf looks at me, I manage to twitch out an agreeable smile, though it is not convincing enough to deflect his sharp gaze.

“Will you not tell me about what is troubling you? Its power is in its silence.”

I shake my head, even though I know I am disappointing him by refusing to confide in him. I cannot speak the terrible conclusion I have reached. All my thoughts have been dashed to death on one sharp fact: it is all Beowulf; it has always been Beowulf. I am existing in the shadow of his mercy, along the knife-edge of his goodness. If anything ever happens to him, I will become what I once was again—I am sure of it.

I barely notice the village or the villagers that greet us warmly as Beowulf leads the way into the hamlet. Clearly, Unferth’s lies have not reached this place.

I only vaguely sense the soft, enclosing darkness of the village elder’s bothy and the fire burning in a brazier in its center. I do not speak, nor do I look at anyone, though I feel them looking at me.

As I sit there, my secret resentment towards the Almighty seeps out of the corners of the confines I try to construct around it. It touches the people around me. As I choke down a bowl of hot soup, the generosity of the woman who hands it to me feels like pity. The curious look of a youth feels like distrust. The vegetables in my bowl turn to earth in my mouth as hatred sparks inside of me: a fire I thought I had killed months ago surges back to life.

The brazier I sit beside is ringed by people who hang on Beowulf's words and feast on his face without shame. Nothing holds them back from loving him. They have never been monsters; they could bear his shield with a clear conscience.

They are just like the people of Trollhattan. They have something I can never possess.

I blink away a bit of ash, and my eyes burn.

I ignore the chatter around me and Beowulf's concerned frown and stare into the fire. Scarlet fills my vision, fills me with a feverish warmth as my thoughts crackle like flames. Has anything really changed after all? Has my life really improved? I am worse than before, for though I have tasted the truth, I can never drink it.

I am jolted from my misery when people begin to leave the bothy, streaming away to their own huts to sleep, no doubt peacefully. Only the elder remains with Beowulf and me—though for a moment I think Beowulf is leaving too, for he rises to his feet.

But he is only moving to look out of the doorway into the night before he comes to sit beside me.

Like a bubble pricked by a needle, my unhappiness bursts and is swept away by his closeness. I lean towards his warmth, and he leans back, and I don't let myself think of anything but that.

"A storm is brewing," Beowulf says to the elder, though he is looking at me, and some of the wrinkles smooth away in his brow when he sees me relax.

It is only then that he looks away, towards the other man. "I think it would be better to press on tonight rather than travel in the snow tomorrow." He turns to me. "If you are willing, Wynnhild."

I uncurl like the bits of bark burning up in the brazier, softening and melting at his consideration and deference to me. As if I matter.

"Whatever you think is best," I murmur, meaning it from the depths of my heart.

"Then we'll be off." Beowulf smiles, rising to fetch the packs we had dropped in the corner. He slips into his, but I linger a moment by the fire, knowing that if I move, this brief happiness will sluice away, and I want to make it last a little longer.

The elder rises to his feet too. "It was a great honor to have you among us, Lord Beowulf." He smiles a little and shakes his head, as if over some great marvel. "How proud your father must be of you, to have sired a son that breaks the hold of dragons."

A twig snaps in the brazier, and so does my happiness—severed in two. The world shrinks around me, too small to live in, too small to breathe. I am being crushed. The bothy seems to sway around me as my head swims. The fire shrinks to a mere thread of light as my vision darkens.

A son who breaks the hold of dragons. It is a paraphrase of the ancient prophecy: the foretelling of a great warrior who will kill the Dragon Below . . . and die in the doing.

Beowulf answers, but I cannot hear him past the roaring in my ears, though I see the modesty in his face and guess that he is deflecting the man's reference to his father, instead of denying that he is the prince in the poem, as he ought to.

I want him to flatly deny it. Why won't he?

I struggle to inhale. Was it only a month ago that the beast I called Mother said to me that Beowulf was the fulfillment of the prophecy? Was it only a month ago that I was glad to hear the words that Beowulf might die?

All is changed now. Beowulf cannot be the person spoken of

in the prophecy: I would sooner face monsters with no one by my side than contemplate such a thing.

I struggle to focus as Beowulf touches my arm. I scour his face with my eyes, trying not to believe what the infernal old man has said.

Beowulf's beautiful face offers no answers. "It is time we were off, Wynnhild."

I sway dazedly to my feet.

"The Almighty be with you," Beowulf says to the elder.

The elder bows. "And with you, dragon slayer."

Beowulf only smiles as he steps out of the bothy.

I stumble after him and then pause just outside the doorway, brought suddenly to my senses by the abrupt lashing of icy rain.

It might as well have been oil poured onto flames for the way it turns my shock into fury.

I turn on my heel and plunge back into the bothy.

The elder looks up, surprised.

"Have you forgotten something—?" He doesn't get to finish, for I take him by the shoulders and shove him violently. His shoulders hit the wattle and daub walls with a thump that sends the herbs on the pegs above our heads swinging, releasing a sharp and stinging scent that makes my eyes burn with unshed tears.

His eyes are wide. I am hurting him, terrifying him—but I can't stop, for I am terrified myself.

"I want you to know something before I leave. Beowulf is not the fulfillment of the prophecy. He is just a man. And if you hear someone talking about Beowulf and saying that again, you tell them it's a rumor, that he's just a simple beast hunter." My fingers dig into his shoulders. "He is not the one the prophecy speaks of, do you understand?"

He gabbles in response, doubtless a promise to obey, but I do not stay long enough to sort out his words. I shove the miserable man away from me and run outside, swiping my face with my forearm and stumbling into the rising wind.

Beowulf is waiting for me, and he knows immediately something is not right. "What is wrong?"

I can barely choke out a single word. "Nothing." Mortification erupts inside of me; my body feels as if it is on fire.

I have lied to him—but if I tell him the truth, what will he say?

Silently, we walk out of the village, pelted by the rain—the bothies like grey tombs around us. I slip once and fall, scrambling to right myself from the hassock of waving grass that reaches up to swallow me.

When Beowulf extends an arm to help me up, I do not take his hand. How can I?

My old monster habits have come surging to the surface, as if all that Beowulf has taught me these past weeks has never happened.

It was so easy to bully the elder, so easy to threaten.

Why did I not speak to him gently, reasonably, the way Beowulf did when correcting a falsehood? Why did I not simply control myself? The more I think about it, the more I convince myself that he was simply a stupid old man that had made an inadvertent reference to the prophecy. He hadn't actually meant Beowulf was the prince of the prophecy: it was simply my own tortured mind leaping at shadows. The old man had chosen his words poorly, and I had made a mistake. That was all.

I cannot look at Beowulf, and I deliberately quicken or slacken my stride so that we do not walk shoulder to shoulder.

If he knew what I had just done, how would he look at me?

The wind and cold are punishing, and my bones ache from lack of sleep, but the misery is almost a relief, for it distracts me from my guilt.

But not entirely, for I didn't just lie to Beowulf. As desperately as I try to convince myself that what happened in the bothy was a misunderstanding, I know I lied to the elder and to myself.

I know the prince of Heofon is more than an ordinary man.

And this knowledge terrifies me.

21

We rest briefly at dawn, finding shelter in a strange formation of rocks as big as obelisks. We curl up in their narrow shelter for a miserable hour, but I only doze. We rest for a shorter period at noon on the open moor, and then a third time in the afternoon, in a narrow gorge formed by a stream that is nearly frozen over.

Three times I try to sleep, and each time I cannot. As we climb from the gorge and into the bitter elements once more, I am nearly sick with exhaustion.

"Wynnhild." Beowulf stops me with one hand and turns me towards him. "Will you still not speak to me?"

I cannot. My misery and shame are so thick, I feel as if I might vomit. I wish I could vomit up all of the fear, all of the inadequacy, all of the doubt, but it merely sticks in my throat.

"Let me pray for you." Beowulf takes my gloved hand in his and we stand shivering on the ridge top, halting our journey to pray.

"Almighty, help Wynnhild surrender her fear to You. You have released her from all torments—let her not take them up again. Shelter her with Your great shield, and show her that You save those You love. Lift her heart and strengthen her, and reveal Your true path for her. Teach her to use her fighting spirit for You, instead of fighting herself. Make our swords strong in Your name. In the name of the Almighty, I pray this."

He holds my hand a few moments longer, standing close beside me, sheltering me from more than the wind.

Tears freeze on my cheeks as my forehead bumps his shoulder and rests there. My hands are limp at my sides, no longer fists.

"I wish . . ." I whisper. "I wish I had your faith."

"Then ask for it," Beowulf whispers back.

I bite my lip. "You make it all sound so simple."

"It is simple. But when one has lived in the shadows for too long, the light can be confusing." He holds me at arm's length, looking into my face. "Forget what is behind, Wynnhild—unless you remember it solely to thank the Almighty for what He has done for you."

The old nightmare slithers through my mind like oil, and I swallow. "I'll—try."

We begin walking again. Beowulf's shoulder bumps against mine.

"Let us sing," Beowulf proposes, despite the terrible wind blowing into our faces, despite the snow that wants to fill our throats. His voice rings out across the plain, and slowly, grasping at the words, trying to claim them for my own, I join him.

"One foot in the grave, one foot in life.
Let us conquer this world of strife,
Bringing praises to our King,
With every strike and every swing.
May every fight His glory bring.
Though our past roars and future quakes,
Those who follow, He will not forsake."

It is nearly evening when we see a village on the horizon, and Beowulf challenges me to a race.

I gape at him in astonishment, and then I am suddenly looking at his back as slush flies towards me from beneath his flying feet.

It splatters me, startling a gasp and a laugh from my throat, and I find myself running after him. The cold air makes my lungs constrict, and my already exhausted legs feel as if they will break beneath me.

"I—I can't keep going!" I shout.

Beowulf looks over his shoulder, grinning. "Yes, you can!"

We run for at least a hundred spear-lengths, yelling with pain and laughing at our exhaustion, our gazes fixed upon the approaching village, until we both finally collapse to our knees in the snow. At least, I collapse—right onto my face. A mouthful of snow nearly chokes me. Beowulf drops beside me, though whether it's from tiredness or to help fish me out of the drift, I am unsure.

"Well run!" Beowulf declares, his voice bright. "And now we are almost there!"

But our spirits drop as we reach the outskirts of the village.

The air is thick with an emotion I know well—fear.

A strange clamor, a kind of bubbling panic of voices, reaches to meet us as we approach, and I look anxiously at Beowulf.

The prince quickens his stride, his eyes focused on whatever lies ahead.

Villagers turn to look as we walk through the narrow street between the bothies. Every face is bleak, empty of hope. Unlike the previous village that greeted us with calm hospitality, no one here stops to speak to us. They all rush past, bowed and silent and trembling, laden with packs that they load hastily onto carts.

They are abandoning their homes.

Beowulf and I stand still in the center of the village, utterly ignored.

I smell something familiar, something I have not smelt since—

My head jerks a little, trying to follow the shadow brushing my spirit, like a dog on an unseen scent. But I am not sure I want to name what I think it is.

At last a man emerges from the crowd, apparently directing the activity—and he truly notices us. He hurries over, and Beowulf steps forward to meet him.

He introduces himself as the village elder, and Beowulf, in turn, declares himself as the famous beast hunter, the foreign prince Beowulf.

The elder's eyes light up for a moment, and then the light goes out, smothered by doubt.

"Lord Beowulf." His voice is as heavy as the snow on the eaves of the bothies. "We have heard much of you, even in this remote village. I would be glad to see you if only it were not too late."

He looks at us, and his gaze holds nothing but utter despair.

"What is it?" Beowulf asks, concern sharpening his normally soft voice. "What has happened?"

"I think it is the end of the world, beast hunter." The elder turns and looks north, and our gazes follow his.

The snow has stopped, but there is a smudge in the distance. I think at first that it is a cloud, but then slowly, with growing uneasiness, I realize that it is really smoke.

The elder's voice is little more than a whisper.

"The Dragon Below has woken."

22

Past the buzzing in my ears, I hear Beowulf calmly asking the elder to explain.

"The Dragon Below has not been spotted hunting in hundreds of years," says Beowulf. "It is said he slumbers, or at least dreams, and sends dreams to the nightmares he calls his children, urging them to do his work and wreak havoc while he rests." Beowulf glances at me, as if to ensure that his words have not wounded me. They haven't—I am still reeling from the blow of the elder's words. "Though I have seen his servants," Beowulf continues, "I have received no word that their master has woken."

My mind scrambles, trying to wrap its thoughts around such a horrible possibility.

The Dragon Below—awake.

"We do not know why he has woken, only that he has," the elder whispers. "We have a witness who can tell you himself—if he can still speak. He crawled here, despite his injuries, and lies on the brink of death. His village was completely destroyed by dragon fire. He speaks of the north becoming a growing wasteland, nothing but an ever-expanding circle of ash. Why the Dragon has not yet come to us, we do not know. We will offer you what food we can spare, but we prepare to flee. Before dawn, this village will be empty. Better to run than be consumed."

A shiver washes over me. Can one flee from such an enemy? No one knows better than me the long shadow the Dragon Below can cast. One cannot escape death itself. I can feel it around me now, in the racing heartbeat of the village.

I shut my eyes, wishing I could shut out the memories so easily. Only a few short weeks ago, I struck this kind of horror in people's hearts. I brought this kind of death and devastation.

Beowulf's hand comes down to rest on my shoulder, weighty and reassuring, as if he is pressing out all my guilt, the way wine might be pressed from grapes.

"Trust in the Almighty. Do not despair of hope," Beowulf murmurs, to me as much as the elder. "Our Lord is more powerful than any dragon. Where is this witness you speak of, elder? I would hear testimony from him."

The elder leads us to a bothy. A woman comes out of the doorway just as we arrive, her face haunted.

"We tried to make him as comfortable as we could," the woman whispers to the elder, with a curious glance at Beowulf, a curiosity that is quickly swallowed by the present worry. "But his wounds are so grievous that the best healer in the world could not help him. I fear there is nothing else we can do for him."

Beowulf is sober as he moves towards the doorway of the bothy. I follow him so closely I bump into his back.

He turns to look at me, a little doubtfully. "I'm sure it will be terrible to look upon."

The sudden insane desire to laugh bubbles up inside of me. Has he forgotten who he is talking to? I have seen hideous bodies before—I have created them.

But a moan from within the bothy turns my bitter laughter into silence.

Beowulf lifts the animal hide that covers the doorway, and we enter.

The man on the pallet hardly even resembles a human being

anymore—he is a great welter of red blisters and blackened sores. His arm is the worst of all. There is a band of pale skin around his eyes that is more or less whole—he must have thrown up his arm to shield his face, sparing his vision but leaving his arm looking like a charred stick, more than flesh and bone.

Guilt floods my throat with bile. This is what the Dragon Below really does. He does not bring freedom—but death.

And I helped him.

I can only be shamefully grateful that my curse did not include fire: a slow and painful torture. At least I killed quickly—not like this long, wretched fight.

But the smell of distress and terror is still the same, and I am ashamed of my attempt to comfort myself when there is true suffering before me. I open my eyes and force myself to look at the man.

Beowulf sits down beside the pallet, not quite touching the man, though his voice clasps the pathetic figure close.

"I am Beowulf. What is your name?"

The man's eyes open briefly, drinking in the face leaning over him.

"Beowulf . . ." he repeats, a note of yearning and sorrow in his voice as he looks upon the face of a legend. He coughs as he struggles to speak his own name. "I am . . . Bjorn."

"Bjorn, I am sorry this happened to you," Beowulf murmurs. "You have a great heart, to have survived so much and come so far."

Bjorn shudders. "My heart fails me." He squints through swollen lids. His mind comes back from some far-off place, and he seems to see Beowulf for the first time all over again. "You are . . . the great Beast Hunter . . . Beowulf."

Beowulf meets my eyes briefly, his gaze full of unspoken sorrow. "I am he."

Bjorn chokes again. Beowulf's hand rests beside his, and his lips move silently until the man can breathe again.

"Can you help us?" Bjorn whispers. "Can you stop it?"

Beowulf does not hesitate, and my heart seizes at his simple promise. "I will try."

Bjorn writhes. "The Dragon Below spoke to me before I escaped. He said . . ." His words trail off as he struggles to form the words. "That he has been robbed. He searched for a cup. He said that since it was a scarlet-clad man that had stolen from him, he would have his revenge upon all men." He shakes his head violently, almost beating it against his pillow, as if trying to pound away the fear and pain. "He is terrible—so terrible! How can any of you escape? How will anyone survive?"

Bjorn begins to weep from pain and sorrow, and Beowulf reaches for him, with that voice he used in the cave when he coaxed me from the shadows.

"Peace, peace."

There is no family left for this man, no neighbor, not even a village. He is dying, and he is alone, so Beowulf holds him, putting his arms around him the way he might a child, and Bjorn does not pull away, though it must hurt to be clasped so tightly. They both weep, and I weep too, watching them.

"You and your village will be avenged," Beowulf murmurs when the storm of tears has passed. "Rest in the Almighty's Hall."

Finally, the man stops fighting and, with one last gasp for air, dies.

23

Beowulf and I sit in silence. Very softly, Beowulf pulls the blanket over Bjorn's face, tucking the damaged hand inside of it.

We rise and leave the suddenly cold hut and stand outside in the little pool of light from the lamp that still burns within, a lonely vigil over the broken body.

It is the first time I have seen someone die since . . .

I shake my head, cringing from the memory and the scent of despair that leaks out of the doorway with the light.

Beowulf does not speak, only watches the people rushing by.

I cannot bear the sadness in his face, or in the room behind me, or in the people that press past us, so I reach frantically for answers—and for anger.

"The man that stole the cup: it must have been Unferth," I say. His name tastes like poison on my tongue. "This was his doing; it has to be."

"There are other scarlet-clad men in the world, Wynnhild," Beowulf says, but doubtfully, for though the deep blood red of Unferth's robes is not impossible to attain, it is difficult, and he is the only man we have seen in all of our travels so far who has worn cloth dyed such a stain.

"He did it on purpose," I insist. "He hoped to incite you to confront the Dragon Below."

"Do not let one man unravel your peace, Wynnhild. There will always be another Unferth. And as for him being responsible for awakening the Dragon, the cup is merely an excuse; the Dragon would have attacked eventually, and for no other reason but his dark dream to destroy the Almighty's creation."

Beowulf looks down at me and starts in surprise. "Wynnhild . . . you're crying."

I duck my head, but it's too late. Tears dribble down my chin.

Beowulf tilts my chin up with one finger. "Why are you crying, Wynnhild? Do you weep for Bjorn?"

"No," I mumble miserably, ashamed that I am not, but my thoughts are tangled too tightly around the man still living to think of anything else.

"Then why?"

"Because you're going to try to fight the Dragon Below." I wipe my face and my voice cracks. "Why? Why must you face him?"

Beowulf wipes one of my tears away with his thumb and studies my face, as if, inexplicably, it is in my face that he finds a purpose.

"Because when I look at you now, Wynnhild, I see clear reason instead of madness—and so much sorrow, so much pain as you try to let go of what you once were."

My tears fall faster. I can't see him anymore, but I hear him.

"Until the Dragon Below is defeated, he will simply go on empowering his servants to keep enslaving people to his bidding—as he did through your monstrous keeper." Beowulf's hands rest upon my shoulders, anchoring me to the ground when I feel like I might fall apart. "Do you really believe I could let this dragon live, to go on pulling souls like yours into a living hell? I cannot stand by and simply let that happen again, not while I have the power to fight it."

I stand there trying to concoct arguments, threats, bribes. The wild, laughable idea of offering to face the Dragon myself leaps into my mind. If I sacrifice myself, perhaps Beowulf will not have to.

Beowulf's next words shatter my schemes like a hammer breaking apart stone. "I want you to stay behind this time."

I suck in a breath, and just like that, my tears stop, as if dammed. "You . . . what?"

Not since my enchantment was broken have I been angry with him, ever. I am furious now.

"You can't make me stay behind, Beowulf. I will go with you."

Beowulf's hands drop from my shoulders. "You have seen what the Dragon can do."

I think of the man in the bothy, but somehow I am not afraid. I can only think that there could be no better death than to die beside Beowulf.

I am nearly yelling at him. "And do you think I could escape if I tried walking south? If the Dragon Below has woken, then it is his desire to destroy everything and everyone—no village would be spared. I would rather see him now than wait."

"Don't make me force you to stay behind, Wynnhild," Beowulf says under his breath.

His sudden exhaustion deflates my anger. I don't want to attack him—enough things attack him—but I must convince him. "I beg you. Let me come."

Beowulf's mouth is a determined line. "I didn't save you just so you could die fighting the Dragon Below."

"We all die, Beowulf," I retort, throwing his words back at him. "All that we get to decide is how we die and what for."

That blow strikes home. Beowulf looks at me with a mixture of dismay and growing resignation.

I press the blade deeper. "Maybe I'm not strong enough to face him, but . . . I won't be fighting on my own. There will be you—and the Almighty. I know he must care for me a little, if he saved me from my curse." I swallow. "I know I can't repay what he did; I don't know if he would accept anything I could offer. But all I have left is my life. I want to give it back."

Beowulf looks at me, and for the first time I see something more than pity, more than kindness, more than hope, more than kinship—I see respect.

Such a gift—from someone like him—is worth dying for indeed.

He sighs and says with little conviction, "I wish you would go back to the coast, to the ship, and wait for me there. And if I do not return, go to my country and begin again."

I shake my head. "I cannot begin again. Not when I have this work unfinished. I will be worthy of my price—don't deny me that. You said it yourself: fate goes on as fate will—and fate has tied me to you, Beowulf of Heofon. Where you go, I go."

Beowulf is quiet for a long, long time. "Have you thought of the cost? Of all that you will never have if you choose this path? Think it through carefully, Wynnhild."

I have. I know I could go back—back to that safe, inconsequential life in the village I was born in. I could grow comfortable and old and fat sitting by a fire. I could make a new life for myself, pretend that I had never been bought and paid for by another's blood, pretend that my life and honor and service was not wholly owed to a foreign prince.

Yes, I could fade away—into comfortable oblivion—a faraway corner where no one knew my past or secret shame. The truth of who I was and what I had done would always be in my shadow, trailing from me like a mantle in my mind—but only I would know. I could pretend myself into a world of comfort and safety.

Or I can follow him—into ruin, into glory, into wild tossing waves to play with sea beasts, into mob-filled halls to shout the truth, into unknown barrows to face trolls. Into the unforgiving north to face the Dragon Below himself.

Because there would be no peace in a normal life—not really. On howling nights, instead of rejoicing in my safety, I would always think of Beowulf and wonder what storms he was fighting.

When gathered around tables and enjoying a shallow companionship, I would think of one who had been a true friend, and how he was all alone, with not even a servant to hold his shield.

There is no choice. I'd rather be swallowed in flames with Beowulf than grow old and safe in a cottage armored with false peace.

I look up at him, and my heart and all that I feel and hold for him is in my ringing words. "If you're going to hell—then I'm going with you."

Beowulf gazes at me, and suddenly his face lights up, illuminated by a kind of joy, as sudden and bright as a sunrise, and I find myself smiling at him—no, grinning—despite the chaos around us, despite the death just inside the door.

"Let's swim with sea beasts," I say, and before the words are even fully out of my mouth, Beowulf draws me close, the way he did in the troll-nest, and clasps me to him with a heavy hand on my back, the way he might hold a brother-in-arms.

I hug him tight, and in that moment, I am not afraid.

Beowulf speaks briefly to the elder, who reluctantly gives us supplies for a week's journey, though he clearly believes he is aiding in our deaths.

"Don't go," he pleads. "You are a great monster hunter, Lord Beowulf. But not even you can think you are capable of destroying the father of all monsters."

"Only the Almighty knows," Beowulf responds simply, and he waves a hand as he walks into the night, his fist closed as if in victory.

And, looking back once more at the villagers rushing to safety, I turn and follow Beowulf willingly into the dark.

24

This is different from all our previous hunts. We both feel it. The moments of laughter and play are gone, though the camaraderie and trust between us is deeper than it ever was before, deeper than I could have ever believed. As deep as death.

Little changes for three days. It is on the fourth day that we first see the Dragon's mark.

Beowulf spots it first. Smoke on the horizon, a heavy haze of death.

We quicken our pace, but by the time we arrive, there is nothing we can do. There aren't even rogue flames to be put out: the wreckage of the charred buildings is silent beneath blackened ash.

And within the ash lies what remains of the villagers.

I want to be sick, and I am sick, behind the skeletal remains of a little barn. I do it carefully, trying to keep Auschere's armor clean of anything as dishonorable as vomit. For some reason I cannot explain, this feels terribly important, the most important thing I can do.

Beowulf waits for me in an empty barnyard and gives me water when I am done, his face as grey and empty as the ash.

"Wash and come away, Wynnhild. There is nothing we can do here."

We do not camp in what remains of the village, although it is the only shelter on these plains. We would rather be exposed to the sky than surrounded by the shadow of the Almighty's enemy.

I am on edge all the next day. But though I scan the skies and flinch at every shadow, the Dragon Below remains hidden, and the skies are full only of fear instead of scales.

We rise the next morning cold and stiff and sober. I don't think either of us slept, but nevertheless we press on quickly, though not eagerly, towards whatever must lie at the end of our path.

The world becomes more desolate with every mile, until we come to a dead forest and a miserable journey through black skeletal trees bearing no growth or life. I cannot wait to be free of it. I do not realize there is worse to come.

When the dead forest falls away, revealing nothing but grey, I stop walking and pull a startled breath into my lungs.

It is as if a line has been drawn across the land. We stand on the edge of nothing. I had thought the dead wood and grey grasses we traveled through had been bleak, but they were nothing compared to this desolation.

As far as I can see, there is nothing but a grey plateau—fine grey rock and earth covered in cool ash. The bones of this country have clearly always been flat, but there should be grass, at the very least, perhaps a few rivulets or streams.

But every bit of life, every bit of moisture, has been pulled from the land, sucked into the enormous flying furnace of a dragon's breath.

And, somewhere on the horizon, so far away it is little more than a haze where grey ground meets grey sky, is the orange and angry glow of fire.

I look and feel a flutter of fear at the evidence of the Dragon's Below's sheer power. Here was a fire so terrible, so powerful, it destroyed everything in sight. The Dragon could do this again at any time he wished. Beowulf and I are standing in a bit of the world he has simply decided not to burn yet, not because he didn't plan to but merely on a whim.

Beowulf looks at me as a rogue wind stirs hair into his concerned eyes. "It's not too late for you to turn back."

My uneasiness snaps like a broken twig, replaced with indignation as I glare at him. "Yes, it is."

"Very well," says Beowulf. And then he suddenly smiles, with that bright sense of glory that was never fully mine, though I bask in its shadow. "The Almighty wills it."

"The Almighty wills it," I repeat.

We step out into the dead expanse ahead, and as we do, we leave behind not only safety but also all of our efforts to keep one another safe. We are both resolved that the other must be here, that it is our mutual destiny to face the Dragon Below.

So we step onto the path ahead and do not look back.

The real world falls away, swallowed up by a strange in-between place. The dim glare of the sun—more like illumination than real sunlight—staring down at an utterly grey world makes it feel as if we are walking through fog.

It seems to last forever. We rest only briefly, and every time I raise my head to look at the horizon, the glow never seems to get any closer.

I think I fall asleep once, upright and walking, or perhaps it is only the sensation of being caught in an endless dream, but I do doze a little, simply because my mind could no longer stand the unbearable tension and sought an escape, even for only a few seconds, from the merciless blaze ahead of us.

Finally, the dim glare around us begins to fade into darkness, and we make camp for the night, kicking aside the top layer of ash on the ground until we clear a space of hard-packed earth for our blankets.

I thought there would be no fire tonight—everything that could be burned in this desolation has been burned already, so I start when Beowulf turns his shield downwards on the ground and pulls out a bit of tinder.

"It will be blackened soon enough," he says, noticing my look with a smile, "so I would rather blacken it first with good fire—fire as the Almighty meant it to be."

But there is little to burn. Beowulf had thought to gather some chunks of wood and bits of moss before we left the dead forest, and he sets it on our makeshift brazier.

It is a small and smelly fire, and we both cough, but it does us good. We are able to warm the last of a little flask of wine, and the spicy liquid tingles in our throats and loosens our muscles as we gulp it gratefully down.

We eat our meager rations and talk of nothing in particular, though everything we touch upon is a happy subject. Our words seem to fill the dark plateau, pushing at its corners, and the smell of food briefly covers the smell of death. For a brief time, we ignore the doom before us, and I can almost feel the shadows writhing at our insolence—at these two upstarts daring to eat bread and talk of ordinary things such as honeycomb and sailing.

But far too soon the last crumb is eaten and the light conversation is swallowed with the last bite of bread. We say nothing more as we lie down and try to rest.

Though I almost immediately hear Beowulf's peaceful breathing, I lie awake in the dark, sleep eluding me, the hard ground digging into my back the way doubts dig into my mind.

I try not to disturb Beowulf, but my tossing and turning wakes him at last. I hear him roll over and sense him looking in my direction, across the shield still resting between us.

"Can you not sleep, Wynnhild?"

"No," I confess, almost guiltily, and then with a sudden flash of irony I add, "You were sleeping well enough."

I hear him smile at my feeble jab. "I often sleep my deepest before battle—the Almighty is faithful in granting me rest."

"How can you?" I marvel.

There is a rustle as Beowulf shifts a little, seeking a more comfortable position on the hard ground. "Years of fighting monsters have trained me to seize moments of rest and to trust implicitly that the Almighty will grant me the grace to lie down and sleep. He has gifted me with the honor of fighting monsters, and part of that gift is an extra portion of slumber when others might be kept awake."

A gift I clearly do not have, I think glumly. I roll onto my back and stare up into utter blackness that seems to press on my throat, smothering me.

The sensation makes me remember the elder that I nearly choked, the one who believed Beowulf to be the one spoken of in the ancient prophecy of the dragon. *A son who breaks the hold of dragons . . .* Once more, the old man's words ignite utter helplessness inside of me. I despair over the warrior I have grown to care for and torment myself over his true destiny.

Who are you really, Prince Beowulf?

I want to ask him—it's on the tip of my tongue to ask him *—Are you the fulfillment of the prophecy? Are you the son that will be slain?*

There is no moon, and the fire has burned down to nothing. No coal remains, we are surrounded by the dark, and I don't know if suns or sons will ever rise.

I roll onto my side, turning my face away from the merciless black above me that does not even grant me a glimpse of stars. I shut my eyes . . . and I try to pray.

Almighty, I know You answer prayer, and perhaps You do not care what happens to me, but I know You care what happens to Beowulf, so please, hear my prayers for his sake. And for Your honor, let Your name grant power to Your servant.

There is a slight crackle of sound and I open my eyes. Beowulf is blowing on the bit of ash remaining in his shield, adding something with a little rustle.

And suddenly there is a spark. A single coal awakes: it's as if a star has fallen into our midst: it burns so brightly in the night. I stare at it for a long time, and then I shut my eyes before I can see it go out. But even though I know it will die any moment, the sudden peace that bit of light releases inside me does not dissipate. It floods my every corner, wraps me in a blanket of quiet.

Almighty, I don't know what to ask for myself. I don't know if I should, but—if I can—please, will You only help me get through this endless night? Will You let this sinner sleep?

I hear Beowulf breathing deeply again, and I listen to it, letting my breath match his, until the Almighty answers my prayer and I fall into a deep sleep.

25

The meager recovery of spirits that we possessed last night fades when we open our eyes to oppressive grey. The realization that the nightmare journey of yesterday will begin anew all over again wraps itself around us like a smothering blanket.

As we silently pack our things, I am shocked by Beowulf's haggard face. Even when I came upon him at the pool where he was mourning Auschere and wrestling over whether he had been sent to kill or save me, I have never seen him look so haggard.

"Are you all right?" A foolish question, but I cannot help asking it.

Beowulf speaks with an effort. "This meeting cannot come soon enough to suit me. I have trained all my days for this. I believe my whole life has led me here. Still, it is a very terrible darkness before me."

I look at him in dismay. His shoulders are almost bowed under some invisible weight that I can do nothing to lessen. Once more, I remember how he looked at the pool: embroiled in an inner battle and fighting things in his spirit that are far harder, far more bitter, than any sword fight.

"I'm sorry." I don't know what else to say.

His next words strike me like ice water. "It is a good end."

My pulse jumps in my throat, nearly choking me. "Don't say such a thing."

Beowulf turns to look at me, his gaze as heavy and still as the sky. "Will you hunt beasts, even if I am gone?"

I let out a breath of disbelieving laughter. "I have no training. I cannot kill monsters as you do."

"You can. And even when you cannot kill them, you can resist them. You can have sympathy for those that the Almighty wishes to extend mercy to. Can you not do this?"

On the horizon, the distant flame burns silently, and my eyes burn with it, tears blurring my vision. "I will try if you want me to. But it will never happen. I don't want to live in a world where I can't follow you. If you go, I will go with you."

Beowulf turns back towards me, and his eyes are wet.

I touch his forearm. My heart swells at the look on his face. "What is it, dear Beowulf?"

Beowulf sighs, and the sound comes from some deep place inside of him that I have never seen. "I am sorry for what may happen to you. But . . ." He meets my gaze, and again I meet that tear-bright gaze. "Thank you for not leaving me."

We do not speak; there is nothing more to be said, and I could not speak even if I wished to, so instead we walk . . . walking ever on towards the end.

There is no sound for a long time besides our breathing and the puff of our feet pushing through piles of ash. I want to run—to get the confrontation, and what must surely follow, over with as quickly as possible—but Beowulf does not hurry, so I force myself to match his steady pace. And, slowly, the fire grows closer.

Neither of us says anything about camping for the evening. We are too close to stop now. Even though we are tired, we push on. I would never be able to sleep anyway, and I can feel Beowulf's eagerness to be rid of the burden in his spirit—an urgency that grows so strong, he simply cannot bear to stop.

Besides, our water and food are running low. We pass the skin between us, sharing a final drink that, despite its coolness, does little to assuage the tightness of my throat.

The prophecy rings through my memory—a death knell. There isn't another sound in this world big enough to silence it, not a single word I can speak to make it stop, though I pray harder than I have ever prayed, until my mind is a tangle of the same broken plea. *Almighty, don't let Your best servant die. He doesn't deserve it. Take me instead. Please, let him live.*

Night comes, and there is no light except for that dreadful glare on the horizon, but we walk on. Moving in the dark holds little danger here, for there is nothing for us to stumble over.

We press forward until black is tinged by the approaching glow. The glow finally brings heat, rising and rising until it is scorching. My heart hammers as we grow closer, closer still, until finally I glimpse a great pit in the center of the earth. We walk on until I can see not just the rim of the pit but its interior, a bubbling cauldron of horror, standing out starkly amidst the bland features of the plateau: a burning, glowing eye-socket in a black face. At last, we stand on the edge of it.

It is perhaps a hundred feet in circumference—large enough for any dragon—and its sides go straight down. It is nearly a perfect shaft, as if burrowed by some giant ancient worm. The pit is roughly funnel-shaped, growing smaller as it descends until it ends in one fiery pinprick far beneath us. The walls of the pit are as lined as an old man's face, etched with wrinkles of fire—thousands upon thousands of heat vents—and it is these cracks that cause the glow to rise up from the pit in a spiderweb of ominous brightness.

There is a half-crumbled path leading down into the crater, a spiral descent of crudely fashioned stone. I wonder how this place came to be. The path was clearly built for humans. But how it was formed does not matter—all that matters is that somewhere at its core is the Dragon Below, and we must go down to face him.

I turn to look at Beowulf, and as I raise my head, I let out a gasp. "Beowulf!"

He looks up too, and as we stand on the rim of a raging, fiery death, we gaze upwards in astonishment.

For one brief moment, the perpetual grey haze above our heads has parted, creating a path through the clouds to the sky beyond.

There is a sunset beyond these eternal clouds, and for a few brief moments, glorious color pierces the stupefying grey around us. Gold spirals before our eyes, followed by scarlet as dark as blood, as if the heavens are depicting the battle before us.

We gaze up at the sky, speechless with refreshment and inexplicable, miraculous hope. The color, the reality of the world beyond this cursed grey land, is like a gift, a sign that we have not been forgotten and a reminder for us not to forget.

Beowulf unsheathes his sword and plants it, tip down, into the soft ash at the rim of the pit, sinking to one knee and bowing his head. I join him, looking sideways at a face that is now perfectly at rest, perfectly content.

He prays aloud, softly. "Almighty use us for Your will." And that is all.

He stands, ready. He pulls his sword from the ground and sheathes it once more, looking up at the patch of sky with a look of joyous anticipation for the violent confrontation before him, and then the clouds close once more, sealing us back into the monstrous dream.

"Now, at last, I come to it," Beowulf says softly. "What an honor to attack the heart of the curse itself. Now, at last, to face the real monster I was sent to defeat." He smiles his brilliant smile, and the burden that has been upon him is suddenly gone, winging away into the shadows. "This will be the most glorious fight of all, will it not, Wynnhild?"

I nod but do not speak, too busy memorizing his face, for I know that in just a little while we shall be too busy to allow me the chance to truly look at his face.

Surely there is still a chance. Just because he is the best and the bravest beast hunter that has ever lived, willing to face the monster no other man has ever dared to face, eager to try his skill against the father of all beasts . . . that doesn't mean that he is the fulfillment of the prophecy.

Surely even in this place, even now, I can still hope for that.

Beowulf holds out his hand, and I take it.

I hold on tight as we step off the rim and onto the path that leads to the bottom of the pit.

26

Smoke curls about our ankles. The heat coming from the pit meets the cool air of the plateau and creates a constant vapor. A noxious smell begins to impress itself upon my nostrils, foul and fetid but like no scent I have known. It is brimstone and poison and death—with something more beneath it. Perhaps it is the scent of dragon. I inhale the awful smell again, and queasiness rages in my belly.

The narrow, crumbling path forces us to huddle close to the wall that bubbles and burns with fiery spiderweb cracks that show molten heat somewhere deep within the walls, heat that reaches out to scorch us like hundreds of hot little claws.

The path winds around the pit in an ever-descending circle, making me sick and dizzy, and I am glad that Beowulf does not let go of my hand. He leads the way, pulling me carefully behind him, never pausing or faltering, until his boot kicks something that skitters across the path and bumps against the wall.

Beowulf stops so abruptly I nearly run into him. "What is it?"

He crouches swiftly, and I look past his shoulder to examine the thing he has struck.

It's a human leg bone, picked almost clean except for a few threads of scarlet fabric that somehow cling to it.

I stare at it, my mind tumbling.

Other men wear scarlet, but there is one scarlet-clad man we know who already crept into the Dragon's lair. Was Unferth really so foolish as to come here again?

We might never know.

Beowulf looks at me, and then he carefully sets the bone down and steps around it, his head bowed, as if from respect or sorrow. Neither of us speaks.

I remember the cursed blade that Unferth gave to Beowulf, and my fingers drop to fumble with the hilt of my own sword.

My blade was not cursed: it was blessed to be carried in the sheath of a warrior as true as Auschere. But I cannot stop myself from wondering and worrying if I myself might somehow curse it.

Beowulf gave it to me without hesitation, as if I am worthy of it, but doubt torments me now. Yes, I have used it before in combat, but killing a troll-beast or a wolf with Auschere's sword is one thing—all monsters kill other monsters. Fighting the Dragon Below is different. Am I worthy to fight the thing I once swore allegiance to? Do Auschere and those other victims curse me from beyond the grave? Will my blade fail me at a crucial moment as Unferth's gift did?

Unlike Beowulf, I am not sure that there is enough inside of me to overcome such a thing, if it does happen.

If, if, if . . . The word runs through my mind, crackling like the fire scorching my fingers.

We continue on, and the pit becomes narrower and narrower as we pick our way along the path, though we see no more bones. At last, when I feel I might scream from the mounting tension, the pathway ends. We have reached the bottom of the pit, and we stand in the narrowest of roughly-rounded spaces. To our left is a massive tunnel. The ceiling of the tunnel is rough and knobbled, and the walls are of a strange aspect, covered in strips of tightly-packed, layered rock—the tunnel itself is scaled.

There is so much heat issuing from the chamber at its end that the tunnel is full of smoke, but it is an unnatural smoke, for it does not waft in the air but sits heavily on the ground in a sinuous pool of fog that obscures the ground our feet will tread.

Beowulf goes first, holding me back with one arm, using his sword to stab the smoke and to feel for sure footing. Though we move slowly and cautiously, I have the irrational fear that the smoke hides pits that will suddenly drop out from beneath us, plunging us into something worse than my own nightmares.

But we pass safely through the tunnel, and each step brings us closer to the bright glow at its end, until at last we step into a massive chamber that I know without a doubt is the Dragon's lair.

We stand in a towering cavern with a ceiling so high we cannot see it, though I sense that the room we are in is not quite as deep as the pit we first entered.

The chamber grows higher towards its center, giving the sense of a vaulted ceiling, and the smooth floor is punctuated at irregular intervals with great columns of stone. At the far end of the chamber are great gaping holes in the wall, roughly-arched doorways leading to darker rooms and darker depths.

But this main chamber is full of light: crackling, licking tongues of fire resting in natural depressions in the rock wall, streaming down the pillars in evil streamers, resting on the floor in strange burning pools, giving the nightmarish impression of candles and braziers.

It is like a great hall such as Trollhattan—but it is the most hellish hall I could have ever imagined.

We stand in the entrance, waiting.

From the back of the cavern, a shape emerges. Dark shadows uncoil and slither towards us as it comes into the light. Heavy footsteps shake the gritty floor beneath us. The Dragon emerges from its barrow into the terrible glare of the cave.

He is massive, with great hunched shoulders above short, powerfully-scaled legs ending in claws as long as Beowulf's sword. He is the color of dull steel, tinged with the orange reflection of flames. His eyes—yellow as night stars—burn like cauldrons in his long, cruel face. The great jaw curves upwards in a fanged smile, and he opens his mouth to reveal a throat of impossible darkness. At the base of his long sinuous neck is a bulbous gland. His fire sac: the source of his most fearsome weapon. It is deflated now, like a folded bellows. He must inhale fresh embers to create his deadly fire—but in a cavern that is ablaze with tongues of fire, it will be easy.

I stare at the Dragon, sickeningly fascinated, expecting him to breathe flame and consume us at any moment.

Expecting that all I have fought and hoped for to be turned to ash.

I have faced evil before—it has been my parent—but I have never felt evil like this before.

The Dragon Below swings his terrible head towards us, and those venomous eyes fix upon me. Then the Dragon speaks in a voice like gathering thunder.

"I've been waiting for you, my child."

The words wash over me, thick as poison, freezing me to the ground. Whose child am I? The daughter of Beowulf's Almighty —or the Dragon Below?

I am afraid—on the verge of vomiting in screaming terror—that this has all been an illusion. Have I been fooling myself? Has Beowulf been indulging me? When the Almighty looks down from His far-off glory and sees me not in the shadow of His servant—but of the Dragon Below, will He change His mind? Will He let me be reclaimed by the Dragon? Oh, but I'd rather *die* than let him enslave me again.

Almighty, are You there? Can You hear me? Please—help me.

Beowulf takes a step forward, shielding me with both shoulder and shield, his voice ringing to the rafters. "She's not your child anymore. Her true Father has adopted her."

The Dragon's gaze moves away from me, and I can breathe again.

I gasp, pulling air into my throbbing lungs. I reach out a fumbling hand, and my fingers find the edge of Beowulf's tunic, and I cling to it. He seems so certain of who I am now, of my true destiny.

Beowulf, I'm trusting you.

The Dragon sucks air slowly inward, pulling it between his teeth, as if straining out something distasteful. "And you are here too, Beowulf." Smoke curls from his nostrils. "I have waited for you also." A dark crimson color ripples across his skin, some unspoken emotion, and his voice grows even uglier. "You have stolen my slave. You have killed the great Mother, my spokesman to mortals. You have woken and stirred up my Hall to rebel against me, to remember their old ways and question their hearts. And for all of this, you will now receive your punishment. You will die, and your precious charge will be mine once more."

Tremors rack my body, even as resolve floods me. I cannot let Beowulf stand alone against any attack—even one of mere words. Once, long ago, I was silent when Beowulf was accused, but I will be no longer. I must be worthy of the price he paid for me.

I step forward to stand beside Beowulf, despite the trembling in my legs, and fling back my head, my voice like pebbles thrown against a mountain. "I will never serve you again. You took enough from me. I serve Beowulf now, and I follow his Almighty."

"Do you really think you can defeat me? Not even a beast killer can destroy death!"

I swallow and look at Beowulf. But the prince from beyond the sea is not dismayed. He raises his sword, and his voice is as inexorable as a sunrise. "Before the day is done, you will discover that there is a power greater than death, Dragon!"

Our enemy opens his jaws, revealing a black maw lined in endless fangs, and then he roars.

The very pillars of the lair shake at the sound. Every piece of flame in the chamber—from pool to streamer—gasps and gutters. That horrible head sinks to the ground, so close I can see the fine lines between each scale, and Beowulf shoves me to one side. Fire as wide and deep as hell itself streams towards me.

I crash to the ground. The clatter of my shield tumbling to the floor echoes shrilly in my ringing head. Hot spittle burns into my back and my arms. My head jars violently on my shoulders. I twist around, and my heart hammers with both fear and awe. Beowulf flies through the air, springing from the top of a boulder. Suspended, surrounded by the flare of fire, he looks like a dragon himself.

The gaze of the Dragon is fixed upon me as he slithers closer to finish me with his flame. He turns to fend off Beowulf a second too late.

Beowulf's blade impales his neck, diving deep into his fire sac.

A hideous scream rips through the chamber. Beowulf hangs grimly onto his sword as the Dragon whips his head, convulsing in pain. The stream of fire meant to harm me disappears into his gaping maw. The red ribbon is rewound on its spool. His fire is gone. He screeches with fury and whips his head in a jerk that sends Beowulf flying to the ground. His sword finally pulls free of the smoking fire sac. The dragon has lost his deadly flame, and now we have a chance.

Terror pulses in my throat and I nearly choke with relief when Beowulf lands safely. His eyes meet mine. With that look, he throws some of his strength to me the way he might throw a sword. My mind clears as if dashed by water.

Of course I'm going to die. That doesn't matter. I came to help fight a dragon, and that is what I'm going to do.

I surge to my feet. My pulse is no longer racing. It is steady, and so are my legs.

I bend and scoop up my shield, grasping it with both hands as I whirl to face the battle raging behind me.

The Dragon swipes at the ground with his claws, roaring as Beowulf drives his blade into his opposite leg. Thick, vile blood—so dark it is almost black—bursts out from between the scales. Beowulf rips his sword free and dives to one side to avoid the snapping jaws.

I ignore the Dragon and race towards Beowulf, sliding in

front of him with my shield raised to block the next attack. The Dragon swipes at one of the fire-filled hollows with his tail. Hot rock and boiling flames rocket towards us.

The world is a cacophony of hissing steam and flame. The missiles strikes my shield, and the metal buckles like crumpled cloth. Beowulf and I press close together, tucking our heads behind the iron, as it grows hot in our hands.

Then Beowulf dives out from behind the shelter with a quick, bright glance at me, before he charges once more.

The Dragon bends down and Beowulf does not flinch as the pointed jaws open to swallow him. I cry out as Beowulf's body is hidden by the descending mouth, half swallowed up—and then the jaws open wider in a scream, revealing Beowulf's sword embedded in the roof of the Dragon's mouth. If he hoped to penetrate the Dragon's brains, his blade did not go deep enough.

The Dragon shakes his head wildly, screeching in pain. The blade finally shakes free, ejected from his mouth like a broken tooth, sliding across the cavern floor towards me.

I scramble forward, my fingers grasping for the sword, and shout Beowulf's name.

"Beowulf!" I throw the sword, and it flies through the air, as light and swift as quicksilver.

It snaps into Beowulf's outstretched palm. His fingers have barely closed over the blade before he swings it upwards, striking at the Dragon's back legs.

The Dragon whirls to counterattack, and I dodge his tail. I strike wildly with my sword and hew the tip of his tail off with my blade. Auschere's sword is still sharp enough to slice through scales. Sticky blood stains the sword and I think, with a surprising jolt of happiness, how pleased Auschere would be to see his sword doing damage against the Dragon.

The Dragon screams, and he turns to lunge towards me, but he checks halfway, and his claws scrabble against the stone as Beowulf attacks him from the rear. I lurch forward as the Dragon turns away and plunge my sword into a scaled foot, earning a spurt of blood and another furious screech.

For several moments, the dance continues, and the Dragon spins in frantic circles as Beowulf and I trade attacks. The Dragon Below twists himself in agitated scarlet knots as we take turns leaping forward to harry the dragon. We are using his weight against him, exhausting him as we force him to evade two separate attacks.

Something like exultation bubbles up inside of me. Such a strategy works only with a pair. I cut and slash at the enemy as new strength floods through me in a sudden rush of assurance. I am using Auschere's sword, and I am standing in Breca's place, and I belong here. This humiliating harassment we are wreaking against the Dragon could have never happened if Beowulf had come alone.

I am here, and it is good.

Beowulf must be thinking this too, for above the crashing of dragon feet and the crumbling rock showering down around us, his golden laughter rings out through the cavern.

That glorious sound snaps the Dragon Below from his panic. With a snarl, he charges out from between our two-pronged attack, leaping for the far wall, striking it with his claws. He springs away from the wall with enough force to twist and then turn in midair to face us both. He swings his tail again, knocking over a column as thick as an oak. The massive stone pillar rolls towards us.

Beowulf and I turn and run for a boulder protruding from the cavern floor. We meet behind the rock, nearly crashing into one another.

Beowulf steadies me with a hand. "Are you all right?"

I am panting for breath, but I smile raggedly at him. I'm not sure how I can smile, but I'm doing it anyway. "I'm all right."

For one brief moment, that feeling that we shared on the beach, when we swam with sea beasts, flashes between us—a kind of giddy joy.

A pillar beside us explodes with a crack of shattering rock. I raise my shield, and white-hot rubble pummels me with a shatter of stone against metal, and my attention is drawn away from the Dragon for the merest instant.

Silver flashes in my vision.

I jerk back, only to be jerked forward again.

The Dragon Below catches me up in one claw, a talon as wide and sharp as a sword that snags me by my mail. My flesh is not broken, but I am as helpless as if he had pierced me straight through.

My stomach plummets as the ground drops out from beneath me. I rush upwards, my feet fluttering helplessly, and I scream like a child when I feel nothing but air beneath my heels. The Dragon shakes me, laughing as I flail like a doll, a broken toy powerless in his unyielding grip. Bile surges into my throat as he slams me down on the rocky floor, with a force that knocks my sword from my hand and the breath from my body.

I squirm helplessly, but his unmovable talon keeps me pinned to the cavern floor. I fight to wriggle free, but all my strength is nothing against his.

My entire body floods with a cold rush of pure terror. The Dragon bends his head towards me. Our eyes meet, and my breath strangles in my throat. I am unable to look away from his smile.

"You have no right to fight me. You have no power to overcome me. I am death, and death was always your destiny. It is over."

His jaws open.

I do not shut my eyes: I look into the darkness of his throat. The dark I had feared would overwhelm me will now finally swallow me. I cannot look away from the fate I deserve.

Then the darkness is pierced with gold.

Golden hair and silver mail mingle together. Beowulf stands above me.

The Dragon's mouth closes on the warrior's shield with a hideous crunch of cracking metal. Beowulf throws himself on top of me, shielding me with his body, as the Dragon's jaw forces him to the ground. I feel his sword arm swing, hear the Dragon snarl. His teeth close again with a second cracking sound—this time not of metal but of bone.

Beowulf's hand reaches behind him to touch me. Then he staggers to his feet, still shielding me with his sword and body.

A cold breeze brushes my arm, and something slick drips down my skin. My arm is wet where Beowulf touched me, and I look down. He has left a handprint of blood on my arm.

Panic erupts inside of me. I stumble to my feet, still half stunned, body throbbing, and I scrabble for my sword.

The Dragon has turned slightly away from me, following Beowulf's limping movements. The prince draws the Dragon's attention away from me. Then the Dragon pounces. He has Beowulf in his claws. His teeth are bared, flashing, and then his head lowers to tear at Beowulf's body.

"*No*!" I run towards them, striking at the Dragon's legs with my sword. I trip and my blow falls short, and I scream in frustration. I leap once, then twice, in a vain effort to reach his tender belly, and then I finally throw my blade, trying to pierce the skin, even though I know it is futile.

It bounces harmlessly off his leg, as I knew it would. As I stand there, empty-handed and half crying, the Dragon suddenly steps back, nearly trampling me. The force of his body shifting beside me sends me to my knees. I am shaking—no, it is the ground that is shaking. The world is falling apart. The entire room is shaking, as if gasping for breath, and in my heart I know.

Even in a cursed place like this, where Beowulf is hated, the earth recognizes when something good has been taken from the world.

Everything is silent.

I raise my head. It is as heavy as iron.

Beowulf is lying on the ground. Unmoving.

"No." Fear wraps itself around my throat, smothering me. I

am so weak, I can barely crawl. I drag myself across the rough ground. "Beowulf!"

He does not smile at the sound of my voice. His face does not turn towards mine like the sun turning to shine on the earth.

I do not know why, but the Dragon suddenly fades away. Inexplicably, he steps away instead of killing me. An invisible hand has cupped itself around Beowulf and me, shielding us from heat and noise and death. The evil flames that line the walls grow suddenly dim, snuffed into mere flickers, holding their breath.

I don't know why, and I don't care—I think only of Beowulf when I finally reach him. I slip my arm beneath his neck and shift his head carefully into my lap.

"Dear Beowulf," I whisper. "You should have let him kill me."

He is broken and bloody and yet, despite his weakness, Beowulf opens his eyes. He looks up at me with a frown of rebuke. "I was always meant to save you or . . . die trying."

A strangled sound somewhere between a sob and a laugh escapes my lips. "Beowulf . . ." I reach for his shredded arm and then hesitate. My eyes travel up and down his twisted body. "What can I do?" *Almighty, please. Not this.*

A shudder runs through his body. "Nothing." He shuts his eyes, and grief rises inside of me in an endless ocean. "I always knew this was how it would end for me."

"This can't be the end for you," I snarl. "I don't believe it."

Beowulf slides a hand towards me, wincing at the movement. "Are you there? I can't feel you."

I know the jostling must hurt him beyond all endurance, but I reach for him anyway. I wrap my arms around his battered body, and he allows it without a murmur. I help him sit up, resting his head against my chest, hoping that it will ease his breathing.

It does. Every rattle seems to go right through me, but Beowulf seems happier upright than sprawled on the ground. His dignity, beautiful and noble, covers him as deeply as the blood.

I press my hand to the most grievous wound in his chest, feeling his life seep through my fingers.

He gently pries my fingers away, interlacing them with his. "You can't stop it."

I squeeze my eyes shut against the tears that threaten to fall. "Are you leaving me, Beowulf?"

Beowulf finally answers. His voice is weak. "I cannot help it."

My breath rattles in my ears, echoing his own rough wheezing. "Are you going to the place you told me of? The Almighty's Hall?"

"Yes." A brief smile flits across Beowulf's battered face. "I will be happy to see it at last." He breaks into a fit of wet coughs. I hold back a whimper, unable to do anything but wait as he gasps for air.

"It's all right," I whisper, even though nothing feels right. "Be at peace."

He stills in my arms and turns his head a little, towards my heart. "It is dark."

I wish I could clean his face: his eyes are half crusted shut with blood. "The Dragon is quiet," I whisper. "The torches have nearly died away."

Beowulf nods. "He won't come near you while I am here. Go now, Wynnhild. You can get out."

He reaches, fumbling, for the ring on his forefinger, a heavy band with a symbol I do not recognize. He pulls it free. "This ring was given to me at birth: it is the symbol of my status within the Heofon court." He slips it onto my thumb with weak fingers. "Go to my home and show them what you wear, so they will know that I leave all that I have to you."

I stare at the ring, shake my head, and swallow a sob. "You should leave it to your kinsmen."

He gives the smallest shake of his head. "I would leave you well-endowed."

"You already have. Someone else will inherit, because I'm not getting out of here alive." I bring my mouth down to his ear and whisper it. "I won't leave you."

His body seems to shrink, no matter how tightly I hold him. Air leaks from his mouth as he answers, "I wish you would."

My voice trembles. "Don't ask me again, dear friend."

He sighs and stirs a little. "It is so dark." He turns his head and smiles up at me with sudden joy. "But think of the light beyond, Wynnhild. True light! Light as we have never seen it—not this cheap imitation—but the real thing. The source of all light. And a Hall, like Trollhattan, but far greater, more beautiful. And a King on his throne—a King who is also a Father."

I do not speak. Tears run down my face, scalding tracks of pain.

Beowulf reaches out carefully and finds my cheek. He touches a tear with a grave finger and then gently wipes my cheeks with his thumb.

"Will I be there in that Great Hall too?" I whisper. "Can I follow you?"

Beowulf reaches for my hand again, and I meet him halfway. "You will."

I do not dare take my hand from his. Even though I can barely see him through my tears, I do not let go to wipe them away. "Will you look for me when I come, Beowulf?"

Beowulf's voice is as bright as the light he yearns for. "Of course I will! I'll be the first one to meet you at the gate."

He smiles at me again. And then, between one breath and the next, he is gone.

27

I trace Beowulf's features with my fingers. His beard tickles my palms. My mind echoes with the single thought that carves me as hollow as the cavern around me.

Beowulf is dead.

But I have only a moment to understand it. The Dragon Below suddenly leaps forward. With his return comes the fire, a hundred torches relit by evil flames, piercing my private pain and illuminating my misery for every evil spirit inside this place to mock and rejoice.

"Turn to face me, Grendel," the Dragon hisses. "Prepare for your death."

I flinch and my grip tightens convulsively on Beowulf's shoulders. "That . . . is not my name," I whisper between clenched teeth.

His tail scrapes against stone as he moves closer. "You have answered to it before, and you will again."

I do not turn around. I ignore him. If I am going to die, I will die looking at Beowulf's face, not the Dragon's.

Beowulf still requires one last service from me.

I do my best to clean the blood from his face and hands by

letting my tears fall on his wounds, and then I wipe them with the edge of my tunic.

It does little good, save to cover me in his blood—an honor that fills me with sorrowful awe.

The Dragon's breath is hot on my neck. It is odd that he does not simply kill me. He could: there is nothing stopping him. I dropped my sword and shield long ago.

But he merely stands behind me, constrained by some unseen grasp. A memory sparks in my mind. An invisible force once withheld me from sitting on a throne, no matter how much power I possessed in my claws.

"It is your fault he is dead," the Dragon sneers. "Your fault! You exploited his generosity, you tricked him into pitying you, and now look what you have done. You have caused his death!"

I swallow. His words dig into my mind like claws. I huddle closer to Beowulf—his body is still warm—some of that warmth seeps into me, like a reassurance, even from beyond the grave.

"It was his choice," I say. "It was his glory to die for someone like me. It was his joy to defend everyone he knew."

The Dragon speaks again, impatient. "Your defender is *gone*, Grendel. Despair and die!"

I kiss Beowulf's scarred hands, and then I lay my head on his chest, searching for a heartbeat.

There is no sound, no movement. Once, that great beautiful heart did beat. It was real. Even though it is gone now, it was there once, and that is all that matters.

"No," I whisper into Beowulf's beard. What I feel now is not despair. I know what despair is, and this is not the same.

This is sorrow—a gift I have never given to anyone before. I have never possessed anything precious, so I have not yet experienced the beautiful pain of possessing and then losing . . . until now.

I answer the beast behind me without turning to face him. "I will die, but I won't despair—how could I? I can't despair, not when I have known him."

The Dragon's voice recedes with a hiss, leaving me to mourn Beowulf alone once more.

Images and words whisk through my mind, memories of our past weeks together, as if I stand outside of myself. The two of us roasting chestnuts by the fire, fighting the troll and then rejoicing, our swords clashing as we trained in mock battles.

The sound of our blades ringing together in my mind is real—I can hear it. My eyes fly open. But there are no bright swords or happy warriors in this place anymore.

The metallic grinding is coming from the Dragon Below.

He is laughing at me.

"You dare to cling to him? You have no right! You arrogant piece of filth! Have you no shame? A vigil should be kept for him by his shield brothers, by family—you are neither. You are not worthy to be trod under his foot, and yet you insist on dishonoring him. Leave him. Let him go before you bring him more insult, before you disgrace yourself further. Beowulf was a great knight—you are a pretender. Your mother was my servant—what does that make you? You are less than a servant. You are nothing."

I close my eyes and take a long, shuddering breath. I remember Beowulf's kindness to me was a gift—I never earned the right to fight beside him any more than I had the right to mourn him. He invited me to.

"I am nothing—it is true," I whisper. "But he made me something."

The Dragon does not answer beyond a hiss. His scales grate against the stone floor of the cavern as he circles me.

I do not look at him. My gaze is on Beowulf, for a memory has exploded amidst my shattered thoughts.

The prophecy—there was more. The verses spoke of the hero conquering the grave and rising again. *A soul too strong to yield to night. . . . Yet in the dark, there comes a light.*

Hope flickers in my chest—a candle that refuses to go out—and I lace my fingers around his still hands.

Beowulf's story cannot be over.

Yet my mind continues to tumble in every direction, trying desperately to unwind the meaning of the verses. How can I be sure what the prophecy means? If it does promise a son will rise again, perhaps it meant Beowulf would come back to life in a dozen years, or a hundred.

Perhaps he will be reborn in a new form.

Perhaps he will not remember me.

I hope for rebirth, and yet I dread it, for what could it mean? One thing is certain: a hero returning from glory would be a greater and different being, and things could never be the same between us.

Either way, I have lost him.

"Ah." The Dragon exhales on a long, low note of satisfaction. Fresh heat scorches my back with bitter pain. "You think he will come back! You truly believe this princeling could fulfill a prophecy? He is not. He is only a dead knight. So why do you still cling to him? He hasn't moved or breathed. His heart has stopped. He has fought his last fight. Was he not doubtful when he first stepped into this barrow? I can see by your face that he was. He's just a man. Why do you cling to foolish hope? Was he not a man of practicalities himself? If you value him so, why don't you emulate him? Face reality—admit that his days are over. Do you really believe that if you sit there he will miraculously revive? Why hold on to foolish dreams?"

Doubt worms through me: a hideous whisper. Perhaps the Dragon Below is right. Is it is foolish to hold on to Beowulf?

My fingers dig deeper into Beowulf's tunic. What do I care what is foolish and what isn't? Wasn't Beowulf himself called a fool many times?

The Dragon dared me to emulate Beowulf, so I will. I will dare to believe, as he did, against all odds.

For what is the worst that can happen if Beowulf was not the hero in the prophecy? My hopes for a future will be shattered, but Beowulf showed me that shattered hopes do not equal a broken heart.

My life has been so short: I was born when Beowulf tore my enchantment from my shoulders, and I truly lived for only a month, but at least I lived beside the greatest warrior that ever walked the earth, in an honored place I could have never dreamed of.

If he lives again, I will rejoice. If he is dead, I am content.

I hear myself speak again: "If he is dead, so be it. But I believe he is the hero of the prophecy, for he is like no man that ever lived. I cannot believe that his purpose was to die like any other mortal."

The Dragon laughs—a hideous sound like chains striking against one another. "Did your great, precious hero burn with purpose? You'll find my flames are stronger than his holy fire! For how can a soul return to earth if there is no body?"

The Dragon's voice draws itself together in a wave of crushing sound. With his roar, the evil light in the chamber grows brighter.

Every flame in the chamber streams across the chamber towards me to blast me free of Beowulf's body as the dragon screams, "I said . . . *let him go*!"

I lie full-length beside Beowulf, clinging to him with my arms and legs, digging my nails into his bloody flesh. I tuck my head into the crook of his shoulder and scream.

I am surrounded by pain—I am pain. It is a torment like nothing I have ever known, not even when I was Grendel.

Holding on to Beowulf is more than hurting me—it is killing me.

But still, I do not let go.

I remember that poor villager in the north, burned to a living cinder. I am living the same agonizing death. But what does it matter? Let the Dragon burn me, for I will then be with Beowulf again.

Death has no hold upon me; pain holds no dread. The wonder of it pierces my agony like water poured over a burn: I do not fear the Almighty or my welcome at His Hall. It is as if the fire burning my skin from my body has burned away all my doubts and terrors of the unknown.

Suddenly, the fire stops.

I open my eyes and look down at my hands. I am still alive, and despite the unbearable torment, I am unhurt. My flesh is still whole.

I look wildly at Beowulf, but he is still there, not burned away to nothing—as if his body is indeed waiting for his spirit to return.

My breath whistles in astonishment in my tingling ears. Though I felt the tortuous heat, neither my skin nor Beowulf's is blistered. We are broken—but still whole.

I turn and look at the Dragon, straight into his astonished face, and unbelievably, I feel myself smile.

"I won't let him go—because you were wrong," I declare. "You're still afraid of him—that is why you stand back. You are still weaker than him and that is why your fire cannot burn him. Even in death, he is more powerful than you."

The Dragon falls silent. The fire goes out as if extinguished by a single giant breath—and I am in the dark.

I had not realized how bright the cavern was until those unnatural pillars of flame disappeared.

I have never known what darkness was until now. It is longer than night, blacker than black. It is not merely a lack of light: it is a thing in and of itself—a slowly ascending weight crushing everything before it. It presses upon me until I can no longer feel Beowulf, though I know my grip has not loosened. It surrounds me until I cannot remember what it was like to see. It seeps into me until I don't know what it was to have a body or a mind. There is only darkness.

I am a monster all over again, only worse, for there is no unholy fire of false zeal to warm me in this darkness—only the cold, brutal assimilation of every thought and feeling. The silence seizes me by the throat in a stranglehold. It is deeper than any silence I have ever experienced: it is dark oblivion.

The darkness is soundless, eternal. And then, without warning, it is broken.

The Dragon begins to hiss—but it does not sound like a single dragon now. There are dozens of voices, hundreds—a strange twisted cacophony of sibilant words. I want to tear my ears off to put an end to the endless whispering that assaults me like a thousand black beetles crawling across my skin.

It is more noise than speech, though I feel the incomprehensible words invade my mind as clearly as if they were spoken aloud. The ceaseless clamor circles around and around me until the darkness becomes an ocean, threatening to drown me.

I can discern only two words amidst the hissing storm.

Give up. They chip away at me; crawling into my mind until it is all I can hear.

Give up. Give up. Give up.

It seems to go on for hours, perhaps days. I do not know time or sense its passing. All I can do is hold on to Beowulf, even when the reason for my resolve fades under the onslaught of doubt.

Finally, the Dragon's voice takes shape amongst the hissing chant, curling around me like thick smoke from a smoldering fire.

"You were formed out of the darkness of my mind. Out of your mother's twisted heart, you were warped into being."

I cannot see Beowulf anymore, so I touch his face, seeing his features in my mind, reaching for the words that seem so hideously small in the darkness. "You only possessed me: you did not make me. I was made by Beowulf's Almighty."

The Dragon inhales savagely. "You dare to believe that you would be accepted by his god? Your bold words are now put to the test! The one you serve is dead—do you still follow his Almighty?" He laughs once more. "Is his Almighty *your* Almighty?"

Doubt floods me again, pressing me, crushing me. The darkness is doubt, implacable, immovable, inescapable. I can't breathe. I have been born in the dark and trapped in it, and now I will die in it. The darkness has even overcome Beowulf. Did I ever truly see or know light? Has it ever been in me? It seems like a dream. Was it a dream?

A single tear slides down my cheek, and I sniff. The sound echoes in the silence all around me.

I start violently awake at that tiny echo. Beowulf's words pour through me like water. *He was my echo. . . .*

I raise my head and turn to where the Dragon's voice had last been,. I cannot see him, but I face him as best as I can.

"Yes, I am a servant of the Almighty like . . . like Beowulf. No matter what happens, He is true. And no matter what happens, I pledge myself to Him."

The Dragon hisses, but there is another sound beneath it, like a groan, as if I have hurt him.

My attention swerves from the warrior in my arms to this new, strange sound. It suddenly occurs to me that, through all of this, the dragon hasn't bitten me, hasn't burned me, hasn't even touched me.

Mother was afraid of the men of Trollhattan, of Beowulf . . . and of me. I smile, and sudden exhilaration sweeps over me.

I now possess what I once feared.

The Dragon Below is frightened not just of Beowulf—but of me—because of the power and the Person that rests inside me. This cannot be pulled from my heart—no matter how deeply claws tear into my body.

Even though Beowulf is dead, I now stand on my own in this truth. When I died as Grendel and looked into the face of all Beowulf has ever told me, the link between me and Beowulf's Master was forged, and it has not broken just because Beowulf is gone.

When I stood in the searing light before that mighty Presence, standing on my own without Beowulf beside me to plead my case, the Almighty reached out to me.

I shut my eyes. Something blooms inside of me: a single coal remains. It sputters to life and rises in my chest in a wave that stuns me but escapes my mouth before I can examine it.

It is a laugh, and the laugh is like a hand sweeping away the soot and the cobwebs that enveloped me. I can see and think and feel more clearly than I ever did before.

The hissing stops, as if extinguished, and I laugh again, this time in triumph.

The Dragon Below reels. He hits the far wall with a crack of stone. He presses back against the wall of his own sanctum as if he has been burned. The flame in the cavern hisses and gasps as if doused by water.

He can barely speak—his voice escapes his throat in a wheezing gasp. "You dare to laugh? In this place, before my very throne, you dare to make light?"

Something presses against my eyelids, but it is not darkness. I open my eyes and look around. A glorious glow fills the chamber.

It isn't firelight—it is *sunlight*, and I am surrounded by it.

Because I made light of his threats, actual illumination has threaded itself around me—it is coming from my skin, filling the cavern with a pure light.

I look down at my hands, radiant and brilliant, and I know that the light I always saw radiating from Beowulf is finally inside of me. It is part of me, and I am part of it. My heart gives a great painful leap, as if it is beating for the first time in all my life.

I rise slowly to my feet. The darkness retreats even further, remaining only at the edges of the cavern as the nimbus around me grows, expanding, radiating from me with a realness, a solidity, that is more than mere illumination. I am smiling and crying all at once as I face the Dragon, still holding Beowulf's hand.

I draw in air—I can breathe again—and my voice echoes in the stunned silence of the cavern.

"Kill me! What is stopping you? I don't care if I live or not—I'd rather die with him than live without him. Go ahead and kill me, you idiotic worm! But you lost. No matter how this ends, you lost. You can torment me for another hundred years—I don't care. You have lost. Your greatest enemy is already in the Almighty's Hall, and I will be there with him too, either in a moment or a century. Beowulf may be dead, but the truth he believed in lives on, and it will always live on. I am the Almighty's, to kill or save, so do your worst—if you can!"

There is a soundless explosion around me. The chamber is flooded with light—light that does not come from me. It is not the evil dancing light of dragon fire. It is clear and cool and heavenly, utterly decimating the darkness.

I stumble and gasp at the change, only half aware of the Dragon's cry of outrage and horror.

And then . . . Beowulf's hand twitches in mine.

I whirl around. "Beowulf?" I rake his face with my eyes, searching for movement. My heart beats wildly with hope, though my mind tells me it is impossible. Trapped in the dark, under this endless torment, my mind has betrayed me.

And yet . . .

I drop to my knees and press my head to his chest, listening.

Nothing.

Tears pour down my cheeks, and I shout his name. "Beowulf!"

Beowulf's heart jumps beneath me.

I jerk upright and look down into his face, and my own heart nearly breaks free from my chest.

Beowulf looks back at me . . . and he smiles.

"No," the Dragon gasps. He stumbles backwards. into a stalactite, causing it to crumble and scatter across the cavern, as if even the cavern wishes to flee. "You . . . you are alive!" the Dragon moans. "You . . . you can't be alive."

"But he is," I whisper. I look at Beowulf, drinking in the sight of him. My heart rises and takes flight. "He is alive."

Beowulf stands up, and I scramble out of his way. I fumble for his sword so that I can hand it to him, but he does not reach for it. He turns and faces the Dragon, unarmed, as the room explodes once more with even greater brightness.

The light pours from Beowulf in liquid shards. It wraps itself around the Dragon as if it is made of cords, entangling his claws, encircling his throat and muzzle, choking him.

It is no longer a roar that bursts from Beowulf's enemy—but a scream—a high-pitched shriek like a thousand swords clashing together. The Dragon Below fights for his life in a blind panic of thrashing claws and writhing scales—but to no avail.

The smoke streaming from his nostrils blackens. It is thick with sparks, as if the fire inside him has been brutally kicked apart, all of its heat escaping.

I stand still, with Beowulf's blood still dripping from my fingers and tears of heat and shock and awe streaming from my eyes. The light pours from the living Beowulf and pierces the Dragon even more deeply.

With a final hideous cough, the Dragon reels upwards in one final effort to break free of the shining band about his throat and chest. And then his claws skid out from beneath him.

He stumbles into a pillar and slides to the ground like a felled tree. The cavern shakes, as if the cavern might collapse around us and I nearly fall. A moan leaks from the dragon's mouth: a low stream of smoke that is no longer hot. The flaming eyes go dark, and the Dragon Below is still, at last.

The licking flames on every wall explode with a deafening crack. Pale blue erupts in the midst of each flame and obliterates the former poisonous scarlet. The flash blinds me, and I shut my eyes.

When I open them again, the flames along the cavern walls have shrunk like blazing strings that have been rewound on a spindle. They burn with a bright, natural light now. The air is clear, even sweet. There is no sound at all, except for the torches now licking happily in the little hollows of the cave, like braziers in a great hall.

I turn to look at Beowulf, just as the bands of light return to their source, like a sword being sheathed. They wrap around him, thinning and fading, and it seems to my dazzled eyes that they somehow go into him.

Then, save for the lingering fires, we are in the dark once

more, but it is a natural darkness—a night emptied of all its specters and shadows—deep and restful and still.

He is still covered in blood, and his face has not changed, but there is something in his gaze, in his spirit, that is brighter and more beautiful than ever. I felt before he was no ordinary mortal, but now I know it.

I look at this face that is both known and new, and I bury my grief. It is enough that he is alive: it should not matter that he is different. I must not expect him to recognize me. He does not need me—not that he ever did, but now less than ever—and yet all is well, because he is alive.

I cannot ask for anything more.

Beowulf turns: a soul too strong to yield to night. He looks at me . . . and then he says my name.

"Wynnhild."

My heart stutters to a stop, seized by joy.

"It is well with you, my friend?" He smiles and holds out a hand.

I blink and swallow, choking out the words past an emotion I cannot name or contain. "Yes. It is well, Beowulf."

I step forward to take his outstretched hand, and he draws me close so that I thump against his shoulder, enfolded in the crook of his arm. I am exhausted and stunned and happy beyond words.

We both laugh, and happiness bubbles from our throats, banishing the shadows and the last lingering doubt in my heart.

"Our battle is over," Beowulf says into my hair. "You did well."

My arms tighten around him. He does not disappear.

I can hear him smiling with all the pride and affection I have only dreamed of. "So very, very well—my echo."

We leave the barrow together. The fiery vents of the shaft have been extinguished, leaving behind cool darkness. We pierce it with a single torch and with our own voices, exultant and powerful. We sing to the Almighty, and my voice rings out as boldly as Beowulf's, claiming and savoring each word, for they are now my own words and not someone else's.

We climb to the rim of the shaft and pause on its edge, blinking in the sudden light. The fog is lifting, and the light is returning to the land. A faint stain of green ripples across the plateau as life begins again.

I turn my head to look at Beowulf, and he smiles at me—a smile that is as brilliant as the sun and even more precious and holy than it was before, and yet . . .

It no longer hurts me to look at it, nor does it make me ashamed. It only makes me glad.

Everything is not just the same between us.

It is better than before.

Don't miss the next installment of ...

CRACK THE STONE

Emily Golus

"I am Valshara, the black stone born of fire. Break me, and my edges turn into knives."

Condemned to a slave camp for her crimes, goblin convict Valshara Sh'a makes a death-defying escape to freedom. But navigating Vindor's treacherous cavern system is only the beginning of her troubles. An encounter with a rogue king turns her world upside down, and a bargain with fairy tricksters leaves her with a human child she doesn't know how to care for.

As she tries to smuggle the boy through the walls of a barricaded city, Valshara can't let down her guard. Because somewhere in the darkness behind her, a bounty hunter rises—relentless as nightfall and merciless as death itself.

Emily Golus re-imagines Victor Hugo's beloved *Les Misérables* as an epic fantasy adventure about suffering, redemption, and the extraordinary power of love.

AUTHOR'S NOTE

To ground the reader more thoroughly in a story that I have twisted into a new shape, I decided to keep the names of all the characters from the historical epic tale of *Beowulf*. The only name in my book that does not exist in the original text is that of Wynnhild.

My main character, Wynnhild, is a combination of the characters of Grendel and Wiglaf. Wiglaf is a young kinsman of Beowulf's in the original epic who helps the warrior defeat a terrible dragon during the end finale. I combined the Old English elements of *wynn* and *hild* to create the name Wynnhild, which means "battle joy"—or "joyous battle." I wanted a name that seemed similar to Wiglaf's name and also summed up my heroine's true nature.

Though I kept the proper names of the characters from *Beowulf*, I did decide to change the names of places and locations. This was partly because words like 'Heorot' are difficult to pronounce—and I have enough of that in this story! I also wanted to emphasize to the reader that this retelling is set in a fantasy world inspired by ancient Britain—and not in historic Denmark.

Even though my story is set in a fantasy version of Anglo-Saxon England, I wanted to use real-world historic names to give the book a sense of reality in the minds of my readers.

Though Beowulf himself is fictional, he comes from a real Germanic tribe in history—the Geats. The Geats were a people group who lived in the historic Götaland region of what is now southern Sweden. The mark of the Geats remains in the name of Götaland, or "land of the Geats."

Because of this connection to the mountain landscape, ancient people, and early history of Sweden, I pulled numerous names from Swedish sources, such as the name of my fictional hall, Trollhattan. Trollhättan Falls is a waterfall in the Göta River in Sweden. The Göta River is still called by the modern Swedish name of *Göta älv*, which means "River of the Geats." The Geats are Beowulf's people, mentioned in the original poem.

Trollhättan is translated as "troll's bonnet." Since I significantly changed the role of the Hall and its people in my book, this meaning felt more appropriate than that of Heorot ("stag").

In the original story, Heorot is in desperate circumstances, but the people are ultimately redeemed by Beowulf's deed, and their King Hrothgar is a nobler person who overcomes his initial failings. In my book, the fate of the Hall is left open-ended, and Hrothgar is a more tragic figure. Beowulf does not leave the Hall in victory—instead, the mood is one of doubt. External burdens can be removed, but some people will forever be locked inside a prison of their own making. "Troll's bonnet" seemed like a good name to represent a people who never quite throw off an infestation of monsters. The image of a monster wrapped around a person's head was perfect for my fictional location, the Hall of Trollhattan.

Frisia, like Trollhattan, is a real place. The Frisians were an ancient Germanic people who lived along the coast of the Netherlands and parts of Germany. But I thought it unlikely that many readers have heard of Frisia, so I concluded it was safe to use this as the moniker for a fictional country. Like Trollhattan, Frisia has a connection to Beowulf. In the original story, Hrothgar's bard sings a song featuring the King of the Frisians. The Frisians are mentioned once more in a brief reference to Beowulf and his past exploits.

Schrawynghop is also based on a real place. Harty is a village on the Isle of Sheppey, near the east coast of England. During my research, I came across one theory that this was the central location of Beowulf. This theory proposes that Harty could have been the coastal town that was the basis for the cliffs where Beowulf makes landfall in the story. In the same theory, the name for the area surrounding Harty could be related to the word *schrawyn-*

ghop. The name consists of two root words: *schrawa* means "demons," and *hop* refers to a place surrounded by marshlands, which is reminiscent of the barren landscape where the legendary Grendel makes his home.

I needed a way to distinguish the great hall from its settlement, so I chose the name Schrawgynhop for my town: first, because it had a loose connection to the original text; second, because the name was thematically appropriate for the location in my story; and third, because pictures of this desolate region closely resembled what I imagined for my story.

Aside from the source material, my choices of names were based largely on words that sounded beautiful or ones that could be pronounced with ease.

ACKNOWLEDGMENTS

First, as always, all thanks and glory to the Almighty. This was all Your idea. You spun this story from beginning to end—both on paper and in my own heart, as Grendel's struggle became my own. Despite all obstacles, Your will was done. May you be glorified in the battle for *Break the Beast*.

The ladies of *A Classic Retold*: Tor Thibeaux, Emily Hayse, Emily Golus, Alissa Zavalianos, Jenelle Schmidt, Rosie Grymm, Nina Clare, and Hannah Kaye. It is a thrill to collaborate with authors I admire so deeply, and it's an honor to call you friends. You are true fellow warriors and beast hunters. Thank you for making this dream a reality.

My twin: How can I even begin to thank you! Your sharp mind, your honest and funny evaluations, and your superior grasp of story never fail to amaze me. Thank you for your brilliant developmental edit. Thanks for having the honesty and kindness to tell me to rewrite almost the entire book—and for having the clarity and wisdom to advise me on how best to do it. I am forever grateful to you for being my partner in crime—in storytelling and in everything else. No one has such good instincts and good taste in stories as you do. Thank you for the many happy hours of ripping apart books and movies with me. Statler and Waldorf have nothing on us!

My beta readers: Thank you, Emily and Anne, for being my advance readers and two of the first people to lay eyes on this book. Your encouragement—and the extra spit and polish you brought to my draft!—means the world.

My sister: Thank you for joining me on this adventure and for giving me the idea for this book series in the first place, with your beautiful retelling of *The Tempest*. I can't wait to hold *Summon the Light* in my hands! You are an inspiration, and I am so proud of you, forever and always.

My brother: Thank you for being a fan and for bragging about me to all of your friends—and for trying to get me to do a book signing at your gaming hangout. Thank you for always supporting me.

My parents: Without your example, I would have never learned the joyous battle. Thank you for the years of prayer, conversations, counseling, reading recommendations, and more. You have been my friends and guides in the pilgrim's way. Thank you for sowing the seeds, for watering and pruning growth throughout my childhood, and for encouraging me to bloom through adulthood. I wouldn't be where I am today—or have written this book—without you.

Mary Herceg: The best copyeditor in the world! Thank you for lending your brilliant mind, tenacious spirit, and meticulous eye for detail to this novel. I might have hewn the rock out of the ground, but you polished it into a shining stone. Thank you for partnering with me so closely in my author journey—thank you for being my Wynnhild in the battle for *Break the Beast*. The Lord increases the widow's mite!

Kimmy Ruth: Thank you for sending me that magnificent video of Benjamin Bagby performing the original *Beowulf*. I celebrated the release of *Break the Beast* by watching the performance in its entirety. It was a fresh reminder, while I was still in the drafting trenches, of how enamored I am with this story—and of these thrilling, mysterious words that are somehow connected to the language we speak today.

MiblArt: Thank you for the lovely book covers!

Declan Rowe and Mike Golus: Declan, thank you for all of your suggestions on cover design and for taking the time to video chat with me when I needed advice. And thank you for the lovely interior formatting for *Break the Beast*! Mike, thank you for such a beautiful website!

My readers: Thank you for your support and for your interest in this book. I pray this story gives you courage to be a beast hunter. Make the Dragon tremble.

ABOUT THE AUTHOR

Allison Tebo is a writer committed to creating magical stories full of larger-than-life characters. She is one of the contributors to *A Villain's Ever After* with her book *The Goblin and the Dancer*—which went on to become a Realm Makers Readers' Choice Finalist. She is also the author of *The Tales of Ambia*, a series of romantic comedy fairy tales. Her flash fiction has been featured in magazines such as *Splickety*; *Spark*; and *Saddlebag Dispatches*, and her short fiction has been published in anthologies by *Inklings Press*; *Rogue Blades Entertainment*; *Pole to Pole Publishing*; *Dragon Soul Publishing*; *Ye Olde Dragon Books*; and *Editing Mee.* She helps run the speculative fiction magazine *Worlds of Adventure.* Allison graduated from London Art College after studying cartooning and children's illustration, but she ended up working in sales before pursuing writing full-time. When not creating new worlds with words or paint, she enjoys reading, baking, and making lists.

THE GOBLIN AND DANCER EXCERPT

Grik the goblin shuffled his feet in time to the music that floated up from the orchestra pit. As one of the janitors of the Metropolitan Dance Hall, he was supposed to be cleaning, but he had crept away from his work to hide in a tangle of ropes and equipment so that he could peek at the dancers from backstage. And at one dancer in particular.

The troupe soared across the stage, their soft, pastel-colored costumes swirling around them. Twelve young elven women bent and swayed and leaped like flowers tossed before a breeze in a delicate display of marvelous skill.

But it was Rosanna, the lead dancer, who was the most magnificent. She danced as if it were more natural to her than walking, or even breathing. Her violet-colored eyes were bright with happiness and her golden curls—the same honey color of the floor in the troupe's practice studio—bobbed around her flushed face. A perfect face, with perfect skin utterly unlike Grik's. But it was her dancing that really made her come to life. It was her dancing that kept her from looking like a perfect doll and turned her into something real and vibrant and gloriously alive. As she performed a dizzying leap and spun effortlessly in front of her cavalier, Grik was absolutely certain that she was magical. She had to be; it was the only explanation.

And he was in love with her.

He thrust his mop into the air the way the cavalier had lifted Rosanna above his head. He wondered what it would be like to have his hands on Rosanna's waist, to hold her close like that. His face went hot at the mere thought of it, and his pulse pounded in his ugly head.

He watched Rosanna dance and sighed to himself as he swayed awkwardly to the music that she danced to so effortlessly. Not only was she the most beautiful dancer in the troupe, she was the most graceful and the most talented. But, better than that, she was the kindest. As a janitor, Grik had observed more than his share of backstage drama. He winced at the barbed words and the accusations that seemed to drift through the air like the powder the dancers brushed across their cheeks before each performance. But then Rosanna would dart into the room like a gentle butterfly, inserting herself softly and earnestly between arguments and soothing hurt feelings. She always had a kind word for everyone, even the lowliest workmen who rarely received even a glance from the dancers.

Even for Grik.

Elves and goblins didn't really mix. They lived side by side and worked in the same buildings, but their worlds, their culture, and their conversations were still largely separate. Some were prejudiced against one another, but, for the most part, relations were friendly, though distant. They bore very little ill will; they just didn't understand one another. And the thought of an elf and goblin fancying one another was unheard of.

That was Grik's secret. He liked the elven world—and he liked Rosanna.

Sometimes he dared to believe that Rosanna liked him too.

He always froze when she looked his way. When she spoke to him, it seemed to take all the breath out of him and he could only mumble awkward responses before running away to hide, utterly overwhelmed that she deigned to see him. Despite his shyness, Rosanna still made a point of singling him out in crowds with her smile.

As if he was something special. As if she cared about him.

If she had been merely beautiful and merely kind, Grik didn't think he would have fallen in love with her—for that would be like falling in love with a pretty statue.

She had a wound. He had seen it in her face. Sometimes the happy smile wavered and her eyes flinched, as if wincing at some secret pain. Sometimes he saw her wiping away a tear and hiding a sob in a handkerchief. Sometimes, when she practiced, she would suddenly miss a step that Grik was certain she knew by heart, suddenly as clumsy as a goblin and looking as if she didn't know who she was. When that happened, she looked like the loneliest person in the city.

Grik knew what that felt like. He had felt so alone in the world; he had always assumed he was the only one to carry a secret wound. But Rosanna had one too. Perhaps they weren't separated by an impassable chasm after all. Perhaps Rosanna was more like a goblin than he had ever dared to dream. That secret pain, and the ugliness of all hurts, somehow bound them together. Rosanna wasn't utterly unlike him. That was what made him love her.

Grik tapped his huge fingers in time to the music and removed the single rose he had slipped carefully into his toolbox earlier that evening. He held it close to his heart, letting the petals tickle his chin. Tonight, he would finally tell Rosanna that he was her secret admirer.

For months he had been leaving little gifts and notes in Rosanna's dressing room. He wanted to shower her with jewels and pretty clothes and sweets and all the wonderful things in the world. But, for now, he had to content himself with flowers, chocolates, and fanciful, homemade gifts that he spent many hours laboring over by candlelight.

Grik scraped and saved to buy the little luxuries. He didn't mind—not when it was for Rosanna. At night, lying in his stone house in Stone Town, he would clutch the thought of those presents to himself as if they were a warm cup of broth. Every hour of work flitted by easily on the wings of anticipation as he thought carefully over how he would surprise and delight Rosanna.

His anonymous gifts caused a great stir in the theater. The backstage gossip was rampant as everyone tried to guess who could be leaving Rosanna presents.

And tonight he was going to admit that it was him.

Grik had thought that he would never, ever be brave enough to confess his feelings to Rosanna. The very thought of it still made him feel sick—but not as sick as it made him feel to go on not telling her. His secret spun and jumped inside of him in its own wild ballet, and it had to get out, to leap onto the stage, despite the audience, a bit of music that had to be danced to.

He watched Rosanna twirl, and the expectation of speaking with her made him as faint and dizzy as if he had been the one spinning around and around. But he was also filled with a strange optimism. Perhaps it was the smile Rosanna had given him earlier that day when he had opened the front door of the Metropolitan for her. Maybe it was the way she had said his name when he had timidly wished her good luck for the performance.

"Thank you, Grik!" The words rang in his ears like the sweet music from the orchestra, giving him hope. Giving him courage.

He blinked and clutched his rose as he looked towards the stage. The music was over, and the enchantment on stage ended. The curtains closed in a whoosh of velvet, muffling the wild applause that still poured from the audience.

Grik pressed back deeper into the shadows as the dancers filed off the stage, complaining of tight slippers, tittering over handsome faces in the crowd, congratulating themselves, or yelling at assistants to help them in their dressing rooms.

Only Rosanna remained behind on the stage. She looked as if she couldn't bear to step off of it. She didn't look towards the curtain and the applauding audience beyond it, as other, vainer dancers might have. She was looking at the floor, as if she were gazing at some invisible pattern that her slippers longed to follow.

Grik waited for her to go back to her dressing room so that he could finally have a moment—one private moment—to tell her how he felt about her.

He looked from Rosanna to the stage. The audience had thrown dozens of flowers at her, and all he had was a rose. He comforted himself with the thought that his rose was the best rose to be had in the flower markets of La Caen—he should know; it had taken him hours to pick it out. And it was her favorite color—a deep, rosy pink. The same color as her mouth, Grik thought, feeling warm all over.

Rosanna twirled half-heartedly in the center of the stage and, for an instant, was almost as clumsy as Grik. He saw the pain travel across her face again, like clouds brushing away sunshine. Her shoulders slumped a little, as if all the euphoria that had made her dance so lightly had been replaced by a horrible weight. Grik's heart lurched as a tear trace its way down her cheek.

Rosanna finally walked off the stage. A stagehand began to tease Rosanna about her secret admirer, saying that he was the reason her head was in the clouds, and they hazarded a guess about who he might be. Grik held his breath, fearing that he would hear some other name on Rosanna's lips . . . and hoping that she might whisper his.

Rosanna didn't respond to the stagehand or make any guess of her own; she only smiled a little at his talk as she headed down the hallway to her dressing room.

Grik shuffled after her, ducking past stagehands as they hurried to dismantle the set. People rushed back and forth, talking, shouting, and working. Life behind the stage was its own little world, but it was one that Grik only occupied on the outskirts, for the fear that he might not actually belong in this place, just as he feared he didn't belong anywhere.

After many years of practice, Grik had become adept at staying out of people's way. He knew how to make himself as small as possible and was fast at giving way to everyone else and tucking himself into corners. But tonight he was so consumed with thoughts of Rosanna that he wasn't paying proper attention to where he was going. He suddenly collided with a hard, tall object.

"Hey! Watch where you're going, you little fool! You nearly made me fall!"

Grik craned his misshapen head back to look up at the man he had bumped into. A dashing and handsome man clad in the scarlet uniform of the National Army towered over him. He was one of the many elves who fought on the borders of Auverne to keep their country safe from marauding orcs and monsters. The epaulettes on his shoulders and the medals next to his lapel showed that he wasn't just any soldier, but an officer and a hero of his regiment.

Grik looked up at the striking face above him and was ashamed all over again by how he must appear in this man's eyes.

Grik had the same pointed ears, but the similarity ended there. Where their skin was pale and smooth, his was rough and mottled and vaguely green—more like the skin of a lizard. His hair was not the smooth, perfect blond or brown tresses of an elf, but black and stubbly. Elves rarely grew taller than five feet, while goblins were far stubbier, a mere three to four feet in height.

The soldier's smooth voice jerked Grik from his unhappy thoughts.

"Goblins," he growled. "I spend my life defending our country from monsters, and then I come home on leave and I'm tripping over them in the hallways of our public buildings. It's a disgrace."

The man's voice was as smooth and rich as cream, and Grik was painfully aware of his own rough and scratchy voice as he muttered a half-hearted apology.

Proud blue eyes looked Grik up and down with distaste from beneath thick, straight brows. He had dark hair and a chiseled face with pale skin and delicate, pointed ears—not like the huge, hideous things stuck haphazardly to the side of Grik's head. The only thing to mar the soldier's outward perfection was his obvious injury. He carried an expensive cane with an ornate handle that he leaned heavily upon. He was slightly out of breath, as if walking pained him.

"What are you looking at?" the soldier snapped.

"Your leg," Grik answered and then wished he hadn't, for he thought the soldier might grab him by the neck and throttle him. For a moment, the soldier flushed as red as his uniform, but then a lordly expression chased away the brief flash of anger and shame.

"A mere war wound. I got this in the line of duty, defending our country from vermin that looked something like you." His gaze skimmed over Grik with open disgust, and he suddenly smirked. "Being a credit and of actual use to my country . . . unlike you . . . janitor."

Grik stared up at the elf, speechless with hurt and fury. He might be ugly, but a goblin was just as much a person as an elf. He wanted to fly at the man, to punch him in the leg, where it would hurt the most, but before he could speak or do anything, the soldier flicked a thin, graceful finger to the rose in Grik's hand.

"Dear me, don't tell me you fancy one of the ballerinas here." The soldier laughed, long and cruelly.

Grik writhed inwardly with outrage, but his shame was greater than his pride, and he mumbled hastily, "It's not from me. I'm . . . I'm delivering it for someone."

The soldier smirked. "Well, that at least makes sense."

He pushed past Grik, but his attempt to strut was pathetic since one foot dragged along behind him.

Grik wanted to laugh at the soldier, to mock him, but as he took a step back he felt his own awkward gait and knew it was just as ugly—uglier—than the soldier's limp.

Grik looked after the soldier and hated him with every fiber of his being, a rage that was swallowed up in helplessness as the soldier stopped in front of Rosanna's dressing room and knocked on the door.

Grik pressed the rose to his chest, mind swirling. Who had he been fooling? How could a goblin janitor compete against an elvish soldier? This man was used to fighting for what he wanted and destroying anything that got in his way. Grik had no doubt that the soldier would easily stomp on him if he dared to interfere in his wooing—and enjoy doing it.

The soldier knocked again on the dressing room door, and it swung open. Rosanna had already changed and was clad in a soft wool coat. Her hair had been removed from its bun and was now spilling around her face and shoulders.

Rosanna greeted the soldier with a smile. "Why, Paul! Hello."

So that was his name. Grik hated it. He wondered desperately if her expression was a shade friendlier than usual. He loved Rosanna's friendliness, but why did she have to be nice to Paul?

Rosanna was exclaiming softly over Paul's wound. One slim hand reached out to rest on the soldier's shoulder.

Grik's gaze dimmed in a kind of red fury and horror, as if his whole vision was swallowed up by that cursed scarlet coat.

Paul's chin was up as he smiled and rattled on in a way that made Grik want to tear him to shreds. The soldier suddenly pressed a bouquet into Rosanna's arms—a bouquet that Grik had been too upset to notice before.

They were dark-pink roses. Rosanna's favorite. The soldier had known.

Grik crushed his own rose so tightly he heard the infinitesimal snap of the stalk.

Rosanna looked down at the soldier's bouquet. For one very brief moment, she seemed sad. Before Grik could wonder why, he saw Paul looking at Rosanna, no longer prideful, no longer showing off, but with his heart in his eyes.

It was like looking into a mirror—only not. For this face was handsome, and Grik's was not.

Grik watched them, and envy nearly choked him. He had never felt uglier in his life.

Paul offered Rosanna his arm to escort her, and she took it.

Grik turned and ran through the Metropolitan Dance Hall, pushing past the workmen. He didn't stop until he shoved against the big door to the side entrance and slipped out into air so cold, it shocked him into breathing again.

The soldier had a pain, not a real one, but enough of one to make Rosanna offer her kindhearted sympathy. He would use his wound to steal her compassion, and then he would steal her heart.

Grik eased down the narrow set of rain-slick steps that led to the alleyway, moving unsteadily—but not just because it was wet.

The lampposts had been lit all up and down La Caen's main boulevard, casting a bright light up into the dark night but doing little to illuminate the alley. The capital of Auverne was far away from the skirmishes along its border, deep in the heart of a country full of beauty and glamour.

At the end of the alley, Grik could hear the talk and laughter of a crowd of theatergoers, saying their good-nights to people who cared about them and returning to something they called home.

Grik hopped off the last step and onto the curb, kicking at a pile of early autumn leaves and wiping hard at his eyes. Rain had fallen the day before, turning the leaves into moldy, wet piles that had been shoved against the curb, where they would be least noticed, all the bright color trampled out of them.

Grik didn't like nights like this so much; they reminded him of himself, as if the whole world had turned into a mirror to show his own ugly reflection.

He looked up at the stars, but all he could see was that horrible memory of Paul gazing at Rosanna with that brief look of curiosity and yearning. He too had seen the wound in Rosanna. Her wound had recognized his own hurt and that shared moment had been like a kiss.

Grik left the alley and stood on the edge of the main boulevard, watching the people go by in pairs—always in pairs.

The city's famous onion-domed buildings were illuminated with the glow of the thousand lanterns that were lit every night to dangle fifty feet above the streets in long, bobbing chains. The domes were gilt, a myriad of soft pastels—and their shape and color reminded Grik of the skirts of the dancers he had seen perform tonight. Everything about this city was as light as the goblin town below was heavy, as bright as his world was dark. A city dedicated to art and scholarly pursuits, trusting in the world beneath them—a goblin culture dedicated to the practical things of life—to keep their sewers maintained, their buildings tidy, and their roads in good repair. Goblins and elves got along well enough, but they were always separate.

He turned to look at the Metropolitan Dance Hall one last time. He could just see them: her hair glowed in the streetlights like a fallen star. Rosanna and the soldier were standing at the foot of the steps and they were catching a hansom cab to leave . . . together.

Grik stood on the corner, hot, furious tears slipping down his face and plinking onto the cobblestones at his feet.

He let the rose drop into the gutter and jumped after it, because that was where goblins belonged.

www.ingramcontent.com/pod-product-compliance
Lightning Source LLC
Chambersburg PA
CBHW020306030826
48979CB00029B/2191/J

* 9 7 9 8 9 8 8 5 0 0 6 2 9 *